THE CORNOVII MYSTERY

BOOK I OF THE ALBA MYSTERIES

DAVID GRIFFITHS

Copyright © 2023 David Griffiths

All rights reserved

The characters and events portrayed in this book are fictitious. Any similarity to real persons, living or dead, is coincidental and not intended by the author.

No part of this book may be reproduced, copied, distributed or adapted in any form without prior written permission from the author, with the exception of non-commercial uses permitted by copyright law.

For Thalia

For what is freedom,
If not the fire of truth;

          DAVID GRIFFITHS

Author's Note

This work is a fictional novel set within the Romano-British framework of Britain in the first century AD.

The novel's events are set amongst a background where the Romans have secured most of the southern part of Britain, much of the east and northern England.

Whilst I have used tribal names to define the basic geography within the book, all of the characters, including chieftains, elders and Roman officers are fictional and not based on any known individuals.

Legio XX Valeria Victrix is recorded as being present within Britain during the initial invasion of AD43 and subsequent decades. They were active within the lands of the Cornovii, covering what is now the Midlands and up towards Chester.

PROLOGUE

Meeting of the Great Council

'What say you Doube?' invited Chieftain Rigari. 'You represent the tribes of the central lands. Your people are largely untouched by the Red empire and their ways. What say you?'

Doube gathered his cloak about him before striding out onto the debating area. Rigari nodded, giving his fellow elder the floor.

Doube had rehearsed his speech many times on the long journey to this meeting of the Great Council. Over two days of travel he had considered his words carefully. Debates were won or lost by the wisdom of words. An ill-conceived speech could lose the day in the same way as poor strategy could lose a battle. He was old enough and wise enough to appreciate both.

Reaching the centre of the large roundhouse, he stopped abruptly, pausing to regard his peers. There was no need to wait, but he knew his audience. The tribal elders of the Great Council were nothing if not dramatic in their debates, to which he would be no exception.

Disagreement, even conflict, was never far away, though these gatherings were designed to prevent skirmishes becoming wars. Chieftains attended in person or by proxy through their chief elders. Disputes, trade and the great issues of the day were all settled here. Agreement was often elusive, playing as it did against personal gain and tribal power. It was not unusual for the council to break up with delegates nursing battered limbs as well as bruised egos.

The moments passed.

Murmurs struck up as the assembly became impatient for his response. Satisfied, he lifted his head to begin his speech.

'The Cornovii do not crave open warfare, but our ways are our own. We will not submit to control by the Red imperialists.'

He paused again, choosing his next words carefully.

'The Red soldiers have so far restricted themselves to acts of bribery or intimidation. Several of our neighbours have already bowed to one or both of these tactics. Some are even willing to give up their beliefs for the promise of wealth and power.' He paused and then added, 'Roman power, not ours.'

He let that sentence sink in, as he had rehearsed, taking time to look intently at each face before him.

'We who inhabit the central lands will not submit to this deceit! It is not our way.' Another carefully choreographed pause followed. 'Neither should it be yours!' he rallied louder. 'We must remain custodians of our way of life. To give it up for material gain is like trading grain for gold.'

'You are living in the past Doube!' he was loudly

interrupted.

Tadc, chieftain of the Dobunni, bounded onto the floor in a flurry of dismissive arm waving.

'We should embrace their ways if it brings us gain. Dancing around a circle of stones and shouting to the stars will not put food in our bellies. These Red *visitors* give us an opportunity to live without trial.'

Though Tadc had the attention of the other elders present, Doube refused to give up the floor. He had, after all, been the one who was interrupted. Such protocol that there was at these meetings dictated that if you already had the floor, you were not expected to relinquish it for an interruption. Only if Toryn, chief elder of the Great Council, interrupted you was that the case.

'You speak of them as *visitors* Tadc, but I say they are invaders, imperialists that will supplant our ways with their own. You are deceived my friend!'

The council erupted. Insults flew freely, beating a path between tribal loyalty and the matter in hand. Tadc seemed encouraged by the uproar his interruption had caused. Maybe that was his intent. Goading the representatives into a frenzy to make your point was, after all, a tactic well used. Many debates were won or lost by the diversion of emotive words, even violence.

'Surely, even the Cornovii must have heard the stories of their great cities, huge villas and massive temples shining with marble?' Tadc continued. He spread his arms out, playing to the crowd, attempting to draw them. 'Consider for a moment Doube. Think how much we could learn from such people. We can leave our roundhouses to become part of a new world. Or, would you rather put all your faith in some outdated notion of appeasing the gods with sacrifice and petition? Will that feed us when our crops fail? Will it save our children when they get with fever? These Romans have medicines and physicians skilled in knowledge from the mysterious east, all of which can pull us out of the old ways.' He turned back to his audience, 'Should we ignore such opportunity when it arrives at our gates?'

Doube could see how his opponent was playing the audience. Several of the council members had fallen silent, perhaps tempted by the vision Tadc had presented. Doube's best weapon was reason. He must attempt to return the council back to their traditions, the value of freedom and the threat that the Romans presented to both.

'The representative of the Dobunni makes a good argument,' he acknowledged.

Surprise briefly registered on some faces, before he whirled back around to counter.

'Yet, the truth in your words has escaped even you, Tadc.'

Tadc flushed at this rebuke, but Doube was not done yet.

'You said it yourself, "*their great cities,*" Theirs Tadc, not ours. You would turn this land into nothing but a province of the Roman Empire and all for what? You would sell us out for power and privilege. Never I say. Not while I still draw beath will I submit to such a future!'

'You arrogant bastard!' Tadc seethed.

'No!' Doube returned. 'You are the arrogant one. Arrogant to suppose your own desires can be hidden from those at this council; arrogant to think we would not see through your motives whilst in the background you connive with the Red; arrogant that you are even here, on this very floor on which the wisdom of our ancestors has heard voice.'

'How dare you!' Tadc flamed. 'You accuse me of conspiracy with empty words and malicious intent. You are old Doube, old like your beliefs. And old things falter, wither and die. That is *your* future and that of those who believe in your tired old dribble.'

'And what of *the Lost*, Tadc of the Dobunni? Should their memory wither and die? Or do you mourn the loss of our warriors that have vanished without trace? Vanished, I may add, since the Red warriors he so admires have been treading our lands.'

Doube almost had Tadc to the point where he had lost control.

Almost.

With great effort, Tadc recovered himself. A flicker of a smile touched his lips as he locked eyes back with Doube.

'Very good,' he acknowledged. 'Well played.'

Turning away from Doube, he re-established contact with his primary audience. The fool Doube had almost succeeded in seducing him into a misstep. Now, he would make good his argument and sow dissent in the council.

'We live in a changing world,' he continued, a steely calmness clamped around his voice. 'Of course, we lament those who have already trod the path to the gods, from all tribes. They shall be missed, but we cannot lay the blame for the odd disappearance at the feet of those that would seek to give us knowledge in return for sharing our lands.'

Doube shook his head. 'There has been more than just the odd disappearance. Our own tribe has lost several warriors and only last week a young boy failed to return from his first hunt. The disappearances began at the same time as the Red soldiers started probing into our territory. Minor incursions at first. Now, they patrol our hills and trackways as though they own them. The pattern is clear if you had the eyes to see it but, maybe, the chieftain of the Dobunni only sees through Red eyes.'

That one struck home.

Tadc lost the façade of control, making towards him, fists curled, capillaries breaking out into a crimson storm across his cheeks. Others jumped onto the floor. It became impossible to say who supported who. Fighting broke out everywhere.

Amidst the brawling, Toryn stepped down.

'Enough arguing! This gets us nowhere. Go back to your people. Talk to your fellow elders, warriors and wisemen. We must have agreement between the tribes on how to deal with the Red scourge. Our choices are stark. Resist and face war, try to reach an accord which may mean concessions or . . .'

He paused, as though tasting the bitterness of his next words.

'Or accept the Red and their way of life, with whatever that means for our own.'

Shouting filled the room at this last option, rivalries broke out once more. Old arguments supplanted what had been discussed. Fists were thrown, daggers drawn.

Toryn grabbed a gnarled staff adorned with black feathers and beads. With surprising alacrity, he sprung at the nearest elder who, having left his seat, had already produced a vicious looking blade in his hand. A loud crack followed by the thud of the elder collapsing to the floor brought the room to order.

'I said enough!' he boomed. 'Go now, to your peoples. We will meet again upon the next full moon. Do not test my patience again,' he added, apparently possessed of more than one set of eyes as behind him the felled elder sought to recover his blade. The staff flashed out again, sending its recipient into a deeper and more bloody oblivion.

'Arsehole,' muttered Toryn.

The meeting ended abruptly. Noone was keen to risk their own skull on Toryn's staff. In the intervening weeks, the elders and chieftains would consult with their respective tribes. What they could not anticipate would be the events that would follow. As the representatives sidled out of the Great Roundhouse plans were already in motion that would change the fate of their world.

***

Doube had left feeling troubled. The usual anticipation of heading home had been replaced by a deep unease. He had hoped the council would unite behind what seemed an obvious danger to their way of life. Instead, they were fractured and at odds. The usual fault lines along personal enmity or tribal honour was subjugated by some other cause which he could not quite put his finger on. The debate had been spirited, even raucous at times. Yet, voices he would have expected to be loud remained quiet. That was unusual, which bothered him more than it ordinarily would have.

Tadc seemed to be swaying several of the other representatives by his flattery of Roman civilisation. Artek of the Brigantes, the tribe north of their own borders, had been strangely quiet. He was usually one of the first to lend his voice to an affray, often bypassing insult, preferring to allow his dagger do some off the cuff bloodletting. During council, he had said nothing, barely acknowledging him even when the meeting had disbanded. A suspicion formed in Doube's mind that Artek had intended merely to show up, make sure he was seen, before disappearing back to his own lands.

He shook his head, a gesture that did nothing to clear that which was obscured.

If he had an ally, then it was Rigari of the Corieltauvi to the east of their own lands. Though not as forthright as Doube, Rigari had spoken eloquently of the rapid spread of the Red imperialists along their eastern borders. His people were already under pressure. Mainly farmers, much land had been lost with the Romans building new settlements with surprising alacrity. As had happened in the south, these new settlements were not temporary marching camps. They were full scale communities being raised up from the earth, solidly built with stone and mortar. Rigari was well aware that his small band of warriors would be quickly overrun should they find themselves in open conflict. To survive, he would need the help of the other tribes. At risk was more than just the land they farmed; their entire identity was in danger of being subsumed within Roman rule.

Doube reflected on the tensions within the council which had not dissipated at its end. They had broken up without agreement or anything settled. That was troubling enough but not so unusual. It could often take several sessions in council to decide a course of action. Yet, something felt different, an undercurrent, some unseen toxicity which corrupted out of sight.

The same unease had followed him since leaving. He tried to dismiss it in the same way as the irrational fear of the night can subvert the mind, but the demon in the darkness still lurked at the periphery of his senses. As a precaution, he changed his route home, returning via the lesser-known paths. Occasionally, he doubled back on himself to check for signs of pursuit. Once, he thought he saw movement near a thicket of blackthorn. Freezing, he crouched down waiting to identify the cause. After a while, a young fox emerged, nose to the ground, tracking the scent of its prey. Relieved, he felt himself longing for the safety of his roundhouse and the warmth of its hearth.

To distract himself, he thought back to the meeting. There was a time when tribal and personal honour would have precluded any thought of appeasing an aggressor. Wealth never used to be entertained as something for the individual. Rather, it was for the good of the community where prosperity was sought. The riches of the land and that of tradition held sway not too far back. They had the Red vermin to thank for the disease that now swept through many of the Britons. The Romans had been cunning in their subversion of the British tribes, choosing bribery, power and personal wealth to secure their influence. Tadc and his supporters were prepared to sacrifice much in return.

Too much.

He was still lost in thoughts when he caught a slight sound behind him.

As he turned, he was yanked violently forward. Astonished, he looked down to see the steel of a Roman gladius protruding from his belly, twisting as it was pushed through his innards. Seeing his own blood running down the blade did not seem real. He continued staring in horror as the blade was yanked out.

His mind could not comprehend his impending

death. It was left to the rest of his body to complete the process. The feeling in his legs went first followed quickly by his chest. Blood jetted out of both sides of his torn torso, pooling into an ever-increasing quagmire of distressed earth. The blade struck again, burying itself deep into his guts. What breath was left in his lungs was ripped out as the gaping belly discharged his shredded organs onto the ruddied earth.

'Is it done?' a voice shouted over.

'It is done,' came the reply

'Good!' replied the Roman soldier. 'The Legatus will be pleased. You have performed well.'

The soldier, a centurion, swung up to his mount before tossing a small leather bag over to the conspirator. It landed with a thump, spilling several silver coins over the damp ground beneath.

The assassin picked it up slowly.

'This is meaningless.'

'The Legatus said you would say that,' returned the soldier. 'He said for you to take it anyway; that you would understand that every act deserves reward.'

The soldier kicked his horse viciously. The beast grunted loudly as its legs sped at the earth seeking traction before leaving a maelstrom of mud and grit in its wake.

The assassin returned his gaze to the dead form on the ground, noting with satisfaction that the pool of blood his foot had stepped into threatened to breach the rim of his boots.

'Our people need order now Doube. Order through those with vision to bring in a new world. Not the meaningless meanderings of the old ways. A pity you could not see that. You can ponder that in the afterlife as your rotting corpse feeds the earth.'

He smirked before kicking the lifeless body. 'Not that you care anymore.'

CHAPTER I

'Are we sure he even came back this way Alba?'

'If he had returned via the main routes he would have been found.' Alba inclined his head, listening to that which could not be heard.

'You picking up something?'

'There is a peculiar depression hanging in the air. We are close.'

'You fear the worst then?'

Alba nodded slowly. 'Death lingers like an unyielding fog. It is different when a man meets his end through natural means. That is ordered, the natural way of all things. The energy of pass-over is light. The body is prepared, ready for the afterlife.'

'So, you feel there is foul play here?'

'I sense the aftershock of violence; the astonishment and surprise of an end. The effect of it ripples upon the air. We must steel ourselves.'

They had been searching for Doube for three days now, travelling by foot over the old ridgeways. These ancient paths were not always visible to the naked eye, but for the indigenous people who inhabited these lands, knowledge of them were passed down, mapped into the minds of each new generation. Thus, despite all of the Red soldiers civilisation, they were oblivious of this hidden knowledge, relying as they always did on their own more materialistic technology. Britannia's landscape was violated with heavy duty roads, forging an unnatural net of criss-crossing highways through which the imperial armies marched.

Up to this point they had not seen or noticed anything out of the ordinary. Were it not for Alba's gift then they would have been oblivious to all but the wet, barren heathland on which they walked. A foulness lurked, suspended upon the droplets of moisture which strove to invade the air they breathed.

Argyll felt uncomfortable, sensing evil. Alba had told him before, on the killing fields of countless battles, that violence requires rebalancing. *Justice* was what Argyll preferred to call it.

The track they were on had been climbing steadily for the last few hours. They were treading an ancient heathland, a *mynd* the western tribes called it. A long flat plateau of gorse and heather stretched out before them. A low mist clung to the heather as though the last shower of rain had been arrested in time. As they moved through it, their clothes became damp, their skin wet, droplets morphing into streams down their clothes and equipment. The sun god tried in vain to penetrate the veil, damp cloud morphing into a luminescent creature determined to smother the light.

Argyll did not need to be a seer to sense how eerie this place was. He shivered, desiring to leave, but knowing their task was not yet done.

A skilled tracker with knowledge of the majority of the Cornovii territory, Alba had been schooled by his father on how to read the land. There were few markers of where one tribe's land finished and another started, so it was imperative that the young were taught such knowledge. Many was the time a young warrior, out on his first hunt, had strayed into an adjacent territory, never to be seen again. Disappearances tended not to be an organised affair, although outlaws and mercenaries were a constant threat to hunters as well as those who simply got lost.

With the appearance of the Red soldiers things had changed, forever. Stories reached the Cornovii and other tribes of a new enemy, one who breached the southern shores on mighty wooden ships from across the great sea. They sailed out of the mist on a scarlet tide, a scourge of warriors who moved and fought as one, sacrificing individual honour for legionary honour. To the Britons who faced them on the shingle beaches, warrior to warrior, this was abhorrent. This new enemy adapted, forming its armies into strange patterns, repelling spear, arrow and chariot. In open battle the Red invaders could not be defeated. Those that resisted turned to ambush and stealth, choosing instead to fight a war of attrition. Other accepted their fate, embracing the new ways, finding a different route to sustain their bellies and, in some cases, their ambitions. Thus, was Roman Britannia born.

The Romans, rich in their own religion, recognised the power of belief. Native deities were absorbed, replaced or blended with their own. A subtle ploy, which they had used throughout their empire. Violence usually came last, reserved for those who could not be bought or turned.

Gradually, those who refused to accept the new order, were squeezed out of their lands, denied its resources and their way of living. This was the crisis which had summoned the representatives to the Great Council to which Doube had attended. He had been missing for over a week. When it became clear that the delay was not temporary, they had sent out scouts. As the most experienced, Alba and Argyll were chosen. It seemed probable based on the elapsed time that their quarry was not alive.

Alba stopped.

Lifting his chin slightly, he sensed the air. The tension he had felt earlier was stronger here. From his satchel he pulled a dark wooden staff the length of his arm. At the top was a natural 'v' shape made by the divergence of two branches. Where the two arms met, a leather braid was tightly wound around the circumference adorned with beads of amber. It held a single jet-black feather to its bole. The bottom two thirds were plain except for several carvings. Argyll did not comprehend the meanings of these marking, save they were of deep mystic purpose; ancient glyphs of power, he assumed.

Alba held the staff aloft, reaching up to the gods who inhabited the sky and stars above. When he was sure of the connection, he brought the staff down firmly into the ground, burying the bottom few inches into the moist earth beneath. Grabbing the middle section he closed his eyes and gripped tightly, inviting the gods of the underworld to meet with those above, a crossroad of divine power. A ripple of energy ascended, rising from feet to stomach. Almost immediately a similar current descended through his crown.

Argyll waited silently. He had seen his friend commune with the ancestors before.

Alba began to tremble, his body struggling to accommodate the elemental energy surfing his own. His mind reached out, connecting with the old ones, ancestor spirits of those that had been before. There was a jolt as the union was made before images, emotions and words filled his inner temple. A voice, a familiar face from previous communion swam into view. Words were given economically, energy never wasted.

And then it was over.

Slowly, his grip on the staff relaxed. Argyll helped him up. Alba was always unsteady after he had communed with the ancient ones.

'We go this way,' he said simply.

They walked to the edge of the plateau before beginning a sharp descent down tufted grass hiding rock and crevice alike. It would be easily to sprain a foot or worse.

'I am not doubting you or the gods Alba,' Argyll noted as for the fifth time his foot and half his calf disappeared down a hidden depression.

'But?'

'I don't see why Doube would have chosen such a treacherous path. This is madness!' he grimaced, taking another stumble.

'He would not ordinarily. I suspect he came this way not from the plateau we have just traversed but from the valley below. There is only one reason a man would chose that more difficult path.'

'You think he was being followed?'

'Yes, I do. He was being very careful.'

'Maybe not careful enough.'

They continued threading their way down the hillside. The section they were descending was a meeting of three separate valleys. Each was steep, two bearing streams that converged into one larger flow that continued down the main basin. Silhouettes of blighted saplings and young trees

THE CORNOVII MYSTERY

that never made it to adulthood were the only breaks to their descent.

'Doube must have gambled that his pursuers would not expect him to take such a roundabout route,' Alba explained. 'The problem is that once you commit to this valley, the steep sides afford little cover with no opportunity for a quick escape. As we have so adequately proved, escape is only possible by climbing your way out, not easy on these rain-soaked hills.'

Reaching the bottom, they were faced with a three-way choice. Argyll started forward, but before he had taken a step, he felt Alba's hand grip his arm, holding him back firmly.

'Wait!'

Alba pointed at the ground just in front of where Argyll had been about to plant his foot.

Following his friend's finger, Argyll looked closer. Pebbles and small rocks which peppered the flood plain of the narrow river beside them had been churned out of place. The perpetrator had left an imprint of its shoe, several U-shaped impressions still etched into the soft mud. As he continued looking, he saw other tracks including the sole of a man's boot.

'This is where he was taken,' Alba broke in.

He crouched down examining the site, his mind framing each imprint, each scuff in the mud timelining the sequence between them.

'There were two of them. One followed on foot, the other was mounted. The rider came from further back, no doubt once the killer had done his work.'

'You said killer,' interrupted Argyll. 'You believe he was murdered for sure?'

'There is no doubt. Look here. See where the

footprints meet? Our killer stood behind Doube when he struck. A coward's way to kill.'

Alba's hand reached out to the mud, his trackers eyes seemingly able to see beyond the layer of earth and stone. His fingers curled around mud and something else. Something not of the earth, tubular and soft.

'By the gods!' exclaimed Argyll, 'Is that . . .?'

'Not by the gods,' Alba corrected. 'By the hand of man.'

They found more pieces of Doube scattered about, rotting entrails trampled irreverently into the sludge.

Alba walked forward, standing in the space where a man had met his end. From here he listened. The air was broken by the sporadic calls of crows, the occasional buzzard supplemented by the flow of the burbling river in the valley base. He moved towards the water. Whilst it flowed strongly, the water was not wide, nor was it deep. The banks on either side were no more than three foot deep. Ample depth to hide a body.

Doube's corpse remained where his assassin had kicked it, partially hidden by the shallow brook that normally gave life rather than conspiring to hide death. The legs were splayed wide, feet pointing towards the lip of the bank, whilst the head had fallen into the water. Animals had already expanded the punctured torso, grabbing the remaining innards for food. Doube's face was unrecognisable, puffed up into a grisly white montage of flesh so that it was impossible to distinguish eyes, mouth or nose from the contorted horror that remained.

They stared at the scene for several moments before together they moved the remains out of the water.

'A foul way for a man to meet his end,' Argyll muttered.

'Foul in more ways than one,' Alba agreed. 'Doube was a Chief Elder, a man of renown, of honour and respect. To gut such a man and leave him for the wild beasts goes beyond mere killing. There is real hate at play.'

'Do we bury him here?'

'No. It is important we show the others how he died. Our chieftain must send message to the other tribes on what has transpired. Someone needs to pay the price for this heavy deed.'

'They should be gutted themselves, when we find them,' Argyll spat angrily.

Alba nodded but seemed distracted.

'Have you seen something else?'

'It's the horse.'

'The horse?'

'The imprints are too heavy. Not what I would expect. Look here.'

Alba pointed at several of the hoof marks.

'I don't follow,' queried Argyll.

'Look how deep the imprint is. When I look at the way the horse stood, how it shifted its weight, then I see that it was burdened beyond what I would expect our native warriors to bear.'

There was silence between them as they thought of the implications.

'Are you suggesting that it was a Red horse, that they are involved in this?'

'That is what it looks like. Our own warriors do not armour our mounts in the way the Romans do. Therefore, had this been one of ours, the imprint would not have borne down so hard.'

'Do you think Doube ran into a Red patrol or a scouting party?'

'I think it less likely he ran into them and more that they intercepted him.'

'If the Red are active here, so far from their usual routes, then they must have had help.'

Alba nodded. 'The other concern is the timing. Whoever killed our Elder knew where he would be and where to pick up his tracks. That means they must have known he was in council.'

'And that suggests involvement of a Briton,' Argyll finished.

'Exactly. I am afraid that there is conspiracy here.'

High above them, grey and black clouds fought a volatile duel for dominance. As the light retreated, the drizzle that had accompanied their journey became heavier.

CHAPTER II

'Your mission was a success, Lucius?'
'Yes, my Legatus. The target was tracked to a remote location before being despatched.'

'You're certain he is dead?'

'Very. Unless he found a way to live without his guts inside him.'

'And no witnesses?'

'None.'

The Legatus, Servius, nodded slowly.

'Our man inside is reliable then?'

'Totally. In fact, it was he who sent their chief elder to the underworld and he is keen to earn further favour. It seems our guarantee of social status and power in the world to come is more than enough to keep him loyal.'

'How very Roman of him,' sneered Servius.

Lucius hesitated, unsure if to wait for any favour that may be bestowed.

His new commander had replaced the previous incumbent only a month ago. Whereas the old Legatus was nothing but a military man, this new commander, Servius, was ambitious, greedy and unscrupulous.

Just like himself, in fact.

Lucius had been assigned to this hell hole two years ago. Initially, he had thought he would find glory and rich pickings. Instead, they had wandered around the middle lands of this miserable, rain-soaked island, moving from camp to camp. He had ceased to count the number of temporary forts they had thrown up. Some became permanently manned, whereas others were levelled after the army had left. Rarely did they establish a formal settlement. His new commander looked set to change that. Lucius had been approached with a new vision for this Britannia. The Legatus had explained to him that there were people in Rome with a different, longer-term concept of Empire. A vision of Imperial Rome that would endure for centuries, millennia even. A new world order.

The seconds ticked by.

'You may go,' replied the Legatus, aggravated by the audacity Lucius so ably demonstrated.

'Now!'

Lucius bowed, drew his cloak around him and took his leave. The Legatus grunted before pouring himself a glass of wine from an ornate terracotta jug. His fingers traced the raised edges of a carving which wound itself around the circumference of the drinking vessel, a large wolf suckling two human infants, a symbolic rendering of Romulus and Remus. He sighed in satisfaction as the dark liquid filled his glass. Both wine and jug were exquisite, having been transported from his own private estate outside of Rome. Servius was not one to travel without his comforts, his luggage alone accounting for three baggage wagons. This was not lost on the soldiers under his command as man and beast struggled to shift a quite unnecessary load alongside their Legion's normal equipment.

Settling back into a velvet padded chair arranged next to his war desk, he let the wine pass between his lips, savouring the entire journey the liquid took from mouth to stomach. Such a vintage had to be enjoyed throughout its transit.

Satisfied, he leaned his head towards a large red drape that partitioned off the rear section of his quarters.

'You heard that?'

'Of course.'

'And?'

'It appears our plan is on track but things can change, Servius. Success or failure is on your head. Do not forget that.'

The Legatus scowled, before downing the rest of his glass.

***

Two nights had passed since Alba and Argyll had discovered Doube's remains. The community had received them back with horror. Given the time that had passed, many anticipated they would return either empty handed or with a corpse.

They had taken the body to the house of Rendrr, the chieftain who held authority over the Cornovii within what was termed the 'central lands'. Like Doube, Rendrr had once been an elder, before winning the vote to become chieftain. Under his leadership, the squabbles which had beset the Cornovii in previous years had disappeared. Stability and unity returned to the hillforts and communities under his rule.

He met Alba and Argyll as they gently unloaded Doube's body from the makeshift sledge to which they had strapped his body.

'It is as we feared?'

'I'm afraid it is much worse,' replied Alba.

'Worse?'

'Doube has been murdered; butchered in fact.'

Since passing through the hillfort's main gate a crowd had followed them through the interior to where they now stood. The murmurings of curiosity were replaced with gasps when Alba confirmed the cause of death.

'Show me.'

'It's not nice.'

Rendrr looked up at Alba. 'I must see.'

Alba motioned to Argyll, who slowly bent down to remove the cloak which had lain over Doube's body since being recovered.

Immediately, they were assailed with the stench of decomposing flesh. Those nearest took an involuntary step back.

Rendrr held his ground. 'Tell me where he was found.'

'We found him a way off of the normal trackways. We think he knew he was being followed and tried to evade his pursuers. He was unsuccessful. Judging by the wound in his back he was slain from behind; a cowardly stroke. Then, they ripped his belly open and you can see the rest.'

Argyll hung his head in disgust. 'This was no bandit attack Rendrr.'

'Enough!' shouted Rendrr suddenly. 'We will discuss this further inside. In the meantime, we will prepare Doube's body for his final journey to the gods.'

He motioned to four men who were standing by. Respectfully, they collected Doube's body, carrying it between them to an adjacent roundhouse. Alba knew this house was used to prepare lost warriors for the afterlife. Within, the warrior was cleansed, dressed as befitted his status and adorned with the marks, jewellery and weapons they had in life. He sighed deeply, still troubled that anyone would attack one of their most respected leaders.

Argyll looked angry. Alba remained quiet, lost in his thoughts.

Rendrr softened his tone. 'You have done well. Come inside and take sustenance with me. We have much to discuss.'

As chieftain, Rendrr held office within the largest roundhouse inside the fort's interior. Alba suspected Rendrr had made sure that this would become his, rather than continuing its former role of providing storage for grain and weapons.

The chieftain waved them to sit around the hearth, the heart of his house. A fire, not long started had begun to warm the interior. However, the kindling must have been damp for soon after sitting on the multi-layered straw floor they were assailed by a fog that clogged their throats.

Annoyed, Rendrr shouted out.

'Woman, this fire requires tending!'

Enica, Rendrr's wife, appeared as if from nowhere, remodelling the hearth so that the flames conquered their moisture rich logs to throw out more heat than smoke. Alba was surprised how she seemed to glide in and out of his view, a trick she seemed to have perfected on the occasional times he had seen her. Within, she was seldom seen unless called and barely noticed when she was. Before retiring, she handed them plates filled with meat, leaving a flagon of beer to the side to quench themselves.

Rendrr waved her away dismissively. Unlike many of the other Elders wives, Enica was reclusive, rarely seen out of Rendrr's company or without their roundhouse. Alba had the impression she was bound to Rendrr through duty rather than love. The wife of the chieftain usually basked in their authority, but Enica had a distance about her. Alba did not think he could ever recall her smile.

'Tell me your suspicions,' Rendrr commanded, interrupting Alba's thoughts.

'I think you know what I am about to say,' Alba replied. 'Doube was not killed by a random act. This was no opportunistic killing; it was a deliberate slaughter.'

'Do you have any clue as to the identity of his assailant?'

'Some.'

'Go on.'

'There appear to have been two attackers, one of which was on horseback. The unmounted one struck the blow and carried out the gutting. The one on horseback stayed back, perhaps watching to ensure the act was carried out.'

Rendrr nodded slowly, all the while keeping an intense focus upon Alba.

'You are troubled by something else?'

'There are several things which concern me.'

'Surely, our chief concern is why Doube was killed.'

'Not just why but how,' Alba replied. 'I am puzzled by the nature of the killing. Doube could have been killed by far less gruesome methods. An arrow fired at distance would do the job whereas this was up close and very personal. It is suggestive of someone who held a grudge against him, either personally or maybe for what he believed.'

'You think his attacker was known to him?'

'Of that, I am sure.'

Noticing Alba hesitate, Rendrr probed further.

'There is something else?'

'The horse was too heavy.'

'Too heavy?'

'The imprints in the mud were deep. Were that one of our own warriors it would not be so.'

'Could it not just have been a bigger horse?'

'Not given the size of the shoe and span of the stride. This horse was carrying weight over and above its own.'

'Any that means what, exactly?'

'It means that the horse and its mount were likely not one of our own warriors. The extra weight could be due to additional armour and weaponry.'

'You mean the Red?'

'That's exactly what I mean.'

Rendrr paused to consider. The implications were potentially far reaching.

'So, you are saying that Doube was murdered by someone known to him, a Briton and that this was at the direction of, or, in collaboration with, the Red?'

'That is what I believe.'

'Are you not forgetting the reason behind this killing?' Argyll challenged. 'Whoever planned this knew where he would be and by association the reason he was there. Surely, our chief elder's murder must have something to do with why he was at the Great Council?'

'Argyll is correct,' Alba agreed. 'As chieftain, I presume you had sanctioned his views to be presented at the council?'

'Of course,' Rendrr confirmed. 'Doube and I were very much of the same opinion concerning the Red.'

'One other thing puzzles me.'

'Yes?'

Normally, Doube would accompany you to the Great Council. How was it that you did not attend in person this time?'

'Enica was ill and with fever. Doube was insistent I should stay. Given that we spoke of the same voice, I acquiesced. Enica can tell you herself of her illness and her desire for me to be by her side.'

'But why did Doube travel alone? There are always bandits or loners willing to chance their luck on the unwary or unguarded traveller.'

'I argued for him to take company,' Rendrr replied. 'However, Doube said that he thought better if he was alone. Something about preparing his speech along the way.'

'Thankyou. I thought it must be something like that.'

Rendrr stood up, signalling an end to their meeting.

'Nothing is to be said of your suspicions,' he commanded. 'For now, you will keep silent. I do not want the community baying for revenge or turning on themselves fearing a spy in our midst. We must proceed with care.'

'You believe this is only the beginning?' asked Alba.

'Possibly.'

'We cannot just ignore what has happened,' Argyll protested, frustration threatening to overcome respect for his chieftain.

'Nor will we!' snapped back Rendrr angrily. 'Alba and yourself will be charged with uncovering this assassin and bringing him before me. No one else is to be involved. I trust that I make myself clear?'

'Bring him before you?' Argyll spat incredulously. 'This culprit must be dealt with in the same way as he murdered Doube. No quarter should be given and he must . . .'

'Enough!' Rendrr boomed. 'You have your orders. I suggest you get started. I will await your progress keenly.' He strode over to the entrance of the roundhouse, pushing open the wooden door in anticipation of their exit. Annoyance or maybe sadness, flickered across his face. Alba could not tell. The Cornovii chieftain could be difficult to read sometimes.

As he stepped through, Rendrr grasped his arm. 'Report to me alone Alba and keep Argyll in check. His anger threatens to overcome him and expose what we know.'

Alba nodded before stepping back into the light.

His mind remained ablaze with questions, his heart dulled by Doube's passing. Yet, they must plan their next steps carefully. Uncovering a conspiracy without raising suspicion would be hard. Their opponents would no doubt be watching for any move against them.

A weariness flooded over him suddenly. As he bade farewell to Argyll, he headed over to his own roundhouse. Without bothering to undress, he sank wearily into the straw bedding, untouched from when he had left it several days ago. As he drifted into oblivion his mind conjured up an image of Doube. The vision had his back to him, walking through the valley whence they had just returned. As Doube turned, his face transformed from the man Alba remembered to the ugly contortion they had pulled out of the stream. The vulgar image stared straight at him until the welcome void of sleep finally took hold.

CHAPTER III

Alba and Argyll did not attend Doube's death rite. Rendrr had sent word that they should pursue their investigations immediately. The day after arriving back with Doube's corpse, Rendrr's personal guard, Rues, arrived at Alba's roundhouse with a message. Without further consultation they were to proceed to seek an audience with Toryn to search for any clue as to Doube's murder.

When Alba informed Argyll of Rendrr's orders he had expressed surprise.

'I thought Rendrr was going to let us follow up our own leads. Now he sends that seedy bastard Rues around with directions of where to start our investigation.'

'It does make sense to start where Doube was last seen alive,' considered Alba, 'and we need to know what occurred at that meeting.'

'I'd love to know how Rendrr thinks we will be granted audience with Toryn?'

'I had considered that.'
'And?'

'We will just have to hope the Chief of the Great Council is in a good mood.'

'In a good mood! Alba, he hates you. We will be lucky to still have our heads on our shoulders by the time we are finished. This is not a good plan. Rendrr knows of the bad blood between you.'

'Rues was laughing when he repeated Rendrr's orders.'

'I bet he was. That little shit seems to know everything that goes on in this fort.'

'Why don't you like him?'

'He's always sneaking about, those beady eyes flicking this way and that. I'd love to gouge them out one day.'

'It's not unusual for a chieftain to have an inner guard. A leader must always be alert to rebellion, particularly one from within.'

Argyll shook his head.

'He's weird. You know he watches the women?'

'Don't most men?'

'I don't mean like a boy sees his first pair of tits. Several times he has been spotted lurking behind a group of our womenfolk as they go down to the river to bathe. He watches them from the trees. Fuck knows what he does to himself. Rendrr's been told but still the man persists.'

'One problem at a time Argyll. We must interview Toryn. As Chief of the Great Council he must have some insight which will be of use to our investigation. His responsibility to the council together with his friendship with Rendrr ought to be enough to get us audience.'

'I hope you're right Alba. It may be enough to get us in but it's getting us back out again which I am worried about.'

'Toryn will not have forgotten or forgiven. I know that,' Alba acknowledged.

Toryn's animosity towards Alba had begun two seasons back, when he had tried to marry off his daughter, Leah. Alba had politely declined the offer, unready for a betrothal to someone he did not know or bluntly did not even fancy. Almost upon her twenty-fifth season, Leah was considered to be past her prime. If that wasn't enough, she was possessed of a somewhat fiery disposition which dissuaded many suitors. Her father had taken to sweetening the chalice by promising a seat at the Great Council. This had been met with anger by the existing council members who protested that only those elected by their respective tribal leaders should be granted such a role. In the end, a compromise was reached, Toryn acquiescing to any such position being an honorary one without the authority to really do anything.

Besides, Alba's eye was already turned by Beatha, a priestess of his own tribe. Beatha was beautiful, practiced in the ancient arts and a healer. Leah was none of those things.

This had not gone down well with Toryn, who took personal afront that someone should turn down his beloved daughter together with a seat at the council. A dispute had arisen. Rendrr had been forced to step in, banishing Alba from ever attending the Great Council, at least whilst Toryn was still in charge.

Alba was rightly nervous about the reception he would receive in Toryn's fort. In fact, just getting through the outer gates would be an achievement. The Great Council was held in one of the largest hill forts in the Cornovii territory. It sat atop a hill protected on all sides by steep banks and ditches, which gave a view for miles out. On a clear day, the mountains of the Celtic west were visible.

A single track led up to the main gates of the fort, sturdy wooden palisades flanking them from either side, a perfect killing ground for the unwary.

A voice bellowed out to them as they approached.

'Identify yourselves and state your business.'

'I am Alba, this is Argyll, sent by Chieftain Rendrr to seek audience with Chief Elder Toryn of a matter of great import'

Silence followed, punctuated only by the call of crows who had been disturbed from their resting place atop the fortified palisade.

'It seems you are still fondly remembered here,' Argyll commented.

'The guards have probably been told that I am a person of disrepute and not to allow entry. I suspect the only reason they are hesitating is because of Doube's murder. Toryn would have been expecting someone to turn up.'

'I doubt he would have thought it would be you

though!'

Alba remained straight faced. 'This will test Toryn. At stake is his personal enmity against me versus his loyalty to tribe and council. He will be unhappy to be in such a position, but, ultimately, I suspect he will grant us an audience.'

'Well, let's just hope he doesn't tell them to send us packing with a spear between our shoulders.'

'Regardless of what he'd like to do to me, to restore his daughter's so-called honour, he knows any attack on us would put him at odds with Rendrr. Our killing would create conflict both within our own tribe and that of the council. Rendrr would be forced to act against him.'

Further musings were cut short as the sound of the gates being drawn open cut through the silence.

'It seems you guessed right.'

'Better prepare yourself for a difficult reception,' Alba replied. 'Let me do the talking and do not interfere whatever the provocation or insult.'

Argyll went to protest but Alba silenced him with a hand in the air.

'My friend, he will fight me with words, not blade. I can defend myself quite adequately.'

'Don't underestimate him, Alba. Insult scars deep the skin of honour.'

They made their way through the open gate. Immediately, they were flanked by two warriors either side, one in front and another behind.

'They're not taking any chances are they?' Argyll observed.

'Toryn's just making a point.'

They emerged into the courtyard and were buffeted along by their escort toward a long bench outside a makeshift wooden hut. A huge barrel of a man emerged, dripping ale from a thick greasy beard which had more hair than what remained on his scalp. It gave the impression that there was no neck between head and torso.

He stomped over to them, belched gutturally, before wiping his mouth with a thick stump of an arm. Satisfied he had their attention, he paraded in front of them looking both men up and down in a play of deliberate exaggeration.

'Place all your weapons on the table,' he boomed.

'We prefer to keep them,' Argyll retorted.

Alba sighed, recognising that Argyll was giving the giant exactly what he wanted. He placed a hand on Argyll's arm and replied for them both. 'As you wish,' he said before Argyll could make things worse.

'It is as I wish. I am glad you get that.'

Argyll went to protest, but Alba's look was firm. Carefully, he placed his sword and dagger lightly on the table. Argyll threw his down loudly. In response, Giant hmphed and blew out disappointed.

'A warrior should never give his arms up so easily. Pair of wimps are you? Or have you been out in the wilds so long that you have gone soft?'

Getting no response, he tried act two of his routine.

'Looking at the pair of you, I wonder if you

no longer look to a woman's skirts for your fun, eh? Maybe you prefer each other's cock for your entertainment?'

He waited, hoping for the expected response. Obviously, this speech was well practiced.

Alba laughed, clapping Argyll on the back hard. His friend took the hint and joined in.

'You are funny my friend,' Alba laughed. 'However, our business is urgent.'

The mass of hair about the giant's mouth twitched, but Alba cut him off before what passed as a brain had formed words in response.

'I am sure that Chief Elder Toryn will be appreciative that we were not delayed on our entry when he hears of the *supremely* important news we bear for his witness.'

Their tormentor relented, the prospect of gratitude from his master something that he drooled over as much as the stale ale that had dried to his beard.

What a two-dimensional brute, Alba thought, knowing that under normal circumstances, Argyll would have knocked this hairy brute to the ground minus several of his front teeth.

In response, Giant shot a huge projectile of phlegm high into the sky in contempt. He motioned to one of the warriors that was in their escort. 'Take them up to the chief elder. He can deal with them, although,' he nodded in Alba's direction, 'I wouldn't like to be in this one's shoes when he lays eyes on him.'

The guard nodded, motioning to his men to reform the escort. Alba and Argyll proceeded in silence till they were outside the chief elder's roundhouse.

'Wait here,' the guard commanded before disappearing inside.

Argyll spoke very calmly, his gaze no longer seeing the world in front of him, but that which he was conjuring in his mind.

'Alba . . .'

'I know.'

'You really don't. I want to kill that slobbering fuckwit with a very blunt knife so far up his greasy, lice ridden arse till I get to his guts, whereupon I will curl my blade around each foul serpent that inhabits his belly and then I will pull them out, wrap them round his neck till his tongue sticks out.'

'Enough Argyll, the guard returns. Forget that excuse of a man; we have a more important audience. Toryn might be a pompous bastard, but we need to get his take on the council meeting.'

They did not have to wait long. Alba already knew Toryn was going to see them, correctly guessing that they wouldn't be inside the fort at all, if not. He would have to ready himself for the verbal tirade that was surely coming.

The guard motioned them to enter and they stepped inside.

'You've got a fucking nerve!' boomed Toryn's voice before Alba had crossed the threshold.

Bringing his entire body into the interior of what was the largest roundhouse in the fort, he forced himself into a passive smile and bowed his head in acknowledgement.

'Greetings Chief Elder Toryn,' he answered calmly.

'Don't you *greetings me* you arrogant bastard!' Toryn flushed. 'How you've got the audacity to turn up at my court must be a measure of the audacious little shit you are.'

This was going well, Alba thought, inwardly smiling at how many insults Toryn could level at him in one sentence. Best he let him have his blow out first, Alba reasoned.

'My daughter has a slur on her good name thanks to you,' Toryn continued. 'And I'll have you know that warriors from many tribes are falling over themselves to take her hand. But she wasn't good enough for you, was she?'

More like warriors were falling over themselves to escape Leah's claws, Alba thought grimly.

Toryn seemed to read his mind, jumping out of his chair, purple faced, rage coursing through his veins like an angry serpent.

'No! Alba, self-righteous, full of himself, fucking arsehole Alba thought he was above the hand of a daughter of the chief elder of the Great Council.'

'I assure you Toryn that I meant no offense to you or your daughter.'

Toryn's rage was threatening to overwhelm him and Alba knew that people do not act rationally when in a rage.

'I should have your fucking head rammed onto a pole at the gatehouse for this you conceited little cunt!'

'I repeat that I meant no slur on your good name or that of your daughter's. Leah is a beautiful, honourable woman who would make any man a good wife and child bearer.'

'But not you, eh?' Toryn replied more evenly.

'Whilst I was honoured with the proposal, I was already betrothed to another,' Alba replied. 'To break that betrothal would have been an insult and a slur on my honour as well as that of my betrothed. I am sure you can understand that, Toryn?'

'I understand that you do not appreciate honour when it is bestowed on you. Leah is my only child, born of a mother who she never knew. She is my only link to her.'

Toryn briefly was somewhere in his memories. For a man such as he, it was a strange moment for an emotion other than anger to show.

'I didn't know Leah was born of another,' Alba replied modestly. 'I thought she was . . .'

'Cor's child?' Toryn interrupted. 'Fuck Alba, Cor is half my age and not old enough to have borne a child of Leah's years.'

'Must make you quite the man having a woman so young!' Argyll jibed.

Alba expected Toryn to explode but instead he just laughed. 'Some of us have the libido of a titan Argyll. Or are you jealous perhaps? Maybe you like older women who don't mind when you run dry, when the mind is strong but the cock is weak eh!'

Argyll flushed with anger, pushing out of Alba's restraint. Toryn bellowed with laughter, teasing him further.

'Yes, come on man. Do you take such insult? Will you not challenge me?'

Alba rolled his eyes. Argyll was giving Toryn exactly what he wanted. Argyll was strong of heart and body but no match for a ruffian such as Toryn. The only good that would come out of their visit would be a cracked skull for Argyll or worse.

The two men were almost together. Alba sprang forward, grabbing the first thing that came to hand, Toryn's staff. He thrust the staff between them just as they were about to collide.

'Enough of this!' he bellowed. 'Argyll, you will desist and return to my side. Toryn, this is getting us nowhere. I need your help, not your fists. Rendrr needs your help!'

Both men paused, two flushed faces braced for combat. Neither wanted to be seen to back down. Alba tried again. 'Come, we are not the enemy in this situation. Let us forgo insult and past misdemeanours. Let us work together, as allies. To work against each other only gives our common enemy victory.'

The last line hit home. Both men relaxed slightly.

Toryn spoke first. Argyll still glared.

'Know this Alba. You are still a cunt and a fucking insult to my eyes, but Rendrr thinks you have worth. That is the only reason you are here.'

His eyes flicked briefly to Argyll, disappointed not to have given him a beating. It was then that Alba suddenly realised that Toryn had integrity. The insult to his daughter was truly felt and not just for appearances sake.

He had taken it to heart as a Father.

'Now get on with it. I can guess what you've come for so ask your questions.'

Careful to avoid any delay which might give Toryn or Argyll cause to face off again, Alba began the interview. Toryn would tire easily, given their history, so he would need to be swift.

'At the Great Council meeting, did you notice anything odd or strange?'

'Well, that depends on your perspective of the people there doesn't it.'

'We're wasting our time,' cut in Argyll, annoyed at Toryn's sarcasm. Toryn glared a challenge. Alba hastily fired off a riposte.

'Was there any friction or dispute?'

'All of the representatives tend to be vocal. There are always vested interests at play. Secret agreements tend to be made before the council meets. Usually, it is obvious if one elder or chieftain is working with another. It is usually who does not speak that indicates collusion.'

'So, there was something?'

Toryn blew out restlessly. 'Fallouts are inevitable between delegates.'

'Did this involve Doube?' Alba interjected.

'Yes, but . . .'

'Did things get heated?'

'There was a discussion about what should be done about the Red. Our own and other tribes have reported increased patrols pushing into our lands. Rigari, of the Corieltauvi, was the one who raised the issue for debate.'

'What happened?'

'Some hate the Red whilst others see them as an opportunity.'

'What do you think?' Argyll interrupted, his tone dripping with sarcasm.

Alba frowned while Toryn flushed red with anger.

'I think your sidekick should keep his fucking mouth shut, is what I think!'

Argyll coloured with rage. 'You arrogant bastard!'

'Argyll!' Alba snapped.

Toryn sprung to his feet, relishing the prospect of cracking skull or breaking limb.

Argyll, back off!' Alba commanded.

With great effort, Argyll took a half step back..

Toryn, disappointed, sat back down. 'You would do well to remember that you are in my roundhouse and my fort,' he fumed. 'One more outburst like that and I will have the guards take you outside, separate you from that wizened piece of gristle hanging beneath your legs, and shove it down your fucking throat!'

Alba was clenching Argyll's arm so tight that he would have a bruise for weeks. Only when he sensed the tension subside did he relax his grip.

'Let's just calm down shall we,' Alba spoke evenly.

'Remember that one of our own has been brutally murdered. So, unless you suspect each other, which I doubt either of you could make a plausible argument for, then let us get on. You were saying Toryn?'

Toryn hesitated for several seconds before answering. Alba knew this was all for effect. No doubt a trick he had learned when chairing the council meetings. Though he could be an arse, Toryn clearly knew his craft.

'I was saying that one of the elders had an argument with Doube and yes, before you ask, it did nearly come to violence. I had to intervene and calm the chamber down.'

'Who was the elder he was arguing with?'

'Tadc, the representative of the Dobunni. Doube had been telling the chamber that he thought the Red's increasing presence was a threat not only to our land but to our whole way of life.'

'And Tadc disagreed?'

'Violently.'

'Blows were exchanged?'

'No. I came between them before that.'

'It was that serious?'

'Tadc took insult at Doube's opinion.'

'How did the rest of the chamber react?'

'There was uproar, briefly. I was forced to re-establish order.'

A smile flicked briefly over Alba's features as he imagined Toryn throwing himself into the fray.

'Did anyone else make any threat towards

Doube?'

'None that I was aware of.'

Alba considered for a moment. There seemed only one person who had shown any animosity towards Doube that night. Was it that simple? Had Tadc been so offended that he had seen off his rival?

'There was one other thing,' Toryn added suddenly.

'Yes?'

'Remember, I said that often it is who does not speak that shouts the loudest?'

'And?'

'Well, usually when there is such a clear dispute, the other representatives will take sides or at least shout for their man. Allegiances are decided quickly in disputes. Sometimes on the fly, and sometimes pre-agreed beforehand. I was clear on everyone's intent except for Artek.'

'The Brigantes chieftain?'

'Yes.'

'Did he not get involved when the floor was invaded?'

'No. In fact, I don't remember him saying anything at all.'

'You suspect his silence had already been bought?'

'Who knows,' Toryn shrugged. 'That's for you to find out isn't it.'

'Was there anyone else who acted oddly that night?'

In answer, Toryn heaved himself up, feet braced

apart, inviting confrontation.

'That is all I recall. I have given you more courtesy than you ever showed me. Tell Rendrr I will not tolerate your presence here again. Now get out!'

They made their way to the entrance of the great roundhouse. His back to them, Toryn had already dismissed their presence as if they had already left. At the threshold, Alba decided to push his luck one last time.

'Just one last thing Toryn. You never said where you stand on this question of the Red?'

There was a long pause before the answer came. 'No, Alba, I did not say. That is my business. Now fuck off!'

Flanked by their escort they were marched out of the fort until clear of the main gate. Once outside, a leather bag containing their weapons was thrown unceremoniously from the palisades.

'Bastards!' yelled back Argyll, following up with several explicit gestures.

Alba was about to yell at Argyll when he noticed an arrow suddenly appear in the ground before him. More shafts germinated, creeping closer to where they stood. He grabbed the bag, shoving Argyll ahead as they sprinted to safety. Behind them, an alleyway of arrows marked their flight.

They took their breath once the thud of penetrated earth had ceased. Alba looked across at his friend. 'Argyll, insults are best thrown when out of range of archers.'

'They'd have done it anyway. That bearded arse licker probably gave the command.'

'Nonetheless, tracking down Doube's killer will be a lot harder if you have an arrow poking out of your own arse. Guards get bored and you gave them sport. That was foolish.'

'I don't like being treated like scum. One day I'll be back to give some sport, as you call it, to that fat, drunken bastard that took our weapons away.'

Despite himself, Alba grinned. 'I'd like to see that!'

They both laughed together, conjuring up the image in their minds. The tension of the last couple of hours evaporated as their guffaws filled the air.

'So, what do you think about Toryn?' Argyll asked once they had exhausted their humour.

'I think that we have a mystery here. Toryn clearly felt that there was an undercurrent of intrigue at the meeting.'

'You think there was a plot? A plan to kill Doube from the outset?'

'You heard what Toryn said. He expects emotions to run high when the council meets. He is used to that, but he also said that not everyone was as open in their opinion as Tadc was. I find that suggestive.'

'Nonetheless Alba, surely our prime suspect has to be Tadc. Afterall, Toryn said he had to intervene to prevent a bust up?'

'Maybe,' Alba mused. 'I'm interested though in what Toryn said about those who didn't speak. Artek was a chieftain. What was he thinking during this spat? And why did he not get involved when the shouting started. Then there's Rigari, the Corieltauvi chieftain. His people are already threatened by the Red. Toryn did not mention him again, even though it was he who had introduced the debate.'

'And Toryn?' Argyll added. 'He has enough anger in him to take to murder. What is more, he did not answer when you asked him for his own position on the Red. Surely that makes him a suspect?'

'All are suspects until we can throw some light on this affair. My gut tells me Toryn is not involved, despite his abhorrence of me. Yet, his position as chief elder of the Great Council would give him a perfect position to pursue a conspiracy. I would be surprised if he was sympathetic to the Red, but who knows. Every man has his price plus it is not always gold that buys allegiance.'

'The mistress?'

'A beautiful young thing like Cor may have been payment for services rendered. She is half his age after all. A girl like that usually wants for a strong, youthful warrior.'

'But you think she settled for power instead?'

'It is just a thought, Argyll. I may be wrong. Matters of the heart are seldom simple. She may simply prefer the older man.'

'She's a bloody fool then!' Argyll laughed, seeing an image of Toryn ploughing Cor and wondering how it could ever be something a woman would want. He shook his head to banish the thought.

'There is some other darkness at work here,' Alba continued. 'As yet we do not see the whole picture, but I feel there is a sense to this whole business which I do not like.'

'You think there is something else behind Doube's murder?'

'It is hard to put my finger on it. Despite this being about a murder, it does not *feel* right. I sense layers; people behind people, energy that hides in the shadows. I do not think this is a one-dimensional killing, Argyll. Something manipulates, shapes and organises in an attempt to control the field. At present we do not see but it is there; I feel its presence.'

'Where do we go from here?'

'First, let us put some proper distance from Toryn's fort. I would not trust that he wouldn't send out a few of his men to give us a bloody nose or worse if we are anywhere near here by sundown.'

CHAPTER IV

The night was dark and very still. Beatha was in front of him, holding his hand, guiding him inside the roundhouse.
Her roundhouse.
'I have missed you sorely, Alba.'
'And I you, Beatha.'
'Come now, warm yourself by my fire.'
A vibrant flame burned in a shallow pit within the centre of the roundhouse. The heat was intense, almost uncomfortable.
Strange there was no smoke accompanying such a hot hearth.
Releasing his hand, Beatha turned to face him, only a couple of paces from the flames. She seemed unconcerned about the heat even though Alba was already beginning to perspire.
Odd that there were no other members of her family present.
'I sent everyone out.'
She must have guessed his thoughts. 'I told them

that I need medicinal herbs for my healing salves.'

'It is late for gathering plants.'

'Does it matter?' Beatha replied. 'You are here and they are not.'

It was true that Beatha gathered many plants and herbs for her healing practice. Gathering plants by torchlight though would surely be a challenge. Some of her relatives were well into their fortieth season.

Beatha usually gathered ingredients herself.

His thoughts were interrupted as he felt her hand slip around his waist, drawing him close. Even beneath her furs he could feel the heat of her body. He had been away from her for a long time and he felt his body respond to the press and warmth of her own. A familiar feeling stirred in his loins.

She sensed the fire within, drawing him closer with long, deep kisses as her tongue explored his mouth, coiling itself around his own. His concern for her family melted away with the intensity of her passion.

Her hand guided his own beneath the folds of her furs till he reached the furnace between her thighs. He became delirious with desire. All he could think of was having her. The lust between his loins was overwhelming and he lost himself to it.

She threw off her remaining clothes, pulling him down to her. The flicker of the flames danced in her eyes. A different flicker danced at the back of his mind, albeit briefly.

Something different, out of place.

Her hand was between his own thighs now, caressing his cock with a frantic vigour.

What was it he was just thinking?

She seemed to sense his distraction and grabbed his hair roughly, moving his head between her breasts. Whatever he had been thinking was lost as her nipples found their way into his mouth. She laughed with delight, a strange laugh he had not heard before.

He barely noticed when something hot and sticky trickled down his back. Their love making had assumed a delirium of passion while she kept urging him to plough her deeper. He had never known Beatha be so elemental or possessed of such an urgency to mate.

The trickle off his back splashed onto the floor beside him. Distracted, he looked down and realised with horror it was blood.

His mind suddenly came back to him and with it, pain. Stunned, he realised her nails were dug inside of his flesh, gouging out deep channels through which his blood was draining out.

He recoiled violently. Beatha tried to pull him back inside her but he was aware now. He blinked, incredulous that he had not realised earlier for the illusion had been almost perfect.

Beatha or whatever it was, let out a piercing scream that almost made him lose consciousness. He resisted with all his might, forcing his mind to fight. In response, she moved away from him, toward the fire, not stopping until her naked form was within the flames.

Horrified, he watched as her skin became liquid, melting away from her bones. Her face, the features he knew so well, dripped off her skull pooling into a dark puddle by the fire. The flames licked at the liquid, drawing sustenance from the gore.

A vile laugher echoed repeatedly and horribly all around him. He jumped back against the wall of the roundhouse, distancing himself from the flames which seemed possessed of an intent. The fire followed as long purple shards of flame attempted too impale him.

Why had he not noticed the colour of the flames before?

There was no longer any Beatha, for that which had assumed her form was now entirely consumed within the fire before him. Avoiding it was proving difficult in such a confined space and he had to quash his own panic at being trapped. He was also acutely aware that his strength was being sapped as the blood flowed freely from the wounds in his back. Horrified he realised it was his core energy that was being drained. The construction of the roundhouse was a trap, one which not only prevented escape but allowed this creature to somehow draw off his lifeforce.

His time was very limited and, if he was to escape, then it would need to be soon. Meanwhile, the creature was increasing its efforts to stab him, screaming with delight each time he was forced to avoid the fiery lances that shot out with alarming frequency.

Quickly, he raised his mental barriers to prevent this thing from pulling anything else out from his mind. It seemed to sense the change, becoming more urgent in its attempt to impale him. There was only a certain number of places he could move within the roundhouse. Maybe he could get out of the entrance, at least outside he could manoeuvre.

The creature laughed, watching his eyes search for the way out. There was none. The entrance through which he had come had disappeared.

He was in a roundhouse with no exit. Trapped!

He would have to deal with the creature where he was.

But he needed a few seconds; seconds which this constant evading daggers of flame were impossible to gain.

'I know you!' he shouted suddenly.

It was all he could think of to say. The one thing that may give him those precious seconds. The creature paused, unsure what he had meant. Alba had rightly gambled that implying he knew its identity would throw it off balance.

That was all he needed. Focusing his mind on the elemental earth force below his feet he drew up energy into his own, feeling the power increase inside him. Too late, the creature realised what he was doing. Alba threw his hands forward, directing the energy out of his palms so that it completely consumed the aberration. There was a sickening scream as the creature, the roundhouse, the entire illusion shattered about him. Shards of the broken image swirled about him and for one instant he saw a face. A face contorted with rage at having been beaten. Soulless eyes without conscience glared back.

Then it was gone, replaced by a different face.

'Alba!'

He awoke to see Argyll bent over him, shaking him violently.

He held his hand up weakly. 'I'm alright now Argyll.'

'But you're bleeding badly!' Argyll answered, still holding him tightly by the shoulders. Alba looked down to see that the ground was soaked where the wounds from his back had discharged his life fluid.

He smiled weakly. 'I will need you to patch me up.'

Argyll nodded, reaching over to a cloth bag where he pulled out an array of dried clothing and plant leaves. Emergency salves and ointments which Alba had packed for their journey.

Supplies Alba had taken from Beatha's roundhouse.

Argyll cleaned Alba's back with water before picking out a small clay pot. The ingredients of this particular salve came from the Elder. *Lady Elder* Beatha called it. From experience, he knew this concoction, made from the leaves, would keep the wound free of infection.

'This will hurt a lot.'

'I know, but the blood must be stemmed else we

will be easier to track.'

'I doubt anyone would pick up our trail, not unless they followed us from the outset. Even then, we are careful and remove all traces of our encampments, as we always do.'

'I talk not just of the removal of the blood fluid itself. Even on the physical plane, there will be an imprint of my energy. Given the nature of the attack I have been subjected to, it is imperative that I do all I can to cloak it.'

'What was it that attacked you?'

'An aberration, sent to kill me.'

'How could it attack out here, in the middle of nowhere, when you were asleep?' Argyll replied incredulous.

'That, my friend, is what worries me.'

Alba winced as Argyll applied the ointment, smearing the salve over the open wounds. A particularly deep gash elicited a sharp gasp as tree and body fluid combined.

'Almost done,' Argyll encouraged. 'What sort of aberration do you mean?'

'An elemental creature, created from fire and spite, conjured by someone with deep knowledge of the ancient arts. One who is not afraid to sacrifice their own spirit.'

'Sacrifice their spirit?'

'Dark magick demands payment. A sorcerer using such energy sacrifices part of themselves.'

Argyll finished the dressing. 'Your wounds are real Alba, as though a wild animal has clawed at your back. Yet, the attack came at you in the dreamworld. I did not know such magick existed.'

'With sufficient ability, anything is possible with the aid of magick. However, this is the first time that I have ever experienced its use.'

'Did you see the sorcerer?'

'I only saw the elemental which they conjured. There was a face, briefly, when it was destroyed, but all I had time to register was the anger at being defeated. It was clever of them to reach into my mind and retrieve Beatha's image.'

'They picked someone you trusted.'

'The trap was baited with someone I was emotionally tied to. It is harder to see the deception when there is an emotional bond, particularly one of love.'

'But who could have sent it,' Argyll persisted. 'And why you?'

'I suspect old friend, that our investigation into Doube's murder has caused concern.'

'Should we warn Beatha or the others?'

Alba shook his head. 'I don't believe Beatha or anybody else is immediately at risk. They fished her image out of my mind so we carry on as we intended for now. Our adversary has made his first move. We have been fortunate not only to survive it but to gain knowledge of what they possess.'

'A sorcerer?'

'We have learned that our enemy is strong enough and wealthy enough to procure such resources.'

'Do you know any that possess those skills Alba? Do the other tribes have someone equal to yourself in the ancient arts?'

'I am not aware of any. It is likely that we would have heard of anyone who possessed the ability. His or her reputation would have preceded them. I believe we may be dealing with an outside entity, one who we have not come across before.'

They both fell silent. The implications that a practitioner of the ancient arts in the employ of another group was disturbing.

'Do you think this leads back to the Red?' Argyll enquired. 'We already suspect their involvement in Doube's murder.'

'There is intrigue here, for sure' Alba replied. 'The tendrils of this plot go deep. If we have collusion between one or more of the tribes with the Red, and if the Red have a sorcerer at their disposal, then that represents a significant shift in the scale of the threat.'

He continued to look perturbed.

'Something else?' Argyll prompted.

'A sorcerer with that level of capability must be hard to find even amongst the empire of the Red. I am surprised that they would even countenance such a thing when they have the physical manpower of their imperial army at their disposal.'

'You mean, why not simply send out a patrol to hunt us down?'

'It would take longer but would draw no more resource than the Red already possess. Unless . . .'

'What?'

'Whenever you use any magick, no matter how small, it leaves an imprint, an impression. Not just where it is used, the physical area, but within the energy signature of the one who casts it. A sorcerer may have detected that subtle energy, whether from searching on the Astral layer or even from a place I had visited. I would be seen as a greater threat in that case.'

They fell into silence, absorbing the ramifications.

'Where do we go from here?' Argyll asked eventually.

'We stick with our plan to interview Tadc. We must ride south.'

'That is quite a journey Alba. The territory of the Dobunni is at least five days ride from here. We will need to restock our supplies and change the horses.'

'We will return home first where we can also update Rendrr on our progress.'

'Will you tell him about the attack on you or make mention of the sorcerer?'

Alba shook his head. 'Not for now. I think it best we keep our knowledge of that to ourselves.'

CHAPTER V

The journey south to Dobunni territory had not been easy. Despite it being the season where the great sun was at its highest, they had been beset by foul weather. Even the horses, hardy souls bought from trade with the western tribes, were hanging their heads with each plodding step through the mud. Their manes had the appearance of being adorned with liquid necklaces as rivulets of water dripped and reformed from the tip of each hair.

Whilst Argyll thought it merely unfortunate, Alba upheld a definite air of suspicion.

'It might be natural. However, I find it interesting that the weather, which has been fine for weeks, choses only now to become wild.'

It was true, that their constant halting to shelter from the worst of the weather had caused them significant delay. Yet, Argyll thought his friend was being over cautious.

'I don't see how this sorcerer could anticipate when and where we would be travelling.'

'Don't you Argyll? Well, remember they got to me in my sleep. They reached out onto the astral level to mount a deliberate attack. If they have the capability to do that, then they may be able to track us on the material plane.'

Since the sorcerer's attack, Alba had been on edge, sensing threat, anticipating further assaults, magickal or otherwise. Each night he would trace a boundary of sand in a wide circle around their encampment. Once marked, he walked the periphery with his staff threefold.

Protecting their space, he told Argyll.

'They could just have spies tailing us,' Argyll persisted. 'The simplest explanation is often the one that gets overlooked Alba. You know this well. Do not let this sorcerer consume you.'

Stating the obvious seemed to hit home.

'They might well be tracking us. I am sorry my friend. I have been so consumed by their magickal ability that I have forgotten the obvious.' He clapped Argyll on the back. 'It is difficult sometimes to clear one's mind when darkness threatens. Thank you Argyll. Let us be on our guard for the obvious as well as the hidden.'

Argyll thought he had made progress but as Alba turned back he overheard a whispered, 'But I must maintain my psychic barriers, all the same.'

He pulled his furs closer around his torso. Like Alba, he was soaked through. The last time he had been dry was on their return home. They had not even had time to wash or take food before the summons had come from Rendrr.

Rendrr had listened with interest when they recounted their meeting with Toryn. Alba kept strictly to the substance of the meeting. Argyll added a few comments of his own, mainly expletives about what he thought of Toryn.

When they had finished recounting their tale, Rendrr spoke.

'You suspect Tadc, then?'

'I believe we should start with him,' Alba replied. 'Assuming Toryn has relayed the events of that night accurately, then Tadc was the one most strongly opposed to Doube.'

Rendrr nodded. 'It certainly makes sense to speak with Chieftain Tadc. His sympathies and that of the Dobunni as a whole are inclined to lean towards greater integration with the Romans. My peers have suspected that for a while. Just because he was vociferous in his argument to Doube does not necessarily make him the killer though.'

'No, it does not and there were others who according to Toryn behaved oddly. If Tadc is innocent, then we can ask him about those as well.'

'Very well, then I support your plan.'

'Thankyou. We will rest for a couple of nights then proceed south.'

'No!'

Startled, both warriors stared back at Rendrr.

'It is vital that you seek out Tadc immediately.'

'It is several days ride to the south!' Argyll objected. 'We need rest, fresh horses and supplies before we can undertake such a journey.'

'You shall have them, but you will leave at dawn tomorrow. I will ensure all you need is prepared and ready for you by the morning.'

'Why the urgency Rendrr?' Alba asked. 'An extra day will not alter the situation unless you are aware of other factors that may affect our investigation?'

Alba knew he was pushing it. You did not just force your chieftain to justify their actions. Yet, he could not understand why Rendrr was so insistent for their early departure.

'Alba, you are one of my elite warriors who also has my trust. Is it too much that I ask you to trust your chieftain in return?'

A succinctly given challenge. Rendrr could be a good politician when he needed to be.

'Of course not,' Alba replied.

'Good. I am glad our trust in each other is reaffirmed. Besides, my concern for this business to be concluded quickly is prompted by reports of skirmishes on our eastern borders.'

'From the Corieltauvi?'

'It would seem so.'

'That would be out of character. We have not had issue with them before.'

'The facts are somewhat vague,' argued Rendrr. 'However, for now, I prefer to be careful. I do not want dispute on two sides, so deal with this issue of Doube's murder quickly.'

They had been dismissed soon after. Alba had missed Beatha who was out on one of her foraging trips. So it was, that on the eighth day they finally crossed into the territory of the Dobunni.

'We must be careful from now on,' Alba warned. 'The Red have many more soldiers in these parts. Not only that, but the natives may be more inclined to report our presence to one of their patrols.'

'You think it's that bad down here?'

'If Tadc's view were anything to go on, then we should be cautious. Men can be bought by loyalty to cause, as well as coin.'

They saw four patrols during the last leg of their journey. Each one appeared to be quartering the land following a pre-determined search pattern.

'Do you think they are searching for us?' Argyll asked during one time they had to hurriedly conceal themselves. The Romans were close enough to hear their commander shouting orders. The two warriors watched silently, laid flat against a slight ridge, the only cover in an otherwise featureless landscape. Their horses, trained from an early age, lay on their side. Man and beast lay still, offering a minimal profile to any Roman eyes which may look their way.

'They are scouting for something,' Alba replied once the danger had passed. 'Maybe it is us. That would concern me if so. We do not want to meet with an untimely *accident* out here in the wilderness.'

Avoiding the Romans had forced them to alter their route. That night, they camped on the side of a steep cliff beneath a large rocky overhang that afforded them protection from the weather. Deep below, a river burbled its way to the coast, thrashing through a barrage of boulders laid down by the steep, crumbling valley sides which framed it. Across the divide, the terrain was similar to their own, large rocky outcrops beneath craggy cliffs along the length of the valley.

Over the fire, Argyll had constructed a makeshift spit over which hung the carcass of a wild boar. There had been no shortage of the creatures on their journey and the only difficulty lay in isolating a single individual, rather than risk injury with an entire pack. Argyll was a skilled hunter, something which Alba was content to let him demonstrate each time they struck camp.

The light had dimmed into the violet of twilight as the oncoming night marched darkness ever closer. Soon they were illumined only by the whispering flames of the fire. Argyll cut up and shared the meat. The warmth and juiciness of the flesh was welcome and they began to fill their bellies. Alba shifted his gaze to the fires of creation that filled the night sky above. For a moment, he was back home, around another fire with Beatha. The unyielding rockface behind him was replaced by the comforting warmth of her belly as he lay his head upon her, sensing the rise and fall of her lungs.

The sanctuary began to waiver, as though the image were being pulled from his vision. His impulse was to reestablish the connection but the link had dissolved. Each time he attempted to get it back, there came a sharp tugging sensation which brought him closer to his mortal awareness. Suddenly, it dawned that it was his other esoteric senses that were trying to get his attention. The realisation wrenched him back to the material world with a thump. The hard rock face pushed at his shoulders, prodding him to action, but why? What had brought him back so insistently?

Suddenly, he was bolt upright, alert, sensing a change. There was no sound or disturbance but the air had stilled, silent in anticipation.

Without warning he shoved Argyll off his seat sending him sprawling onto the chalk floor.

'Alba, what the . . .'

A whoosh like a kiss on the wind flew past them.

Alba threw himself down. Loose shale skittered away as his body crashed to the floor whilst his open mouth became host to a torrent of grit. His cheek stung where a silent assassin of wood and iron had sliced the skin open.

Impacts resounded on the rockface where they had sat moments earlier.

'Stay down!' Alba shouted.

'What are they?' cried Argyll

'Arrows. Kill the fire quickly!'

Desperately, Argyll threw dirt, stones and even the discarded boar skin at the flames to quell the light. Projectiles sliced the air above them including one which hit the spit, causing it to recoil and bounce off its V shaped retainers. It clattered off to Argyll's side, the head of the boar coming to rest a hands width away from his own. The dead animal's eye sockets stared at him as he lay prone to the ground. An arrow, still with its white fletching, was embedded neatly in its forehead, killing it twice.

'Can you see anything?' Argyll shouted.

'Archers over the other side of the valley. We will have to move. If we stay here they can keep taking shots at us and whilst the distance is long, they may get lucky.'

Keeping low, they grabbed their things and scrambled out of their hideaway. With the loss of the fire, their attackers were shooting blind but several shafts flew dangerously close as they made their escape. The number of projectiles suggested a sizable force the other side of the gorge. Alba hoped that meant any patrols on their own side would be smaller and less frequent.

Finally, they clambered their way up to the rocky plateau above where they had left the horses. The ground here was devoid of vegetation, offering little cover for their flight. The sound of arrow impacts had receded, but they were faced with a dash across open ground partially illuminated by the multitude of suns that burned high above.

'We may still be visible to their archers once we strike off,' Alba warned as he mounted. "The starlight may give them a target so ride fast and swift.'

'Even in this light, it would take a master shot to hit us,' Argyll replied.

As if in answer, the sky above lit up with a multitude of shooting stars.

Except these were no stars.

'Shit! Those cunning bastards.'

'Let's go!' cried Alba.

More fire arrows streaked across the heavens, illuminating their escape. Loosed from distance, they dropped from a high angle peppering the ground with a line of blazing saplings. Desperately, the two warriors charged across the plateau, zig zagging their mounts through a hailstorm of death. Only when they were well out of range did they stop to catch their breath and rest the horses.

Alba realised they had been lucky. His ability to detect subtle energy change had given them a precious second to save themselves. He cursed himself for thinking they would be safe high up on the steep side of the gorge, protected above, below and what he mistakenly assumed from the side. It had not occurred to him that their enemy would attempt an attack from the other side at such distance. Once more, the enemy's resourcefulness had caught him off guard and his carelessness had nearly cost them.

They had no sleep that night, moving rapidly to throw off any pursuers, stopping only when Alba was sure they were safe. Their senses were stretched, constantly alert to signs of pursuit or the risk of running into another patrol.

'I have been careless Argyll. You even warned me that we could be followed. I was convinced an attack would come magickally rather than physically. That was arrogant and stupid of me.'

He rubbed his cheek, still weeping, where the fletching of the arrow had split open the skin.

'You are hurt?'

'A scratch. No more than I deserve.'

'At least we should be safe now. They would have to detour some distance to cross the gorge.'

'They would,' agreed Alba, 'but we cannot assume just one party is hunting us. We have just learned, firsthand, how resourceful our enemy is.'

Their flight had brought them across open heathland. The light of the stars shed just enough illumination for them to see ahead. A thin line of trees, formed in a wide semi-circle separated the heathland from what lay beyond. Alba was staring at it.

Instinctively Argyll crouched lower, hand on sword, anticipating danger. All he could see was the dark smudge of the trees contrasted against the night sky. Trees that could hide a patrol.

'What do you see?'

'An opportunity.'

'A working?'

'An illusion. I can use the energy of the trees to form a boundary, a barrier to those without the sacred sight. It should confuse their trackers and buy us time.'

'You think they are still following?'

'I think someone is very determined to arrest our progress.'

They crept forward, watchful for ambush, fearful of the shadows within the trees. The still of the night remained unbroken. For now, they were alone. Once within the boundary Alba threw his satchel down before mixing several herbs and powders into a small mortar. Satisfied with the result he held his hand over the mixture, repeating a long incantation using a language Argyll had heard before but had long since given up trying to comprehend.

'Are you ever going to tell me what that means?'

'It is meaningless to the uninitiated.'

'That helps.'

Alba cast a disdainful glance at Argyll. 'The language is determined by the focus of the sorcerer. The words form around the objective.'

'So, I could do it?'

'Focus and intent are not enough. The key ingredient is energy, a force that works sympathetically with the focus, the language and the environment it is cast out to. This is not a learned behaviour my friend. A sorcerer is usually someone who has the ability from birth; a person who intuitively feels the elemental forces around them and who can channel them to his or her will.'

'I'll stick to my sword then.'

'Probably best.'

The contents of the mortar began to emit a strange incandescence pulsing to a low crackling sound which gave the impression the bowl was about to explode. Alba nodded to Argyll to stay clear before proceeding to walk the treeline from right to left, scattering the mixture as he went. Finally, he walked back to his staff, held it aloft before planting it into the ground. A cloud of grey mist erupted from the dark earth, spreading out to the tree boundary, circling like a flock of crows. Alarmed, Argyll hunkered down lower, unsure whether Alba's magick would distinguish friend from foe. The grey mists swirled in increasingly wider and rapid circuits before dissipating suddenly into a thousand tiny fires, briefly flaring up before fading back to darkness.

Alba gathered his staff and returned to his friend.

'It is done.'

'Can we rest for a while?'

'No. The illusion will hold for several hours and hide our progress, but if they have a sorcerer with them then it could be dismantled. Even if they don't, then we have to assume there are other patrols looking for us.'

'At least we now know for certain that it is us they are searching for.'

'We do and we can see just how much effort they are willing to expend in our capture or death. Why though? I keep asking myself why all of this effort, Argyll?'

The question went unanswered, consumed by the vast emptiness of the cosmos above them.

CHAPTER VI

In the early morning mist of the following day, they entered through the gates of the Dobunni fort. The Dobunni held several hill forts in the area but they had headed to where Tadc was ensconced as chieftain. Argyll had been disappointed not to have spotted the ocean but they were too far east of the coast, although a day's ride would get them there.

On arrival, they had announced themselves to the sentries to find they were admitted without challenge. Tired, they steered over to the stables intending to make themselves known to Tadc once they had watered and bedded the horses.

'I thought we'd have more trouble gaining entry,' Argyll remarked as he led his horse to an empty pen.

'I'm surprised we didn't. Maybe we were wrong about these people.'

He turned to lead his own horse away when he heard Argyll exclaim.

'Alba!'

He whirled around, sword already in hand.

'Don't!' a voice rang out. Several spear points suddenly appeared at his throat. Argyll was already pinned against the stable fence.

'What is this?' declared Alba.

A man shoved his way to the front. If they expected it to be Tadc then they were disappointed. What came next was an even bigger surprise.

'You are under arrest for the murder of Chieftain Tadc. Drop your weapons now. I will only ask once.'

Alba nodded to Argyll. Two swords clattered to the ground. Immediately, they were shoved hard against the stable wall, searched and relieved of their daggers.

'Hoping to slip in quietly were we?' their captor queried.

'There is no quietly about it,' answered Alba. 'We announced ourselves at your gates with no intent to conceal our presence.'

The man seemed to take insult that his prisoner had remained calm. He walked up to Alba at the same time as bringing his knee hard into his crotch. It forced the wind out of him and it was all he could do to remain upright.

'I tell you what I think, shall I? I think that you thought you could sneak within our walls and murder a few more of us. That is what I think. But do you know what? Your devious little plan has been thwarted by me and my men. You will realise that you can't fuck with me so easily.'

He turned away, making out he had finished before bringing a fist into Alba's guts. This time

Alba did collapse to the floor. The man spat at Alba before aiming a kick that sent him sprawling backwards into the mud.

'Fucking northern scum!'

He motioned several of his men forward to grab hold of the two Cornovii warriors.

'Throw them in the pit and don't bother lowering the ladders. Chieftain Gruenval will interrogate them shortly.'

They were tussled towards an oblong pit covered by a lattice of interlocking tree boughs which were secured by iron rings pegged along each side. Once the covers were removed they were shoved forward. The drop was significant, roughly three men deep. Alba landed awkwardly, a sharp pain in his side catching as he breathed in. Feeling his ribs he was relieved to find no break, though they were obviously bruised. Argyll had fared no better with a wound on his forehead bleeding profusely where thick roots protruding from the walls had hooked and torn away the skin.

'What the fuck is going on Alba?'

'I don't know. I did not expect an over friendly welcome for sure, but this . . .'

'Tadc's dead!'

'So it would seem.'

'We came all this way for nothing!'

'No journey is ever wasted.'

'This one will be if we are left to rot in this pit,' Argyll replied grimly.

Alba looked around their prison. Simple but

effective. Even standing on each other's shoulders they would not be able to reach the lattice above. The only way out would be via rope or ladder and that would be dependent on their captors.

'I'm afraid we will not be going anywhere until our friends above desire it.'

'This is a disgrace,' Argyll spat. 'We are the representatives of the Cornovii but we are treated like common criminals. I'll have someone's head for this.'

'Steady Argyll. Shouting will not release us for there is much anger in this fort. The news of Tadc's death is both new and raw to them.'

'But Alba, we came here to talk to Tadc, not kill him.'

'We know that, but these people do not. We must use our heads, not our anger to recover freedom.'

'They should use their own heads if they think we'd walk into their fort after just killing their chieftain.'

'I suspect confusion and disbelief clouds their judgement.'

They both fell silent. Argyll fumed and thought only of demanding apology whilst Alba looked inward, turning over the reason for their arrest in his mind.

Tadc's killing had been unexpected.

If he were innocent, then had he been killed as a further part of the conspiracy? Yet, that seemed contrary to the views he had aired at the Great Council. Why kill a supporter of greater integration with the Red? Or, had he been killed to silence what he knew; did he know too much of the enemy's plans or had he threatened to expose them?

Too many questions with too many answers.

His thoughts were interrupted by movement above. The great lattice was removed and a ladder was lowered down.

'You will make your way up.'

'You can go fuck yourselves!' Argyll shouted back angrily.

'It may be best to save the insults till we are out of this hole,' Alba said dryly.

'But Alba, these bastards cannot be allowed to treats us like this.'

'If we are left here to rot then we will not fulfil our mission. Think about what has happened. Events are moving rapidly, even before we arrived here. We need to find out what relation Tadc's killing has to Doube's murder, for linked they must be. Our adversary has acted, once more with blood. Make no mistake my friend, we are in real danger. We must, therefore, temper our anger and help all parties see who the real enemy is; one that conceals themselves with deceit, misdirection and mistrust.'

Argyll acquiesced, settling for aiming his best, *I'm going to kill you face*, skyward.

'You should listen to your friend,' boomed the voice above, 'I was only told to bring you up. The manner in which you do so is up to you. It matters not to me whether you climb up alive or whether we skewer your arsehole on the end of a spear. Either way, you will do as instructed.'

As they climbed back onto normal ground their hands were roughly bound with tight leather straps. Argyll bristled with anger. Alba hardly noticed, his thoughts still wrestled with the sudden demise of Tadc and the speed events had proceeded.

Once more the unseen hand had acted.

They were jostled all the way up to another roundhouse escorted by a guard of six warriors. No sooner had they crossed the threshold than they were unceremoniously thrown down to the floor, landing almost on top of the fire that burned brightly in its heart.

Alba tried to get up but was immediately pushed back down to the ground.

'You will stay down in the dirt where you belong,' bellowed a voice.

'Scum!' yelled Argyll. 'Is this how you treat representatives of your fellow tribes?'

A spear cracked over his head and he sank to the ground, stunned. Alba moved to help him, but another spear quickly barred his way. He looked up in disgust. As his eyes focused, his gaze settled on three warriors sat together. The one in the middle watched him keenly. The other two seemed more intent on enjoying the entertainment of Argyll receiving a beating.

'What are your names?' demanded middleman.

'I am Alba and this is Argyll, both of the Cornovii.'

'If you are Cornovii then you are far from your own lands are you not?'

Before Alba could answer, the one on the left cut in.

'Gruenval, this is no coincidence. Surely their guilt is obvious given what we know?'

Gruenval, nodded in agreement. 'It would seem so. Well, what have you got to say for yourselves? Do you deny you came here to murder our chieftain? Why else would you be so far from your own territory?'

Three questions, all with an answer already clear in the minds of these three.

Alba attempted to stand but was immediately shoved back down. He hadn't noticed the guards behind them. The intimidation was thorough; bound, on their knees and accused of murder, their chances did not look good.

'If you will permit us to speak, then maybe we can clear up this misunderstanding.'

'Misunderstanding?' laughed Gruenval. 'You understate your predicament. You stand accused of a most heinous crime and one in which you were in the vicinity to have carried out. Added to that, you are a foreigner in these parts and your excuses run very thin.'

The one on the left cut in. 'Let us waste no more time with them Gruenval. Kill them now and let our enemies see how we deal with those who would murder our own.'

'Jovnah is right,' agreed the one on the right. He had remained silent up until now, but it seemed he had made up his mind over their involvement.

A warrior entered and handed Gruenval a leather satchel. Alba recognised it as his own.

'Ah,' Gruenval noted, tipping the contents onto the floor. Herbs, powders and other items were cast about the ground as if attesting to the guilt of their owner.

'You are a sorcerer?'

'Is that a question?'

'A sorcerer would have found it easier to kill. It is known your *type* have ways to deceive a man's mind. You would, no doubt, have found it simple to have weaved your illusion magick in order to disarm our chieftain.'

'I do not use magick to murder. Besides, we came to your gates of our own choice.'

'Bollocks did you!' shouted Jovnah. 'You were probably cornered by our patrols and felt you had no choice but to bluff your way out.'

'Bluff our way out?'

'Obviously. You saw that you could not escape and decided your only recourse was to enter our fort on the pretence of innocence.' He kicked the items on the floor sending Alba's equipment skittling off in all directions. 'No doubt you would have deceived us with your magick had we not deprived you of your freedom and your tools of the trade.'

They are convincing themselves with every second that passes, thought Alba wearily. Meanwhile, Argyll had pulled himself back up to a kneeling position having recovered his senses. The blow to his head had done nothing for his temper and he was casting around at the guards trying to decide which one had struck him. If Alba could not get them to listen then he feared both Argyll and himself would be gracing the halls of the underworld by nightfall. But how could he get through to them? The anger at the death of their chieftain was clouding their judgement and revenge favours a quick riposte before rationality has time to recover.

'My own tribe has suffered a recent loss,' he said, attempting to switch their sympathy. 'Doube, our chief elder was at the same meeting Tadc attended. He was murdered and gutted like a beast before he could get home. That is why we are here. We are sent by Chieftain Rendrr to investigate Doube's murder. Tadc was vocal in the debate in which Doube was a part. We came here to ask for his help and gain insight to the proceedings of the Great Council.'

'Lies!' shouted Jovnah. 'You insinuate our leader was involved in this man's killing. You bury yourselves deeper in your own mire Cornovii scum.' He walked over to Gruenval, addressing him direct. 'We have surely heard enough and now they attempt to avert their guilt by accusing our chieftain, the very man whose blood lies on their hands.'

'Doube is dead?' Gruenval asked.

'Yes,' answered Alba. 'He was killed on his journey back from the Great Council. A cowardly killing from behind. He was gutted like a wild animal and left to rot. Argyll and I discovered what was left of him in a stream.'

Having sensed Gruenval's demeanour change, Alba deliberately fed him the details of Doube's killing. For now, he omitted their suspicion of Roman involvement to avoid any accusation of shifting the blame. He would get to that later, should they still remain in the world of man.

'I knew Doube,' softened Gruenval. 'He believed in things I could not. Yet, he was a fair and honest man. His passing casts a shadow even down in these parts.'

'This is bollocks!' Jovnah stormed, rounding on Alba. '*You* killed Tadc and for all I know you probably killed Doube as well. Nubvaan, do you not agree? They must be put to death as our laws demand.'

Nubvaan shook his head slowly. 'It makes no sense that these men came down here to murder Tadc given their own chieftain despatched them on the back of one of their own being killed. Let Gruenval rule on it, Jovnah.'

'Are you a fucking sucker for any old shit that comes out of their mouth,' protested Jovnah. 'Never mind, I will do it myself.'

He drew his sword in one swift motion. Alba tensed, waiting for the blow that would end him. Instead, there was the clash of steel against steel as Jovnah's blade was stayed by Nubvaan.

'Fuck you Nubvaan!'

'You are out of control Jovnah. Stand down!'

Gruenval finally pulled himself from his thoughts. 'Jovnah, sit down!'

'But Gruenval, they are outsiders and murderers. They must be killed.'

'Outsiders yes,' spoke Gruenval, 'but murderers I think not.'

'This is an outrage!' declared Jovnah. 'They must be made example of.'

'You will stand down.'

'Would you allow them to walk free? You, as our new leader would pander to their lies?'

'Do you question my word or doubt my authority, Jovnah?' boomed Gruenval, his hand already tight around the hilt of his sword. The two men stood squared up against each other. For a moment, Alba thought they were actually going to fight.

Finally, Jovnah shrugged his shoulders. 'As you wish Gruenval. You *are* chieftain now.' He turned and left the roundhouse leaving the rest of them to release a collective breath of relief.

'He challenges you,' noted Nubvaan.

'I know,' replied Gruenval. 'Yet, I would not begin my time as chieftain by striking down my fellow tribesman due to a difference of opinion. I must hold myself to higher standards of leadership than those of simple pride.'

'I hope Jovnah sees it in the same way. What you say is leadership, he interprets as weakness and that can be dangerous.'

'I am aware of the dangers Nubvaan,' growled Gruenval. 'Should we turn against each other then we bring instability to our own and risk the status quo with the Romans. Whilst I will honour what our dead brother Tadc agreed with them, I will not see us consumed; not least as a result of our own infighting.'

Gruenval motioned to the guards to release Alba and Argyll.

'As you can see, feelings are running high in the wake of Tadc's killing. My position as Tadc's successor is but a day old and already my rule is in danger of the instability that comes with hate.' He rose to his feet wearily. 'It grows late and I must attend my wife. Nubvaan will arrange quarters and see that your weapons are returned to you. We will speak further in the morning.'

CHAPTER VII

They were woken early by one of Gruenval's guard.

'Chieftain Gruenval sends greetings and wishes you attend him.'

Wishes, thought Alba. The guard had spoken it as though he meant *commands*.

'Wake yourself Argyll. We have another audience with Gruenval.'

Argyll, still fatigued, groaned as the first rays of daylight struck his blood shot eyes.

'Getting up early seems to run in the blood of chieftains,' he grumbled.

'I am surprised by the early hour,' Alba replied, an unsettled feeling growing in his gut.

The guard waited outside whilst they got dressed. When they emerged, they were surprised to see a second guard stationed outside with the first.

'Seems our change in status from *villain* to *guest* is still not without suspicion,' Argyll remarked as their escort led them up to the chieftain's roundhouse.

'Gruenval's being careful. Despite his acceptance of our story he has to be seen to be cautious. He is newly ensconced here don't forget. His opponents will be watching for weakness.'

They were ushered inside the roundhouse whilst the two guards took up position either side of the door. Argyll glanced a concerned expression to Alba as they entered. As before, Gruenval was seated in the centre with Nubvaan on his right. Jovnah's seat was vacant.

'Welcome,' Gruenval opened. 'I trust you are rested?'

'Thank you, yes. Has something happened?' Alba enquired, sensing a change.

'Jovnah has vanished.'

'Vanished?

'He has not been seen since yesterday evening, since leaving our *interview.*'

'Could he not have just sought space to reconcile his thoughts?'

'Maybe, but Nubvaan has some additional information of which I was not previously aware. It has import on both Jovnah's disappearance and Tadc's killing.'

There was annoyance in Gruenval's words. Nubvaan looked awkward, though Alba was unsure whether this was to do with the information he possessed or the fact that his chieftain was frustrated at being kept in the dark.

Nubvaan left his seat, walking slowly before

them, deciding how best to frame his next words. Finally, he stopped, pulled himself up proudly and began his tale.

'I say this to you first, so that you all bear witness to my truth. I am a proud warrior of this tribe, loyal and willing to give my life for my chieftain and this community. I speak my truth rather than remain quiet, but I do not go against my chieftain; that I would never do.'

'But you know somebody who would or who did, perhaps?' Alba probed.

'To answer that, I have to relay what I know about Tadc.'

Gruenval made to interrupt.

'No!' Nubvaan barked. 'You must hear me out Gruenval.'

Alba could see Gruenval was irritated, but he was also getting the measure of this new chieftain of the Dobunni. Gruenval acquiesced, no doubt deciding that the information Nubvaan possessed was of greater value than taking offence.

This man has wisdom, Alba thought.

'Very well, continue.'

Nubvaan inclined his head, respectfully before continuing. 'You will recall the day when Tadc returned from the Great Council?'

'Yes,' answered Gruenval. 'He was agitated when he arrived.'

'Was he still angry over his encounter with Doube?' Alba asked.

'I do not think so. He never mentioned him or the

meeting. He appeared upset over something else.'

'You do not know what aggravated him, there was no clue?'

'None,' replied Gruenval.

'There was something,' Nubvaan cut in. 'I was hunting on the day Tadc returned. I had been out most of the day, but on my way back I saw him. He was not alone but in the company of Roman soldiers.'

Alba stiffened with interest.

'Hold on,' Gruenval interrupted. He turned to Alba and Argyll. 'We have a somewhat different relationship with the Romans down here than perhaps you do up north. We have, shall we say, an agreement that they leave us alone in return for certain rights.'

'Rights?' Alba queried.

'The Romans are not interested in outright conflict. That does not serve their purpose. They want resources; metals, minerals and raw materials that we have in abundance here.'

'I thought the Red were used to taking what they wanted,' Argyll said cynically.

'You get something back as recompense perhaps?' suggested Alba.

Gruenval nodded. 'Mainly trade, security, an undertaking not to accost our people.'

'How is that working out for you?'

'It is not perfect but the peace has held. We do not force our people to live the traditional ways of the past. They are free to leave if they so wish.

What we accomplish here is an accommodation with the Romans to not interfere with that choice. They encourage us to participate in their society but not at the point of a sword.'

'But Tadc was more involved?'

'There was always a hint that Tadc may have had a deeper association, one that was outside of the boundaries agreed by our council of elders.'

'That was never proven,' interrupted Nubvaan.

Alba turned back to Nubvaan. 'Did you see something else?'

'I saw him take a bag of coin.'

'You think he was being paid off?'

'Possibly, I don't know.'

Alba sensed Nubvaan was holding back. 'There is something else you are not telling us?'

'I was loyal to Tadc. I thought him a good leader. It is difficult for me to entertain that he may have been conspiring with the Romans outside of our own council. It may, after all, have been an innocent transaction; a sale of something perhaps.'

'It is irregular though,' grumbled Gruenval. 'Tadc was always his own man, but this smacks of some intrigue. The tribal council would not have been happy to learn of this, Nubvaan. You should have spoken up earlier.'

'We've been through that. I accept my conduct was incorrect, but Tadc was our chieftain. To speak out against him would have been difficult without specific evidence.'

'Nevertheless, you did notice something else that

cast doubt on his motives?' Alba persisted.

'It was who he was talking to that surprised me. The man who handed him the coin was an officer, not the normal type; this one wore polished armour and they appeared familiar with each other.'

'How do you mean, familiar?'

'They talked on their own, away from the main body of soldiers. They were *friendly*.'

'I see,' answered Gruenval.

'Is that normal down here?' Alba asked.

'No,' murmured Gruenval, lost in his thoughts. 'The accommodation reached with the Romans is done openly within our ditches, inside the great roundhouse and in front of all of the tribal elders at council. No single elder, including the chieftain, should conduct any form of meeting with the Romans on their own.'

Nubvaan continued pacing. 'The thing is, Tadc was not the only Dobunni present.'

'Jovnah was with him?' Gruenval guessed.

'Yes, though he did not take any part in the discussion between the Roman officer and Tadc.'

'Then in what capacity was he present?'

'That I cannot say. I can only assume he had accompanied Tadc on this clandestine meeting.'

'Is it possible they ran into each other by accident?' Alba asked.

'I do not think so. I watched them after the Romans left. They talked as though they were in agreement, not as though Jovnah had surprised him.'

Gruenval looked thoughtful.

'It does look like there was some conspiracy between them then,' Alba suggested.

'But to what end?'

'I do not know yet. However, you have not informed us about the circumstances of Tadc's death. We must surely start there and I sense there is something you have not told us concerning the fate of your predecessor.'

'You are very perceptive.'

Gruenval took a deep breath. 'On the day of his disappearance, Tadc had called a meeting, here in this roundhouse, to discuss granting the Romans permission to take over the running of two of our lead mines. Only the management of them, you understand. We would still benefit from the metal extracted, though there was suspicion from some of us that the Romans planned a tax on it.'

'Did you suspect Tadc's judgement was impaired?'

'We were concerned enough to give him cause to call the meeting to thrash out the details.'

'So what happened?'

'We met outside, awaiting Tadc to call us to council. After a while we had still not received his summons. Eventually we grew restless, admitted ourselves and discovered he was not present. After a search of the fort it was determined he was missing. The alarm went up and scouts were despatched to search the surrounding area.'

'Was he found quickly?'

'Relatively. We received word several hours later

from one of the scouts. Jovnah, Nubvaan and myself rode out with him to where the body was discovered.'

'And what did you find?'

'Well, for a start he was found in a place which most people tend to avoid; a barren, rocky wound in the land which is difficult to traverse. Some say it is an accursed place. We may not have found him for weeks had not the horse been discovered wandering nearby.'

'Now, tell me,' continued Alba, 'for it is important that you describe in detail how he was killed.'

'Well, that's the thing,' replied Gruenval, 'He was found together with one other man. It appeared each had killed the other. The unknown man was a little distance away from Tadc. A trail of blood lay between them so we reasoned he had tried to stagger away before succumbing to his wounds.'

'Do you have any idea who the other man was?'

Gruenval looked uncomfortable. Alba had an inkling of what was coming.

'We thought he was one of yours?'

'One of ours?'

'His body carried the markings of the Cornovii.'

'And that is why we received the welcome that we did,' filled in Alba. 'This business begins to show us a shard of truth.'

'A setup,' Argyll said simply.

'There is a conspiracy here that works hard to conceal itself. They go far indeed, if to implicate us, they risk conflict between neighbouring tribes.'

'But who would gain if war broke out between the tribes?' asked Gruenval. 'The Romans would find themselves drawn in and they would need be careful not to overstep or instigate a general revolt. Britons do not tend to care whose blood graces their blades once our blood lust is up.'

'The Romans would ultimately benefit though' mused Alba. 'A diminished native threat would be easier for them to rule over. They could tear up your agreements, for example, then just take what they wanted without fear of any serious revolt. It would take some time for the British tribes to recover and by then they would have cemented their control.'

He paused, considering all that had passed. 'However, there are other factors at work which make me sense a different influence.'

'The magickal attack?' prompted Argyll.

'Yes. That is not standard practice from the Red. A malign force is set against us, but always it hovers at the periphery, watching our movements and planning its own.'

'Are you saying that there is sorcery at work?' Gruenval asked, surprised.

'Alba was attacked by a dark sorcerer in his sleep,' Argyll replied.

'That is indeed concerning,' Gruenval acknowledged. 'Do you know the identity of this sorcerer?'

'Not yet. I suspect they are working with the Romans though. However, let us return to Tadc for a moment. You said earlier that you were worried about his judgement. I get the sense something like this may have happened before?'

Gruenval nodded slowly. 'It was many summers back, long before he was chieftain, but you are right, there was something.'

'Something that called his judgement into question?'

'Most have forgotten or pushed it out of their minds. However, those of us who were close with Tadc remember. You said about questioning his judgement yet this was more about loyalty.'

'Go on,' prompted Alba.

'Well, Tadc never took a woman. By that, I mean he did not have a permanent wife, but he did have several women who he took to his bed over the years. Their favour normally only lasted a few days before he would tire and seek the belly of another to spread his seed. But there was one who he did stay with longer; Arietha was her name. It was known within the tribe that she was his, but he never formalised their bonding. Arietha was never allowed to live in his roundhouse and after he had enjoyed her body she would always be sent on her way. We suspected she meant more than the others.'

'Did something happen to change the arrangement?'

'Arietha became with child and after the course of things bore a daughter. Everybody knew it must be Tadc's, but he would not acknowledge her or the mother. This drew surprise and some disapproval from the elders, including myself, but Tadc just shunned it off. Arietha never returned to his bed and died several summers after. The girl had nowhere to go and rather than face more disquiet Tadc reluctantly took her in.'

Gruenval look at Alba. 'There was no love between him and the girl even though she was his own. He took her in just to avoid more criticism. It was a shame. She grew into a fine young woman.'

'Do you remember the girl's name?'

'Eith, I believe she was called. That was what her mother named her.'

'What happened to her?'

'She disappeared. I suspected Tadc had sold her into a marriage but nothing was ever proven.'

Alba was shocked. 'So, rather than be a father, he betrayed her and Arietha's trust. Do you have any idea what became of the girl?'

'No, I don't. One day she was here, the next she was gone.'

'And how did Tadc explain this disappearance; surely there was concern?'

Gruenval frowned. 'Tadc did what he always did. He suggested that the girl had wondered off on her own or had an accident. He was singularly dispassionate about the whole affair.'

'But you suspected he had profited from her disappearance?'

'It was the only time I really questioned Tadc and his motives. I remember he flew into a rage, accusing myself and several of the other elders of baseless accusations, even going so far as to threaten us with expulsion. He could get very enraged when pressured.'

'So, what happened?'

'Despite his anger, a few of us organised a search. There was no sign of the girl although we did find tracks. He threatened me personally after that, as it was I who had instigated the search. But, in the end, with no evidence and no sign of the girl, we had to relent. He was affected by it though. He was careful not to openly flaunt his position after that. Since then, he has ruled with the tribe's blessing.'

Before they could continue they were interrupted by the sound of a horn blasting through the early morning silence.

'What now?' Gruenval grumbled getting to his feet.

A warrior appeared at the door.

'The sentries report a troop of Roman soldiers approaching. What do you command?'

Gruenval turned to Alba. 'This will have to wait and you must hide. If they find you here then it could cause complications.'

'Our options for hiding seem limited,' Argyll observed gloomily.

'Indeed,' agreed Alba. 'Gruenval, we have no time to flee on horseback, they would spot us and hunt us down. It will have to be here.'

'I have an idea,' Gruenval answered. 'Follow me.' He turned to Nubvaan, 'You know what to do?'

'Of course.'

Nubvaan left the roundhouse whilst Gruenval said nothing more, intent on leading them towards whatever he had planned. They followed him outside, weaving between the many roundhouses and animal enclosures. Whatever they were hoping for, finding themselves staring at the lattice of the prison pit again was not it.

'Oh no!' grumbled Argyll.

Alarmed, Alba turned to Gruenval. 'We will be discovered here. They have only to remove the lattice.'

'We can make them see what we want them to see.'

'How do you mean?'

There is no time to explain. You must climb down.'

'But . . .'

'Trust me, Alba.'

Alba stared at the Dobunni chieftain. He believed he could trust him, but if he was wrong then their mission and most likely their lives would be over. Unfortunately, there was no time for any other course of action. Resolved, he climbed down first, knowing Argyll would not hesitate to follow. He was too good a warrior and a friend to do anything else.

Argyll stepped down beside him, angry, throwing his arms against the sides of the prison. 'There is no way they won't check here. Gruenval might as well serve us up on a plate. He's betrayed us Alba.'

'Maybe but look here.'

The ladder was still in the pit. Looking up they

were surprised to see Nubvaan climbing down, halting only just above their heads.

'What are they doing?' Argyll whispered.

'I think, my friend, that magick is not the only way to carry off an illusion.'

'Send it down,' Nubvaan shouted up.

A second lattice was lowered down, but this one fitted the diameter of the hole exactly, apart from two poles which protruded either side.

'You will need to crouch or lie down,' Nubvaan warned them.

With much cursing Nubvaan manoeuvred the lattice so that it was wedged horizontally above them. Once the lattice was in place a cloth bundle was thrown down. Nubvaan opened it up to produce a heavy, thickly woven blanket which he spread out across the lattice before climbing out.

In complete darkness, the two warriors heard muffled shouting before the sound of dirt striking the cloth thumped above them.

'We are being buried alive!' Argyll shouted in anger.

'I do not think so. Gruenval is carrying out a deception and makes a false floor above us. Only if they climb down might they discover the illusion.'

'I hope you're right Alba. What's to say he doesn't just leave us here once the Red have gone.'

'If that were the case he could have had us killed before now. Our corpses would be a strong symbol of his continuing loyalty. As a newly installed chieftain, that would buy him some credit with the

Romans. But no, I think Gruenval is a canny leader who will make his own path with the Dobunni. Let us be silent and stay still. We have sufficient air to hold out for a while.'

***

Gruenval climbed the ladder to the palisades before walking across to the main gate. Nubvaan joined him as they watched the Roman patrol approach the outer ramparts.

'Is it done?'

'Yes. They are safe as long as no one climbs down.'

'And their possessions?'

Nubvaan shifted uncomfortably. 'I brought them to your roundhouse and mixed them up with your own. I apologise, but I had no time.'

'You have done well. Let us hope the Romans do not stay long.'

'Why do you think they have come now?'

'We will find out shortly.'

'Do you think it is to do with the outsiders?'

'The timing would suggest so.'

'You know, of course, that if Jovnah is with them then he knows about the false floor.'

'That is a risk we have to take. If he is and he gives them away then we have a much larger problem to contend with. For now, let us bluff it out.'

As they watched from their lookout, the column of soldiers came to a halt. They consisted entirely of mounted troops, two abreast. At the front rode their senior officer, immaculate in white plumed helmet and polished armour.

'Let them through,' shouted Gruenval, choosing not to wait for the Romans to announce themselves.

He stayed long enough to observe the column of men restart their synchronistic march into the fort's interior. This was an unusually large force, out of proportion to the scale of patrols they were used to. Tactically, he had thrown away any defensive advantage should things go sour. He would need all his skills and the loyalty of men like Nubvaan to navigate the next hour or so successfully. He did not want to be remembered as the chieftain who led the Dobunni to historical oblivion. Quickly, he left the parapet, hurrying to his roundhouse before the expected audience arrived.

Gruenval only just made it. Keeping to an indirect route via the outer houses he managed to enter his roundhouse undetected. Moments later, the Roman commander entered. Gruenval suspected he had deliberately sought him out quickly to catch him off guard. He had not waited to be invited in.

'You are Gruenval?'

'Yes.'

'I am Lucius, centurion of the Legio XX Valeria Victrix.'

'I see,' Gruenval returned evenly.

Lucius stood completely still, not taking his eyes off Gruenval.

The moments passed in silence.

Gruenval remained quiet. This battle of silence

was a tactic he had experienced before. He thought it pompous that the centurion would revert to such a childish device. Had not so much been at stake then he would have found it mildly amusing.

Lucius shifted his attention to the roundhouse interior. Unexpectedly, he walked across to where Gruenval's personal possessions were stacked. Amongst them, lay Alba's staff. It must have looked out of place compared to the other trappings of the Dobunni chieftain. Nubvaan must have put it there when he had tried to hide Alba's belongings.

Lucius picked up the staff, his eyes roaming over its weathered surface, pausing when a symbol etched into the wood turned into his view.

'A strange object,' he remarked. 'I have not seen one of these before.'

'It is ceremonial,' answered Gruenval, trying not to betray the alarm in his belly.

'Indeed! And what is its purpose?'

He was testing him. Gruenval had to think quick. Though his eyes never moved from the centurion's face, his mind was rapidly processing plausible answers.

'It is used when our juveniles become men,' he answered finally. 'The ceremony demands they swear an oath upon the staff of our ancestors.' He spread his hands in a play of reverence. 'It is sacred to our people,' he added, gently removing it from Lucius's hands.

Lucius said nothing, once more weighing up his man.

Did he see it as a challenge?

Apparently satisfied, he continued.

'I expect you are wondering why we are here?'

'It had occurred to me, yes.'

Lucius smiled. He enjoyed the sparring.

'We have been tracking two fugitives.'

'Fugitives?'

'Yes.'

'How does that concern us?' Gruenval replied evenly.

Lucius smiled. 'Hopefully, it does not. However, we have come by certain *intelligence* that suggests they may have headed this way.'

'I assure you that this fort does not harbour fugitives.'

'I am glad to hear it. However, my superiors are, shall we say, very *by the book* and if I were to inform them that we had come here without searching . . ., well, then I would be seen as remiss in my duty. I am sure you understand?'

'Oh, I understand very well. Of course, you must conduct your search. I would not want your superiors to think that we would allow any unforeseen event to compromise the agreement between our two peoples.'

Lucius nodded. 'A wise choice. We would not want any misunderstandings to get between us.'

He made to leave, when Gruenval unexpectedly grabbed his arm. 'One thing though.'

Unaccustomed to having his arm seized, Lucius briefly looked alarmed. He regained control quickly, levelling his gaze in challenge.

'I expect your men to search *carefully*, to avoid any *misunderstandings.*'

Lucius snatched back his arm. 'Very well. Let us hope that we find nothing.'

He turned swiftly, unable to conceal the annoyance of physical contact. Once he was out of earshot, Nubvaan entered in his place. Gruenval could not suppress a smile at having scored such a simple victory over the Roman. Pride was a weakness and this new officer had plenty.

'Did you hear Nubvaan?'

'Yes. He is arrogant, that one.'

'Arrogant and full of himself. You noticed what was said?'

'I heard what he said about Alba and Argyll being fugitives.'

'No Nubvaan, that is not what I meant.'

'Then what?'

'The first words out of his mouth.'

Nubvaan still looked lost.

Gruenval sat down heavily, forcing a long sigh as the demand on his leadership weighed heavier. He looked up at Nubvaan, the impending explanation finding route through the meandering creases in his forehead.

'He addressed me by name, which means he already knew that Tadc was dead!'

CHAPTER VIII

'Your attack was unsuccessful then?'

'Yes. It appears this warrior who threatens us is one of their mystics.'

'Is it a problem?'

'More of a surprise,' Adrionix answered. 'This one appears to have ability.'

'Stronger than yours?' probed Servius.

'Of course not! These are barbarians after all. It just makes it more interesting.'

'Interesting or not these two barbarians are still on the loose trying to discover why one of their own was killed.'

'And what have *you* been doing about it Servius?' sneered Adrionix.

'I have despatched Lucius to track them down.'

'And has he?'

'His last report stated they were heading southwest.'

From behind the heavy drape another voice cut in. 'This is unacceptable so I suggest you make sure that these Britons disappear quickly. Our agent reported that their deaths would strengthen his position and therefore by association, our position. I would hate to have to recommend your replacement and all of the *disadvantages* that go with it, Servius.'

Servius suddenly found his mouth was very dry. 'I assure you they will be dealt with very soon now,' he offered.

'They had better be.'

Adrionix grinned at the Legatus, enjoying his predicament.

'And you Adrionix,' continued the voice. 'You were brought here to assist Servius in his task. Instead, I hear that you were countered by this barbarian mystic. Your particular skills were recommended, but do not think you are the only sorcerer that our organisation can call upon. I expect better returns on the substantial investment in your services.'

The smile left Adrionix's face as Favius walked out from behind the drape. He was a thin man, with dark brown hair topping a face whose features were unremarkable, a trait that served his purpose well. Most citizens would not give him a second glance unless they happened on his eyes, for the two dark discs that occupied the skull were soulless.

'This operation must succeed,' he continued. 'If the Britons discover that we are behind these deaths then we risk open warfare across all of the occupied lands of this godforsaken island. We would need to commit more men and materials whilst the barbarians would harry our supplies and sabotage our efforts. Whilst it goes without saying that we would be victorious, my masters prefer a more subtle approach.'

'Killing two of their elders was hardly subtle,' bit back Servius.

Favius walked up to him till there was but a hair's width between them. The two dark orbs drilled into the Legatus's own eyes.

'No, Servius, it was not subtle, but it was necessary.'

'*Two* of the barbarians were despatched?' queried Adrionix, surprised.

'Oh yes,' Servius rallied. 'The first was killed to prevent his polarising views spreading beyond the central lands of Britannia. Favius and his friends were very happy to have my men do their dirty work.'

'Who was the second?'

'One who had become too greedy to be trusted,' Favius answered before the Legatus could finish.

'You risk much Favius,' sneered Servius.

Favius held up his hand, quelling further discussion. A small hand, the skin appeared translucent and strangely stretched over the bony framework below. Servius noted the long spindly fingers. Had he been an ordinary citizen, he might have shivered.

'We employ our agents to nudge the Britons into a Roman way of life,' Favius returned. 'That way we absorb their culture, their religions and their wealth.

Oh, I do not speak of material wealth but that of the land itself. We want their resources, all of them.'

Favius smiled, a tight, thin smile that gave the impression that his face had absorbed what little flesh which passed as lips. 'But more than anything, Servius, we want their minds; their stupid, dumb, senseless minds.'

Servius stared at him, confused.

'You don't understand?' Favius laughed. 'Well, I said we need resources of the land but we also need those that farm, mine and control it. Servius, our enemies and friends alike see us as the *empire of Rome*. That is what we want them to see. We do not care whether we use them as an enemy of Rome or a citizen of Rome. To us, they are all the same. It is just the effort expended that makes the difference. Friend or foe, they see the empire that we want them to see. Ours is an empire behind an empire, run by the unseen few, one that feeds on the public flesh of the many.'

Servius looked shocked.

'Yes Servius,' continued Favius. 'Do you think we care if two Britons die at our hand or a thousand? The very army you command is but an expendable resource, a tool for us to use. Ours is a victory of control, of mastership of the masses. We shape the world in *our* image, around *our* desires. Such an empire then becomes unconquerable and unstoppable. And do you know why we are unstoppable?'

The Legatus shook his head.

'Because most do not even know they are part of it. We manipulate unseen, behind the public face of our empire and those we subject to it. We look over years, centuries, even millennia to our continuance. Ours will endure, unseen, unknown and unchecked, for you cannot stop that which you do not know.'

***

'They must be done by now,' Argyll whispered.

'The Red commander takes his duty seriously. Their search is thorough.'

Argyll was about to reply when they heard voices, much closer, above them.

'What's down here?'

The two Britons tensed. A different voice answered in reply; Alba thought it may have been Nubvaan.

'That is where we keep prisoners. It is used for storage when we have no occupants.'

'Let me see.'

The sound of the uppermost grate being removed came moments later.

'See for yourself.'

When Nubvaan had placed the false floor above them he had also carefully placed some lightweight jugs, bowls and a couple of storage vessels. Ironically, one container was a Roman amphora emptied long ago of its wine.

Alba hoped it would be enough. The deception was only as good if it prevented a man from climbing down. Once a man's weight stepped on the false floor it would be all over.

In the dark, time stretched out, as did their hearing, straining to catch the sound of discovery.

'It looks clear,' came the soldier's voice.

Alba and Argyll breathed out. Then came the words they feared.

'Go down and check.'

A different voice, sharp and full of authority.

'But sir, it's empty!'

'Go down and check. Now!'

Lucius shoved the trooper forward so hard that he almost fell into the pit. Loose soil fell onto the false roof above them. Discovery hovered close.

'Lower the ladder,' Nubvaan commanded.

Unknown to the Romans, Nubvaan had replaced the original ladder with one that was several feet shorter. This was only used when the deception was in play. Had they used the original, the Romans may have wondered why it was over long. To an enquiring commander, like Lucius, such a detail would have raised suspicion.

Nonetheless, when his warriors returned carrying the shorter ladder, Nubvaan was careful to wedge it diagonally across the pit. This was an attempt to dissuade anyone who climbed down from walking across the false floor, which would betray its secret below.

The trooper began to descend while Lucius did not take his eyes off Nubvaan. All now depended on the Roman staying on the ladder. From below, Alba and Argyll braced themselves against the damp wall.

'Well?' shouted Lucius.

The trooper, who had descended across the ladder, now halted hallway, an arm's length from the false floor.

'It is as he said. Just old pots and containers, nothing else.'

'Are you sure?'

'Yes, sir.'

Lucius snatched a spear from one of his other troopers and passed it down to the soldier in the pit. 'Use this,' he commanded.

'What for?' asked the puzzled soldier.

'Check the storage baskets you idiot!' barked Lucius.

He turned back in challenge to Nubvaan, '. . . in case they are hiding something.'

Nubvaan kept his gaze levelly on Lucius as the act played out. Within the confined space the soldier could not level his spear, which, ironically, served to keep him on the ladder. From here he could better manoeuvre the head of the spear towards its target but only in a stabbing motion. Nevertheless, jars and bowls spilt their contents as the spear penetrated their shell sending shards of pottery across the false floor.

Helpless, the two Britons below could do nothing but wait it out. The roof held, helped in part by the loose soil Nubvaan had spread earlier, enough to cushion the impact of broken vessels.

'Just grain and loose items,' reported the trooper.

Lucius, still watching Nubvaan closely, nodded. 'Very well. Climb up and continue your search.'

In the darkness below, the welcome sound of the ladder being dragged up followed by the top grate banging back down finally allowed Alba and Argyll to breathe freely.

Gruenval remained in his roundhouse while Lucius's men conducted their search. He knew better than to go outside and watch. The Roman commander would have been suspicious otherwise. He assumed the occasional sound of breaking pots and shrieking animals was a ploy to draw him out. Lucius was arrogant indeed if he thought such simplistic tactics would work.

Eventually, the disturbances subsided followed soon after by the centurion's return. Lucius entered in his usual composed manner, but Gruenval noted his cheeks were slightly flushed.

He is annoyed, Gruenval noted. *He thought they would be here.*

'My men found nothing,' Lucius said simply.

'I am glad.'

Silence fell between the two men.

Lucius's eyes, ever furtive, fell on Alba's staff once more. Some part of him sensed it was different, out of place.

Watching him closely, Gruenval marked the slight shift of body weight and moved to block his way. The movement caught the centurion off guard causing him to sway before recovering his balance.

The two men were practically face to face. Lucius's hand moved to the hilt of his sword.

Unmoved, Gruenval brought his own hands up in front of him.

A dagger with fine golden metalwork entwined around the handle lay flat across his two palms. Lucius, the alarm still in his eyes, kept the grip on his sword.

'A gift,' Gruenval offered, his voice steady. 'A gift to you personally and a sign of the alliance between us.'

Lucius relaxed. Gently, he lifted the dagger from Gruenval's hands. 'A fine object indeed,' he muttered, turning it over in appreciation.

'It is yours,' Gruenval answered, stepping back. 'But next time, I hope you will do me the courtesy of taking me at my word. A search of this fort was unnecessary.'

Lucius smiled, enjoying the rebuke. He would have been disappointed if the gift had been given without strings. Then, he would have been suspicious. 'Trust is a tricky thing to come by, Gruenval. However, I will ensure to communicate your cooperation back to my Legatus.'

'I am glad we understand each other,' nodded Gruenval.

'Then, I shall take my leave.'

'I wish you and your men well in your search.'

Lucius nodded, turned and strode towards the entrance. There he stopped while Gruenval suppressed a smile.

I knew he would stop for one last go, he thought.

'Gruenval, I trust we can rely on you to send word should these fugitives come your way?'

'We will send word immediately should they enter our lands. My men have already been advised to apprehend any that match the description of those you seek.'

'Good. I am pleased we can count on your continued loyalty.'

Lucius strode out, making sure to whip his cloak around him in another show of his self-importance.

CHAPTER IX

Gruenval did not trust that Lucius would return to try and catch him out. Only when scouts rode back to report that the Romans had indeed cleared the area did he send word to free the Cornovii men.

'I am sorry you had to wait so long. I had to be sure they had really gone. Their commanding officer is arrogant but cunning.'

'I gathered that much from down the pit,' replied Alba. 'We were almost discovered.'

'There is something you should know. When the Roman centurion first arrived here he addressed me by name. He must have known Tadc was dead because he has not visited here since I have been chieftain.'

'That is informative and confirms our suspicions of collusion between Britons and the Romans.'

'What will you do now?'

'We will continue our investigation, starting with where you found Tadc.'

'Will you send word to Rendrr about what has

happened here?'

'For now, we will use silence as our weapon of choice.'

'Very well. I have ordered that you be provided with provisions. You will find them with your horses.'

'That is good of you.'

Gruenval smiled, but his features belayed anxiety. 'Alba, if you do come across Jovnah, be careful. Though it pains me to say so, I think you should view him as hostile. We do not know yet what the extent of his involvement is in this affair.'

'I will be careful, but if it comes to a fight we will defend ourselves.'

'Do what is necessary. Nubvaan and I will handle things here.'

Alba nodded before taking his leave.

He found Argyll with the horses. True to his word Gruenval had seen to it that they were provided with at least five days' worth of provisions.

'Have you seen this?' Argyll remarked, spreading his hands out in the direction of the supplies.

'Yes. Gruenval has been kind to us.'

Argyll turned back to his horse, placing his palm to the beast's neck. 'You know Alba, when I came down to my horse this morning I realised I had missed its scent. It is the smell of a friend but also of more familiar things.'

He turned back, securing tackle and supplies that were already secure. Alba smiled. It was Argyll's way of saying he missed home.

He went to his own horse and buckled his half of the supplies to its back. The beast looked well enough rested. It would need to be, given they were likely to continue playing a cat and mouse game avoiding the Red patrols. He too felt a longing to get back to his own people, familiar landmarks and the smell of home. Beatha's face floated into his memory, but it seemed a distant desire, so, for now, he buried the emotion.

'I assume we will be heading out to look at where Tadc was found?' Argyll said, breaking into his thoughts.

'Yes. Although much time has passed, there may be something we can learn.'

'The Red centurion will be looking for us.'

'That one is devious and determined Argyll. I do not believe he will give up easily.'

From the wooden stockade, Gruenval and Nubvaan watched them leave. His position as chieftain had become more complex over the last few days. Though he had defended the Dobunni treaty with the Romans to Alba and his friend, he found himself with an uneasy feeling in the base of his gut. The old arguments of trust and tribal values briefly filled his head, together with a memory of Tadc vehemently defending a new arrangement with the Romans.

A treaty for future generations, Tadc had said.

Climbing down from the palisade, Gruenval wondered just how many generations it would last. The stability of previous years seemed in flux with recent events and the security of his peoples' futures was no longer as solid as he had once thought.

***

Nubvaan had given Alba a map to the location of where Tadc's body had been discovered. The journey took them to within sight of the coast. It was the first time Argyll had seen the ocean. He brought his horse to a halt, balancing on its back, marvelling at the thin blue line that floated across the horizon.

'I do not think it natural for a man to float on water,' he said quietly.

Alba laughed. 'There are many things that seem unnatural my friend, but I assure you there is no mystery or magick to sailing on a wooden vessel.'

Argyll grunted and settled back on his mount. 'I hear the Red have vessels of great size that wage war on opposing fleets.'

Alba nodded. 'Stories speak of huge naval battles far away to the east with large fleets bearing hundreds of warriors engaged in combat. They say ships try to sink each other with huge bronze rams on their bows. The loss of life can be terrible and huge.'

'I do not think I would like to die on water. They say the gods of the oceans do not give up their dead like those of the earth,' Argyll muttered grimly.

'Then it is good that we are not planning to tempt fate. Our destiny lies within the bounds of this Isle, upon the earth itself.'

THE CORNOVII MYSTERY

Argyll fell silent. Alba mused his friend was no doubt conjuring the horrors of a watery death. He did not like the thought either.

Their progress brought them up to a heathland, blanketed by low lying gorse and fern. This was a different place to the mynds in their own lands. Here the vegetation was dry and brittle. Thorny bushes, only a few feet high, struggled skywards with berries glistening orange in the bright sun. Nubvaan had advised them not to eat this apparent bounty.

'A man dies contorted with spasm and froth from his mouth, should he eat the golden berry,' he had warned.

They passed on, ignoring nature's deceit. Beyond the heathland they turned east, travelling parallel to the ocean which teased them, appearing and disappearing beyond the horizon. The Sun had passed its midday point when they began to descend into a 'U' shaped valley, carved from a glacier long since vanished. Large boulders appeared randomly on the valley floor, rooted where they had been deposited thousands of years ago. Their progress echoed around the valley sides, bouncing from side to side so that the effect was quite disorientating.

'I do not like this place Alba,' said Argyll.

Alba did not immediately answer. A wisp of the etheric brushed against his senses, a delicate, featherlight caress against his magickal field. The touch of an ancient energy seemed tangible in this place. He had the disturbing sensation that it detected him too.

'This place has known magick,' he finally replied. 'I do not think it was used well. There is an after effect of dark sorcery which leeches into the stone and the space between. I am not surprised there has been death here Argyll. This place has a corruption embedded into its fabric. We should do what we came to do and not linger beyond what is needed.'

They dismounted, preferring to lead their mounts cautiously over the increasingly uneven, rocky floor. Each walked their horse to a different side of their body, protecting that side from long range attack by arrow or spear. Unless they were ambushed from both sides at once, at least one of them would have a fighting chance to resist.

'We are almost there,' declared Alba. 'The map shows it as just beyond the next turn.'

'I don't like it,' Argyll moaned. 'This place is perfect ambush territory.'

'I don't think ambush is the thing we should fear most.'

They rounded the bend in the valley floor. If they expected anything to be different then they were disappointed. More of the same stretched ahead of them.

'This place is accursed,' Argyll complained. 'A man could go mad walking this valley. It plays with your head.'

'We are in the right spot,' Alba replied, ignoring his friend's complaint. 'Let us deploy our skills to read the land.'

There was little vegetation, so they secured the horses by looping the reins around a suitable boulder. Then they spread out, scouring the valley floor for evidence.

Argyll was first to pick up the trail. 'The ground is difficult being so rocky, yet there has been disturbance in several places. I see multiple tracks leading in and out.'

Alba moved across to his friend. He identified at least four distinct set of tracks, which converged between two massive boulders which gated their section of the valley to what was beyond.

Like giant sentinels, they would have made an obvious reference point for anyone choosing to meet in this godforsaken place, he thought.

'It becomes difficult here. The tracks are all mixed up. If anyone had arranged to meet then this would be an easy landmark to head for. I can single out the later tracks, probably Gruenval's party searching for Tadc. These others are impossible to determine given the rocky nature of the terrain. I do not think there were many men here, no more than say seven or eight. That rules out a Roman patrol but not necessarily their involvement.'

While Alba considered, Argyll wondered over to a smaller boulder set further back near to the valley wall.

'Alba!'

Alba could smell the corpse before he saw it. There was no attempt at concealment. The man had simply been left in the place he had succumbed.

'This must be the other,' Argyll noted.

'Looks like it. The progress of decomposition would be about right.'

'I wonder why they did not bring this one back?'

'They accepted the evidence of their eyes and assumed this was the killer of their chieftain. Why treat your enemy with respect after such a crime?'

Alba bent down to search the corpse. Skin still adhered to the bony framework below, though it was stretched tight and sallow. The eyes remained, frozen open with the sight of death.

'I can see why they thought he was one of ours.'

'The markings on his arm?'

'They seem to have made their minds up just on that one singular piece of evidence.'

The dead man's arm had discoloured, although they could still make out the blotchiness of the skin where the stagnant blood had pooled. His skin was a dark tan, the colour of decay. Though hard to see, a tattoo was still visible, the swirling knots of the Cornovii.

Alba continued inspecting the man's body. Turning the corpse over he peered at the man's back. 'Strange,' he muttered.

'What is it?'

'This man has only superficial wounds to his chest. The real damage was done here.' He pointed to two cuts at the man's side. 'These would have sliced into the kidneys. Quite an accurate blow in the frenzy of battle. Either that or our friend here was unskilled with a blade.'

'A warrior would not have shown his back,' Argyll pronounced.

'No, a warrior would not.'

Alba turned the man back over on to his back. 'Look at his arms and legs. I would have expected other minor or defensive wounds to be present but there are none. In fact, his limbs do not look like the limbs of a warrior at all.'

'Now you point it out, they do not.'

Argyll reached for the man's hands, inspecting the palm and fingers. They were worn and calloused. 'This man has a labourer's hands and yet his markings argue he is one of our warriors.'

'It would have been easy for the Red to have snatched some unfortunate from Cornovii territory, bring him down here, then dress him up to look like one of ours,' said Alba.

'So, this is another falsehood, a hoax?' Argyll said, shaking his head in disbelief.

Alba nodded. 'Only in so far as this valley is the stage of the deceit. Tadc was still killed here. The accuracy of the kill suggests it was probably by an experienced fighter.'

'Maybe our friend who searched the fort?'

'A distinct possibility.'

'But then that would mean the Red killed Tadc as well.'

'Once again, our enemy goes to great lengths to further their deceit.'

'They sow unrest between the tribes to conceal their own actions.'

'Yes, but unrest risks conflict spreading,' remarked Alba. 'I wonder if that truly is their intent or whether there is another reason?'

Whilst they had been investigating the corpse their attention was focused away from their immediate surroundings. Unseen, another stepped quietly from concealment and stole slowly towards them. Below, the dark energy stirred, anticipating the drawing of blood, lusting for the red life force to wet the valley floor once more.

This man was no labourer. He set about his business carefully, lightly moving across the uneven floor, choosing his steps carefully. In his line of sight, almost within strike range, was Argyll's back.

Though he made no sound, keeping out of sight until he lined up his attack, his presence had caused a disturbance. The same dark energy which perceived his threat, hungering for his success, now gave itself away by the greed of its lust.

Alba perceived the energy change a moment before the blade struck. He whipped around, pushing Argyll to the side in one motion.

He was a moment too late.

Argyll cried out as blood was spilt. His own sword in hand, Alba found himself facing Jovnah.

'You murdering bastards!' Jovnah sneered.

'We have not murdered anyone. This is a falsehood Jovnah!'

'Lies! You speak deceit Alba of the Cornovii. One of your warriors lies dead at your feet and you try to deny it.'

He lunged at his gut, Alba quickly parrying the blow. He decided not to counter but to try and talk sense to Jovnah. It would be hard; Jovnah's blood lust was high and threatened to overcome him in delirium. At the periphery of his senses he detected the hunger of the creature, growing in intensity.

Jovnah took half a step back, inviting Alba to attack. Alba stood his ground, unwilling to be drawn in. Incensed, Jovnah attacked again, feinting a blow to Alba's legs, then following up with a swipe aimed at his side. Once more Alba countered, moving in a circular motion to keep his guard and his opponent in line.

He tried again. 'Jovnah, this man on the ground is not a warrior. Look at his hands. They are not the hands of an assassin. This was staged to make it look like an attack from one of ours. The deceit lies elsewhere and not with us. In honour of your dead chieftain let us make peace, join forces, uncover the true evil that lies behind this foul deed.'

'I hear not the vile deceit that spews from your mouth,' shrieked the reply. 'Tadc would have brought us wealth, civilisation and power. I, Jovnah, would have been part of that world, but you, an interfering cunt from up north had to spoil it all.'

Jovnah had now lost all sense of sanity. His eyes shone with madness and hate as the dark energy seeped deeper, coursing more hatred through his blood. Alba saw the insanity stare out of his opponent's eyes and realised that there would be no reasoning.

Jovnah attacked again, bloodlust sustaining an endless strength to each strike. Alba found himself forced back as blow after blow reigned down. The creature's energy seemed to give Jovnah the strength of a titan. Its vileness was within him now, subduing reason and energising hatred.

The dark energy drooled in anticipation of Alba's blood, sensing the magickal energy within him. A sorcerer's blood would be prized above all others by the formless demon that inhabited the valley. It could barely contain its desire at such a prospect. The addition of Alba's life force to its own may even be enough to allow it to break its bonds to the place that had contained it for so long.

Jovnah's attack was sustained, possessed of superhuman strength. Defending a particularly strong attack to his head Alba lost his footing. Unable to recover, he crashed down hard onto the rocky floor, his sword arm bent over on itself so that his only defence went skittling down out of reach.

His head had taken a nasty blow as he hit the floor so that his vision blurred. He could hear sounds but not locate their source. A figure swam into view. Desperately, he tried to focus, but this just caused his head to hurt more. His brain told his legs to move, but the signal seemed to take ages to reach them. As the first twitch of movement finally returned the shadowy figure before him savagely stamped down on his leg causing him to cry out.

'So, Alba, finally I have you. I don't have your skills in the dark arts, but I can sense enough to know that this place wants your blood. I feel it within my own. It craves your suffering and drools over the thought of drinking your essence. I will not deny it the prize it seeks. In fact, I believe I will enjoy it just as much as it will.'

Powerless, Alba watched as Jovnah raised both arms, the tip of the sword positioned directly above his heart.

CHAPTER X

Alba braced for the strike to fall, angered for allowing himself to be made helpless and not meet death in battle. But fate is friend to no one and instead of the cut of the blade, the man above him fell heavily upon his chest. His breath, rather than his life, was crushed out of him.

Another figure flopped beside him, breathing heavily.

'Alba, do you still live?'

Dazed and gasping to recover air into his squashed lungs, Alba nodded weakly to his friend. Together, they sat against each other, neither moving or saying anything for several moments.

When Alba finally recovered his wits he tended to Argyll's injuries. His companion had suffered a deep gash to his left arm which had left him pale through loss of blood. His own wounds amounted to a lacerated tear to his right temple which had not cut deep but had left him with a throbbing head which took some time before it ceased spinning.

Whilst they lay recovering, Alba looked across at

Jovnah. He was quite dead. Argyll's blade had struck him precisely between the shoulders, piecing the heart. Another pair of sightless eyes stared up to the grey sky above.

There was a lot of blood running out of the corpse.

Below the man's body the red liquid did not pool. As Alba watched, it seemed to melt into the rocky ground as though being absorbed.

'We cannot stay here.'

'I know,' Argyll replied weakly.

'You were right that this place is accursed. Just before Jovnah attacked you, I sensed the evil react to his intent. It is sentient Argyll. It lives in this place; in the stone, the dust, the rocks themselves. It lives on hate and lusts for blood.'

Argyll did not answer. His head dropped before slumping to the side. Alba quickly slapped him hard across the face.

'No! You must not sleep. This place will draw your lifeforce should you do so.'

Argyll nodded, the weight on his eyes heavier than he had ever known. They made their way back to the horses. The beasts were nervous, wide eyed and stamping at the ground, sensing the growing malevolence. Relieved to have made it, they led their mounts back the way they came. After a while, Alba looked about him puzzled.

'What's the matter?' Argyll asked, his voice a little stronger.

'We are being played with. I am sure we came this

way already.'

Suspicious, but not quite willing to concede they had gone in circles, Alba took up a small rock and inscribed a mark onto the nearest boulder to their left. They continued on, each watching for landmarks with Alba marking every third boulder they came to. Eventually, he stopped. On his left was a boulder that looked familiar. Sure enough, when he inspected its surface there was the mark which he had left earlier.

'We are not allowed to leave,' he said simply. 'So be it.'

'You thinking what I think you are?'

'Probably. Let us tie up the horses and return to that clear area over there.'

Alba pointed to a section of the valley floor that was relatively clear of boulders. After securing their mounts they returned to where he had indicated.

'What now?' Argyll asked, glancing around nervously. Above him, the light had dimmed to a subdued grey, adding to his sense of foreboding.

'We must gather as much firewood as we can.'

'There's hardly any tree or plant growing here Alba!'

'We will have to make do with the blanched branches that pass as trees in this place. They are scarce so we must gather all we can find. Go now, quick as you can and return on my whistle. We need to start before the dark of night overtakes us.'

They each went their separate ways, hunting for every scant piece of sun scorched scrub they could find. When Alba's whistle came, Argyll had barely collected an armful.

Seeing his friend's anxiety at the lack of wood, Alba attempted to reassure him. 'Do not distress yourself. I possess dry moss which mixed with some of my powders will kindle a flame that will burn long enough for our purpose. Come now, time is short and the night breathes down our neck.'

They moved over to the centre of the valley floor where Alba unloaded his supplies.

'I will need your help for this Argyll.'

'Of course.'

'Are you sure you are up to it?'

'Are you?'

'I will have to be.'

'I assume you are going to deal with this thing, whatever it is?'

'It has made its intentions clear. It wants me Argyll. I am a prize that it desires very much. My magickal energy would not only sustain it but increase its power. For now, it is bound to this place, but it desires more. It wants to live out in the world of men, searching and feeding on hate, on spite and on blood. We cannot let that happen. This evil must be defeated here.'

He looked across to Argyll, concern stretched across his face. 'This will be dangerous. You must do and say everything I tell you to without question. No hesitation must hinder your actions for the stakes are too high. Either this creature dies . . .'

'Or we do,' completed Argyll grimly.

Alba nodded. 'I said earlier that the energy or presence in this valley is sentient. It has a mind with a singular intent. What it does not have is conscience or mercy. Therefore, we must show it none.'

'I understand.'

'Good. First of all we must create a sacred space; an area where I can expedite my work without this dark energy interfering. Grab this and follow me.'

Alba took two leather pouches out of his satchel. Both were tied at the top with a leather thong. He tossed one over to Argyll.

'Untie the thong and open the bag.'

What's in it ?' Argyll asked, untying the bag.

'Brine granules. Beatha regularly visits the brine springs on the south-eastern border of our lands and therefore carries a large stock, so I always have some. We are going to make a wide circle. I will lay my brine down first, then when we return to this point, we will go around again. You will lay yours next to mine so that we have a wide, clear border.'

Argyll moved into position, waiting for Alba's signal.

'Oh, and one more thing. Do not be distracted by anything you see or hear. This thing will try to distract us from our purpose. Ignore it all. Keep your focus on me at all times.'

Alba set off, tipping the white brine to his side, so that as he moved a circular marker formed behind him. As in all his magickal work, Alba had taken care to start from the east, moving anticlockwise through the cardinal points until arriving back where he had begun.

Moving out of the mundane world and into the spirit world, he had called it.

'Now your turn.'

Argyll made the same circuit, laying his brine to the side of Alba's track. When he returned, Alba moved them to the centre.

'That seemed to go unhindered,' Argyll noted as they repositioned.

'Yes, but listen . . .'

Argyll strained to hear, but whatever Alba was alluding to was silent to his ears.

'I hear nothing.'

'Precisely,' Alba whispered. 'Do you not sense the stillness that has befallen this place. Since we made our circle, there is no wind, no bird noise, nothing. It knows what we are about. It waits to see if it needs to fear me or fight me.'

Argyll frowned. The place was deathly silent.

'We must ignite the beacons of light,' continued Alba. 'Take care to stay within the boundary and do not go outside of the circle. We are only protected within, not without. Do not forget that. '

They gathered up the brittle branches from the scant vegetation they had found earlier, taking a bundle to each of the cardinal points. Constructing a torch out of these decrepit branches was difficult. Alba had to bind what little wood they had before surmounting the top of each with a dry moss from his satchel. To this he added a thick, tar like substance.

One by one they lit the beacons. The spark from Alba's flint took easily to the black gloop lighting the wood below.

'That's the easy bit done.'

'Those sticks will not burn long,' Argyll said, concerned.

'Do not fear. I only need their physical fuel long enough to light the spiritual flame.'

'What next?'

Alba looked intently at his friend. 'Now Argyll, I need to summon special help. Are you aware of the myths of the winged serpents?'

Argyll looked blank, unaware to what Alba was referring.

'The Romans call them Dracones. They are elemental creatures that protect and look after all of the realms. Their presence is not limited to the unseen; they can be felt here too, in the physical realm. They inhabit the energy centres of this land, guarding the pure energy that flows through the earth. You may have felt their presence in the stone circles we sometimes visit.'

Seeing the confused look still inhabiting his friend's face, Alba continued.

'Either way, we need their assistance for this task. The aberration that has corrupted this valley has been allowed to fester here for too long. My magick alone will not be enough to combat it.'

Alba picked up another torch, lit it and passed it to Argyll. The daylight had already dimmed.

Twilight fast approached.

'I am going to call in the fire Draco. Its energy is required to consume and purify the demon. This is something I have not done before. I only hope that my summons will be answered. These elemental creatures demand respect so if I get something wrong then they may not show up at all.'

'What happens if they don't?'

'For this to work the Draco must be present, else . . ., well, let us not dwell on that eventuality. Once the Draco is present, the darkness will try all it can to resist. It will not give up without a fight. Be ready.'

Argyll nodded. 'I am ready.'

Alba took the staff, the same one which a few days earlier Lucius had found so intriguing, holding it aloft. Grasping it with both hands he shouted:

'Here stands my Power, at the crossroads of my circle.

Here stands my Light, at the crossing of the ways;

Here stands my Right, at the centre of creation.'

He brought the staff down, driving it into the ground with all his strength. Below, the darkness stirred, sensing challenge. Etheric tendrils snaked out towards the circle. Where it made contact with the boundary it recoiled as the energy of the circle gated its presence, pushing it back. Incensed, its anger began to oscillate with increasing amplitude.

A deep, ominous rumbling took up through

the valley reverberating along both its length and breadth. Loose rock and shale began to slide down the valley sides. Tumbling debris fell toward them from all directions. Gravity appeared overcome by some other force as the onslaught seemed possessed of an intent, directed straight for where they stood.

Ignoring the impending landslide, Alba signalled for Argyll to pass the lighted torch. Holding it aloft, he began to swing it back and forth. As his movements became more animated an unearthly hiss emanated from his mouth so that the impression his body gave was of a serpent weaving with the flames. Argyll remembered Alba's words about not interfering, but he had not seen his friend like this before.

Alba began to run around each of the beacons waving the lighted torch in complex patterns, their rapidity creating geometric shapes from the track of the flames. He began to speak, a strange language which seemed to be hissed out rather than spoken. Yet, Argyll noticed, it was having an effect. There was a sympathetic reaction to this fire dance from the four beacons, their flames becoming bolder, increasing in intensity as they began to mimic the shapes Alba's torch traced in the night air.

Where was the twilight?

The violets and indigos of a few moments past had been replaced by a cloak of obsidian, blanketing out the torchlight of the stars. The only light came from the beacons. The creature who inhabited darkness draped it over their physical space. Shivering, Argyll suddenly realised how alone they were.

He tugged at Alba's arm. 'Alba, the sky, look!'

Alba turned toward him but the eyes that reflected his image were alight with fire, each iris mirroring the patterns of the torch. Alba seemed to be looking through him rather than at him. The valley was shaking; no longer a deep rumble, the creature had increased its power to match that of the sorcerer that dared stand against it. Huge boulders were loosened from their ancient seats and sent cascading down toward the valley floor. From every direction, rock tumbled towards the two men below.

Argyll saw no escape. The energetic barrier had been effective against the landslide of rubble that had initially assailed them. Yet, he could see no way that it would stand against such huge opponents which, even now, were thundering toward their position.

Yet, a strange thing occurred. Each time he thought that they were about to be pulverised, smashed into shards of flesh and bone, the boulders would stop or veer off in another direction. None fell against or penetrated the brine perimeter.

It seemed their protection was working. Immune to the threat of rocky oblivion, Alba continued his fiery dance, weaving between the four perimeter torches, spewing forth more outlandish verse.

The creature was outraged. Only now did it begin

to realise what Alba was about. More tremors hit the valley, as though a resistance was resonating between the circle and the demon below. It resisted, clinging to its lair, unwilling to be wrenched from the shadows.

As Argyll watched, the four beacons flared up brighter than before and he found himself staring at the face of the fire Draco, one within the flames of each beacon. He could only see the head. The body of these creatures was not visible. Each Draco became larger, growing in size so that they reached from the beacon to the apex of the energetic circle above them. Their mouths were agape with huge curving teeth and their faces covering in a type of bony plate. Each one was possessed of vivid amber eyes housing a slim oval pupil that seemed to hold him in its glare wherever he stood. From the midway point of the head, huge curving horns reached back over their necks. Even though he could only see their heads, the countenance of these creatures was immense.

He stumbled back in fright, truly petrified at the awesome sight before him. Though unskilled in the dark arts, he could nonetheless sense the energised air around him, feeling the elasticity of the tug of war taking place between the Dracones and the creature below. For the first time in its existence the formless evil felt threatened.

A huge crack rented the air as the ground on one side of the valley split open as though a sword had sliced through the fabric of the ground. The creature was sucked out of the rocky wound and pulled into the centre of Alba's circle. Exposed, the demon appeared as a dense, green fog accompanied by a putrid smell. It tried to escape its imprisonment, repeatedly ramming itself against the magickal boundary.

Incensed at its inability to escape it turned instead toward Alba. Forgetting the warning of not to interfere, Argyll jumped into its path, sword ready. Creature or not, he would defend his friend to the death. As he watched the green mist before him, it began to coalesce into a defined shape. He could make out multiple limbs protruding at odd angles, contorted and bent with huge backward curving talons. In the centre of the monstrosity was a maw that snapped with long, narrow, twisted teeth dripping venom.

He gripped his sword harder, taking courage from the grip, trusting his sacrifice would allow Alba to finish. The demon advanced upon him, its vile breath seeping down his throat, causing him to retch. The stench was constricting his lungs too. His brain sent the signal to his arm to sweep the sword down in an attack, but before the arm responded he was thrown violently backward, out of reach of the creature. Alba had whirled around at the instant Argyll had made to attack, sending him flying into a heap several paces away.

'No!' Alba boomed, before returning his attention to the creature.

Bruised, Argyll watched in horror as it

approached Alba. It thought it had won. Even Argyll could feel the swell of anticipation as it closed to within an arm's length of his friend. It reared up, limbs pulled back with each vicious talon held vertical ready to be pivoted and swung down to impale its victim. Anticipating how it would rip Alba apart the creature started to click its claws together at the same time as an opaque, viscous liquid slobbered out of its mouth, burning the soil where it fell.

Desperate, Argyll made one last ditch attempt to intervene. He was out of range of a sword strike, so he pulled the dagger from his waist and flung it with all his might at the monstrosity before him.

The creature never flinched. Almost flippantly it flicked an arm out deflecting the puny blade. But it was annoyed. In spite, it lashed out at Argyll throwing him to the perimeter of the circle. Dazed, all he could do now was watch the end play out. He could see no hope for Alba and whatever his friend had intended by the summoning of the Dracones had not worked. There was no sign of them doing anything to help. The evil before them sensed their impotence to intervene, anticipating its victory. The sorcerer before it would make a fine addition to its own energy once it had sucked out the lifeforce. The thought made it almost feverish in its desire to kill.

It was draped directly over Alba with all of its limbs forming an arch above him. Cocooned within the centre of its span, Alba seemed oblivious to his impending doom. Argyll cried out, imploring his friend to action, but Alba stayed still without any attempt at escape.

And then it struck. Argyll saw it move, but in the split second of its strike the four Dracones emitted a blinding golden light. His eyes were burned by the intensity, but he saw the creature literally pulled apart, consumed within each quarter amid the purifying flames.

A deafening shriek tore through the air before all fell silent. The beacons withdrew to their normal size, the Dracones disappeared and Alba sank to his knees. Unsure whether to move Argyll stayed put. Alba eventually pulled himself to his feet, walked over to his staff and pulled it sharply from the ground.

He stood still for a moment before bowing his head. Finally, he walked over to Argyll and helped him to his feet. 'You alright?'

Argyll dusted himself off, still shocked at what he had witnessed. His mind seemed unable to rationalise what had happened. 'Alba, that thing. I did not think it would be so *real*.'

'Steady yourself, my friend. The formless vileness that infected this place is destroyed. I am sorry *we* had to force you away but you would have been killed.'

'*We?*'

'The Draco and I were as one Argyll. The demon thought we were separate, which was its mistake. We were never separate. The fire Draco took form within the flames of the beacon, but its energy flowed through me as well. We wanted it to attack me. That way its attention and its guard was distracted from the four beacons. Once it made its move the Draco literally pulled it apart, consumed within the four flames. Four flames, one Draco. Despite what you saw there was only one of them. They are immensely powerful elementals.'

'But Alba, at the end I saw the creature take shape,' Argyll exclaimed. 'I could see its form materialise in the green fog, before it was consumed. I will never forget it, such a despicable thing.'

Alba said nothing for a moment. Then, of all things he smiled. 'The best way to forget the bad is to focus on the good. Listen . . .'

Confused, Argyll kept silent. There was nothing save the feel of a gentle breeze and the call of a raptor gliding somewhere high above. Gradually, he became aware of other sounds, the ambient noise of nature returning.

These were sounds that had not been in this valley for a long time.

Alba nodded. 'You hear it don't you? The light returns to this place. Nature will do its work and restore.'

Later on, as they emerged from the valley, heading out into open countryside Argyll asked Alba: 'Where did that creature come from? Was it sent by the sorcerer that attacked you?'

'I do not think so. It is possible that my adversary

may have known of its existence, but I do not believe they created it. The demon, for that is what it was, had infested that valley for a very long time.'

Argyll, still confused, persisted. 'How did it come into being in the first place?'

Alba shrugged his shoulders. 'I do not know. I have only rarely come across things like that. In most cases, it has been where the living have experienced some kind of emotional trauma, usually anger. Rage is a strong emotion and if released often enough can leave an imprint in the area where it is vented. The energy of such emotion can sometimes take on a mind or a sentience of its own. However, these energies, though unpleasant, tend to be localised to a small area and can be cleansed easily enough by sorcerers like myself.'

Argyll sensed there was more. 'But that thing we just experienced in the valley was different; stronger and darker than what you have previously encountered?'

'That vileness was not created by accident or by some small-scale emotional outburst.'

'You believe it was created deliberately?'

'I do.'

'If the Red or their sorcerer did not create it, who did?'

'We may never know the answer to that. A sorcerer, like the one sent against me, could in theory create or *conjure* that creature, but it would leave the one who created it very weak physically. The energy required to bring it into being and sustain itself could even kill its creator. I believe that demon had its origin elsewhere, maybe outside the realm of man.'

They both fell silent, each contemplating their experience in their own way. Despite the fact that the valley had been restored, it was some hours later before they struck camp for the night. As their conscious minds bade farewell to the day, only the assurance that they were many leagues away from the valley allowed sleep to finally overwhelm them.

CHAPTER XI

At last, they were on their way back home. Alba found himself daring to hope that he would finally be able to spend time with Beatha. He longed for her embrace and the warmth of her bed. Often on the return journey his mind drifted to imagining his time with her, running his hand through her long dark hair, holding the smooth strands to his cheek, caressing the hidden regions of her body. Argyll did not need to be a mystic to guess what was putting the smile on his friend's face.

They had managed to evade any Roman patrols thus far. Alba assumed, correctly as it happened, that Lucius would have tracked back to Gruenval's fort in a move to entrap them. The centurion had been thwarted in this belief and realising his mistake, had taken his men off to the valley where they had battled the demon. Alba took some pleasure in imagining Lucius's frustration at having missed them once again.

On the return journey, they had made steady progress so that the borders of their own lands were but a few days distant. Here, the terrain varied between open grassland and thick forest. They allowed the horses to walk at their own pace, the dangers of the last few days lost amid the sanctity of a fresh breeze and the relative security of the guardians of oak, birch and chestnut which stood tall around them. The path they followed would have been invisible to any but an experienced tracker so they felt relatively safe, at least from the Roman patrols.

'The Red seldom venture into our great forests,' said Alba. 'They are all too aware that we Britons would have the upper hand.'

'It is a shame that they have ventured into our lands at all.'

'An event which unfortunately cannot be undone. Their continued presence is the biggest threat our way of life has faced in the memories of our people.'

'It cost Doube his life.'

'It did, but I am still puzzled why.'

'Surely the motive is clear,' Argyll replied. 'Doube spoke out vehemently against letting the Red push further into our lands. They killed him to remove his opposition and prevent him from gathering more support amongst the other tribes.'

'Maybe and yet I feel there is some other hand at work here. Why go to the trouble to arrange a Red sorcerer to attack me? That makes no sense and also how did they know so quickly about what we were about.'

'You think we were betrayed; that the Red were

informed about our mission?'

'I think the wolves were given our scent very early on.'

'Then why kill Tadc?' argued Argyll. 'He supported the Red and Gruenval will still hold to whatever agreement Tadc made with them.'

'I think Tadc's killing wasn't part of the original plot. You are correct that it flies in the face of reason to kill an advocate of their strategy. Unless . . .'

Alba tailed off, pondering a thought that had just come into his head.

'Unless what?'

'Unless his death became a necessity. Think about what we know about Tadc. Both Toryn and Gruenval told us the man was clearly determined to bring in a new era of cooperation with the Romans. I sense he wanted the power that went with it too. Maybe his masters thought his ambition was superseding his worth.'

'Or maybe he threatened to reveal some secret?'

Alba fell silent for a moment, considering his friend's words. He felt sure there was a deeper plot at work, a conspiracy that he was not yet seeing.

'You might be onto something there. Perhaps it is not a thing but a person he threatened to expose. There are many things about his death that are puzzling.'

Whilst they had been talking the trees had begun to thin out, giving way to patches of heather and gorse. The soft springiness they had enjoyed traversing the moist earth of the forest was replaced by an unyielding sandstone bedrock, where coarse sand found its way between their toes, and hidden cavities waited to twist ankle of human and beast alike. The path started to descend, winding its way towards an exposed ridge, navigable through a narrow, winding cut, gouged from a stream or rivulet that had long since dried up.

Loosening the ropes to their mounts, they allowed the horses to navigate the narrow slippery path of their own accord. The descent was tricky, requiring constant adjustment of their balance to help the horses. It would be all too easy for one of them to lose its footing or lodge a shoe within the narrow cut, either of which would result in a lame beast.

Once through, they emerged onto a square of land which was covered in deep red sand, the eroded sandstone particles that had weathered from the ridge over centuries. Dismounting, they lead their horses through the sandy hollow. Suddenly, Alba tensed, holding up his hand for Argyll to stop. Both warriors instinctively laid a hand on the hilts of their swords.

'What is it?' Argyll whispered.

'A sound. One that is not of nature.'

'The Red?'

'Maybe. They draw close. Ready your blade.'

Quietly they withdrew their swords, once more using the horses as protection on alternate sides. The deep sandy ground would not allow speed of movement and there was no cover. Behind them was only the sandstone ridge.

Not the place to survive an ambush.

'Alba, we are dead meat here. There is no cover and our manoeuvrability is compromised.'

Alba knew they were in a perfect kill zone. At this distance, spear or arrow could cut them down easily. He decided on bluster as their only hope.

'Show yourselves!' he yelled firmly. 'Or do you hide in the trees like Roman cowards?'

Almost immediately, the voice of another rang out from beyond the boundary of sand.

'We are no Romans! Sheath your blades.'

'Then come out into the open or have you not the balls to face us?' Argyll sneered.

Several moments passed. Alba's instinct told him that this was not a Roman ploy. If it was, then why announce themselves; they could have easily surprised and overcome them. His gut told him this was something else.

But it might be another ambush. They had suspected native involvement from the start. This could be it, a trap sprung by the traitor who had dispatched Doube. Yet, they were still alive, unless they were to be captured so.

Ahead of them, a man emerged from the trees. He was tall, well-built and looked like one of their own. He held his hands out, free of any weapons.

'You finally find courage to face us!' yelled Argyll in challenge.

'Hold fast Argyll,' Alba interrupted. 'He speaks the truth that he is not Roman, though he may be something else. Sheath your sword but keep your hand ready.'

'Alba, they could cut us down.'

'They would have done so already if they wanted us dead,' replied Alba.

'Your friend speaks the truth,' returned the advancing warrior. 'Besides, I would not sully my honour with such deceit. I assure you that I would fight you honestly, were that my intention. However, I do have more important matters to impart to you.'

'Go on,' Alba encouraged, relaxing his grip just a little.

'My master, who I believe is known to you, awaits your company.'

'And who would that be?' shouted back Argyll, unconvinced and unimpressed.

'Rigari, chieftain of the Corieltauvi,' returned the warrior. 'He bids your urgent audience.'

'How could Rigari know where we were?' Alba exclaimed, somewhat taken aback.

'We have had scouts out searching for you. You were spotted yesterday, but, I'm afraid, it has taken us this long to intercept you with the rest of our party. My name is Horva and I am one of Rigari's inner circle.'

Horva's eyes flicked down to where both Alba and Argyll's hands were resting on the hilt of their swords. 'Rest assured this is no trap, but maintain your weapons if it makes you feel easier. Now, please follow me as my chieftain is most keen to take counsel with you.'

'Alba, this man may not be who he says he is,' Argyll warned. 'What's to say that Roman centurion and his troop are not hidden in the trees. We could be walking into a trap.'

'If they meant to kill us then we would already be gracing the halls of the gods by now Argyll. I think we can trust Horva, for now.'

Horva nodded before proceeding to guide them forward. As they crossed the tree line Argyll tensed in anticipation of a double cross. None came. As they walked deeper into the forest they were joined by two more warriors. At Horva's orders, they walked ahead of them, taking care not to encroach on Alba or Argyll's personal space. Alba noted the courtesy.

They were brought to a small clearing where some six or seven warriors were camped. Horva introduced them to a stocky man, well into his fortieth summer, who was in the process of kindling a fire.

Rigari regarded them keenly from two crystalline grey eyes which danced quickly over the Cornovii men before a sympathetic mouth smiled a greeting. Whilst youth had passed its zenith several seasons past, those eyes shone with an intensity which belied both character and strength.

'You and your companion certainly get around!'

'As do you,' replied Alba evenly. 'You are far from your home territory.'

'Quite so.'

'We were charged with investigating Doube's

death.'

'By Chieftain Rendrr,' Argyll added for effect.

'So I deduced,' Rigari answered, mildly amused.

He motioned to his men, a signal. Alarmed, Argyll shot to his feet, sword drawn.

'My friend, sit down,' Rigari countered. 'I am merely summoning us some sustenance.'

'I am afraid we have seen much to give us concern over these recent days,' Alba explained. 'Trust is harder to come by than when we began our journey.'

'Well, then we have much to discuss.'

A warrior walked forward, handing the Cornovii men two decent sized slabs of meat. Argyll contemplated the meat before raising his eyes in question to Alba, who, in turn, stared a challenge toward the Corieltauvi chieftain.

Rigari laughed. 'You certainly are careful aren't you? I assure you that I would not stoop so low as to poison you.'

He tore off a piece of meat from Alba's portion before putting it into his mouth. The two warriors watched as he bit into the flesh. Juice ran down his chin as he chewed and despite himself, Argyll felt his stomach yearn to sink his own teeth into the meat.

'A bit seared, but an excellent piece of meat,' their host announced.

Satisfied, the two men tore hungrily into their portions.

'I apologise for our caution. We meant no offence,' Alba replied once he had finished.

'It is understood,' Rigari nodded. 'Now come, tell

me of your travels and what you have learned. Then I will share my side.'

Alba recounted their tale, joined and occasionally embellished by Argyll. Rigari was surprised when they came to Tadc's death.

'A complex tale indeed,' Rigari said once Alba had finished. 'I see why you are so on edge. We had not heard of the death of the Dobunni chieftain.'

'Neither did we until it was too late,' said Argyll. 'We ended up in a pit for it.'

'Indeed so,' smiled Rigari. 'What do you make of his successor, this Gruenval?'

'He seems fair,' replied Alba. 'More *balanced* than his predecessor.'

'Does he hold the same political views?'

'I suspect he will maintain the status quo with the Red. Certainly, he will not want any existential threat when his rule over the Dobunni is only just beginning. I think we can expect stability from him, for now at least.'

'I suppose that's something,' Rigari acknowledged. 'Let us hope he does not get tempted to dip his feet too deep into the Red cesspit.'

'You have not told us why you made such effort to find us,' Alba asked, changing direction.

'A fair question,' Rigari acknowledged, calling Horva over to sit with them. 'I believe I may be able to fill in some gaps and also grant you some additional knowledge which you will not be aware of.'

'I would like to start with the Great Council meeting, if you don't mind?' Alba interrupted.

'Patience my friend,' Rigari replied. 'I will, in fact, begin *before* the council meeting.'

Surprised, Alba acquiesced. 'Please continue.'

'As you know, the chieftain and elders of all the main tribes receive a summons whenever the Great Council is to be convened. A courier is despatched to each tribe, the chieftain informed verbally, who will then give his response before the courier returns to Toryn.'

'That is how it is done,' Alba agreed.

'Well, in this case it was different.'

'Different?'

'The courier who sought me out that day was Tadc.'

Alba was shocked. 'Tadc!'

'Yes,' Rigari continued. 'He was the courier.'

'That is most unusual.'

'Indeed. But there was cause to his visit.'

'I think I have an idea what.'

'Tadc was vehement and brazen,' Rigari continued. 'He attempted to usurp my views on the Romans to bring them in line with his own. He was very animated and very determined.'

'He tried to bribe you?' guessed Alba.

'He was loaded with coin. In fact, I was surprised by just how much coin he had, plus he was brazen enough to say he possessed more, much more.'

'You suspected he had been bought?'

'I think his allegiance had already been procured

by the time he met me. He seemed obsessed with granting the Romans title to our lands. He was animated about how much money and gold would come my way if I allowed the takeover of farms, mines, even our peat bogs.'

Alba considered for a moment. 'That would certainly tie in to what Gruenval told us of his recent behaviour.'

Argyll, impatient as ever, interrupted. 'How did you respond, Rigari?'

'I told him no,' Rigari answered, ignoring Argyll's directness.

'As simple as that?'

'As simple as that.'

'Then Tadc would have seen you as an adversary when he left.'

'Yes. He was most displeased and by the end of our interview he was protesting so loud that I summoned Horva to escort him out. To be honest, the man seemed irrational. He was consumed by visions of power and wealth.'

Alba considered for a moment. 'I am minded to believe that you have been lucky. I suspect that it is only because Doube was more openly defiant of his views in the Great Council that you were not targeted first.'

'That was mine and Horva's opinion too. However, with Tadc dead, do you think that threat has gone?'

'I think we are all in danger. Tadc appears to have been removed because his aspirations had grown too big for his masters liking. He may not have been getting the rewards he so desired quickly enough. I suspect that was what vexed him on his return from the council. His ambition and probably the irrationality which you detected made him a liability.'

'But are we any closer in determining who his masters are?'

'We know part of the story. Tadc was certainly in league with the Roman centurion we met at Gruenval's fort. We suspect that the Red were involved in Doube's murder too, although whether they wielded the blade that so viciously gauged out his innards is uncertain.'

'And who do you think killed Tadc?'

'My guess, would be the centurion he dealt with. He probably received the order to despatch Tadc and to make it look like it was in retribution for Doube's death.'

'What about this valley creature which you battled. Was that instigated deliberately?'

'My own feeling is that the creature had dwelt in that accursed place for a long time. I suspect that it was known about, most likely by their sorcerer. He probably picked the location as a failsafe in case Lucius did not kill us first. A risky strategy because that thing would not have cared less whose blood it fed on, Briton or Roman.'

'So, that still leaves the question about who killed Doube,' Rigari replied.

'It always comes back to that and I must confess

my sight remains clouded over who did the foul deed.' Alba answered.

'Could it not just have been the Romans or even Tadc?' Rigari ventured. 'Gruenval said he could get enraged and I well remember his anger when Doube thwarted his attempts to convince the council into a closer relationship with the Red.'

'The thing that bothers me is the violence that was done to Doube's person,' Alba replied. 'The man was gutted so that his belly was hollow when we found him. It seemed personal, either through hate for the man or for what he stood for. Tadc, as we know, was motivated by greed. Whilst he was undoubtedly offended at Doube, I cannot see the hatred running so deep as to stoop to evisceration. However, I have to concede that both his anger and political views give him motive. He could be the killer even if his masters removed him later.

'I suppose the Romans would be careful to avoid direct involvement. Such an obvious act attributed to them would bring immediate retribution and conflict,' Rigari mused.

'And that is where we come back full circle,' Alba replied frustrated.

'What will you do now?' Rigari asked.

'We will return to Rendrr and update him personally with what we have learned.'

'Personally? Are your other elders not fully aware of all of the details?' Rigari asked, surprised.

Alba shifted uncomfortably. 'We were instructed not to tell anyone of the specific details of Doube's death, particularly the manner of it.'

'That is unusual. Rendrr will be forced to tell your people now. Too much is at stake and there is still danger.'

'And an unknown assassin,' agreed Alba.

'Let us hope the assassin does not challenge your own chieftain. Incidentally, can you be sure of Rendrr's position on the matter of the Red?'

'He has not given us cause to think anything other than a continued resistance to Red expansion. He did, after all, send us on this quest to uncover Doube's murderer.'

Alba regarded Rigari. 'You are suspicious?'

'I have attended many councils in my time Alba. As a consequence I know what makes men tick. It is not always obvious to the unskilled eye when a man has hidden motives. Still, given Doube was sent to the Great Council with Rendrr's blessing then it is reasonable to assume they shared a common and settled position.'

'Aren't you both forgetting Toryn?' Argyll interrupted. 'He chairs the Great Council. If anyone would have his hand on what lies beneath mens' words then he surely would.'

Rigari nodded. 'Ah yes, Toryn. Your companion is right. He would be very well placed to conspire with both Roman and Briton alike. An ideal collaborator to sow the corruption that precipitated these deaths.'

'And he has a wife roughly the age of the girl that Tadc sold off,' Argyll added quietly.

'He certainly has temper enough,' conceded Alba.

'Toryn has the temperament for sure. His *enforcement* at the Counsels are somewhat legendary,' joked Rigari. 'However, he is like my hillfort; he has been around for so many seasons that I would find it difficult to believe he would sell out to the Romans. I suppose it could happen, but if he was the one then there would be little hope for any of us. Of course, let us not forget that there was one other at the Great meeting.'

'You mean Artek, the Brigantes chieftain?'

'Exactly.'

'We have not heard much about him at all,' Argyll remarked, 'except that Toryn described him as strangely silent during the meeting, which he thought peculiar.'

'It was certainly out of character ,' Rigari agreed. 'The man was usually at the forefront of everything. He would be first to produce his blade should anyone take offence with his views. I had never known him remain so quiet as that night.'

'Then once we have taken counsel with Rendrr, we must seek out Artek. His behaviour remains under suspicion,' Alba decided.

'Will you travel back with us to Rendrr?' Argyll asked.

Rigari shook his head. 'I will accompany you as far as the great fort at Bredon, then I must return to my own. But know this, I stand with you on this issue of the Red and Doube's murder. If you need my assistance then myself and my warriors stand ready to fight.'

CHAPTER XII

'Our agent is becoming increasingly vexed at your inability to protect his interests and his identity,' fumed Favius.

'The barbarians have been lucky thus far,' Servius conceded. 'However, luck is a fickle friend, and theirs is running out.'

'We have heard your excuses before and yet these two barbarians remain stubbornly at large. They have learned much already. Too much!'

'I have instructed Lucius to pursue them northwards,' the Legatus blustered. 'He assures me they will not escape again.'

'Do not attempt to be subtle with me Servius. It is not Lucius who bears the brunt of this fiasco. *Your* failure has caused our agent to take matters into his own hands. He does not trust us to deal with it. Do you hear what I am saying Servius? A Briton does not trust *us!*'

'I am confident we will endure and that Lucius will find them.'

Favius cut him short. 'I care not whether Lucius kills them or our agent. The point is, by forcing our agent to act, your failure is risking our whole operation. If the Britons rise up or worse if they unite several of the tribes then we will have a rebellion on our hands. That is not what my masters desire.'

'Sir, I assure you that . . .'

'Silence!' yelled Favius. 'I will hear no more of this. One more time, Servius and you will reap the penalty of your constant failure.'

The Legatus stayed his tongue. Considering it best to retreat, he bowed and turned to leave. As he was about to step outside, Favius called him back.

'Servius . . .'

'Yes?'

'You would do well to remember that my masters are not as forgiving as I am, but if you need a reminder of the consequence of failure, then I suggest you have a word with Adrionix.'

Favius turned his back. Unseen, a cruel smile flickered across his narrow lips.

The Legatus let out a breath of relief when he exited Favius's quarters. He had expected a grilling. As a soldier he was used to that, but Favius was a man with connections; associates who you did not want to upset or prove that you were incompetent. The organisation to which Favius belonged worked in the shadows, their influence only visible via the actions of those they directly commanded or puppets who cared not who pulled their strings. He,

Servius, was but a small cog in the machinery of their empire, but he had been promised much. He did not care what their grand plan for utopia was as long as he benefitted. Should his actions succeed, then he would retire a wealthy man, content to run his family winery, maybe even expand it to other areas of the empire. Should he fail, well, then he doubted he would have much need of wine any longer.

'A Legatus is only as good as the men that fight beneath him,' he thought. Yet, here he was, Legatus Servius, commander of the Legio XX Valeria Victrix, a mere foot soldier, a paid employee of an unseen organisation who held his future in their hands.

And Foot soldiers are expendable, he thought grimly.

Approaching the sorcerer's tent, he noticed the usual guard was absent. That was odd, but maybe Adrionix had sent him away to obtain food or wine. He would probably need it if Favius had given him a bollocking. That thought gave him cruel satisfaction as he strode through the entrance, walking in unannounced, as was his way.

He was a Legatus after all.

Adrionix's plan to lure the barbarians into the so-called cursed valley had back-fired dramatically. Favius had obviously disciplined Adrionix for his failure. The enemy had guessed their ruse, and to Adrionix's deficit, had nullified what lurked in the shadows. Clearly, Adrionix was not so powerful as he made out. He had shown weakness and Servius was determined to extort his own advantage from the defeat of the sorcerer's plans.

Enjoying the thought of benefitting from Adrionix's misfortune, he looked about the sorcerer's tent. The interior was dark, the atmosphere subdued. All but one of the candles were spent. The remaining taper cast a weak, transient light. The Legatus halted, allowing his eyes to adjust. It was disconcertingly quiet, broken only by the occasional sound of the goatskin panels catching a breath of wind. Gradually, he made out a form in the centre, unmoving.

'Adrionix,' announced the Legatus. 'Favius had bid me . . .'

He stopped mid-sentence, his mouth dropping open as his eyes focused on the sight before him. Facing him, Adrionix was naked, bound hand and foot to the tent's central supporting strut. He was also quite dead.

The face was frozen in a look of abject horror. As Servius struggled to take in the grotesque image before him, his gaze ran over the rest of the body. The cause of death was obvious enough. He counted no less than nine arrows buried up to their fletchings within the sorcerer's punctured torso.

One arrow had hit low. The Legatus wondered if it had been deliberate. What was left of Adrionix's balls were slowly dripping down his left leg in a collage of blood and gristle. Servius wondered if he had been dead before or after that shot.

Someone had enjoyed this killing.

Someone with a fancy for the dramatic.
Someone like . . .

A movement caused him to whip around. Favius was stood right behind him.

How had he not heard him before?

As a soldier, Servius both appreciated and feared that Favius had got within strike range before he had been aware of his presence.

He could have killed me easily.

The fact that I am still breathing is because he wishes it so. I have a chance still.

Favius flicked his eyes from Servius to the sorcerer's pierced body. 'A little dramatic, but I think it makes the point. My masters paid handsomely for his services but it appeared that money did not buy quality. Let us hope his successor proves more reliable.'

He leaned in to Servius's left ear, close enough for his warm breath to tickle the hairs. 'Unless you wish a similar fate, no more failures. I granted Adrionix a relatively short suffering, but this would pale against that which my other associates enjoy inflicting.'

That night the Legatus consumed many glasses of the family wine. The image of Adrionix took much of the red grape before Servius finally succumbed to a restless sleep.

***

Wyeval Woods, Cornovii territory

Beatha moved slowly and very deliberately through the trees. Her quarry was cunning, difficult to find and given to growing close to the ground in the places of darkness. A fungus, it preferred the damp shade found beneath rock or fallen bough. She sought it out for her salves for when warrior or farmer required a wound healing.

The search for the prized fungus had been long and, as yet, unsuccessful. Her horse was a distance away, tied to a large birch on the outskirts of the wood through which she hunted. The sun was several cycles past its prime and she would have to return soon or risk travelling at night.

'A little longer,' she said to herself. *'I know it must grow somewhere hereabouts.'*

Several rocks of the correct size and disposition presented themselves, but each time she overturned them, it was disappointment which grew in its place. Only woodlice, who scurried away as their refuge was suddenly exposed to the light, lived on the dark side of these stone habitats.

Frustrated, she stood up, stretching her arms out wide to release the tension from her endeavours. This ancient wood was one her favourite locations to seek medicinal herbs. Often, she would visit just to walk idly amongst the trees, lie down within the ferns and feel like she belonged to this place. To be part of the very fabric of the wood, listening to the wind play through the trees, the call of raven, the shriek of fox; all these things gave her pleasure.

She blinked herself present, suddenly realising something felt different. Silence had crept up, unseen and unexpected, deadening the wood. She stood quite still, unsure and listening for some indication of the cause.

'How quickly a place of beauty changes,' she thought. Even the empty space between the trees seemed filled with an invisible, ominous presence all of a sudden. Involuntarily, she shivered. The air had become heavy, burdened not by the freshness of nature, but as though reality was being cocooned around her. Amid the stillness, the thumping of her heart seemed so loud it would give her away. But give her away to what or to who?

She knew well the beasts that roamed the forest and woodlands. Wolves were an ever-present danger, but only if you were perceived as a threat or were close to death. Wild boar were also prevalent and could inflict a severe injury with their tusks. Yet, both boar and wolf were natural predators, part of the fabric of the wood. The feeling she had now did not feel natural. Her instinct told her this was man, not beast, which disturbed the balance.

Then came the sound she feared, a twig breaking under the weight of something moving very slowly and stealthily. She slipped her hand to her side where a small dagger was suspended in the ropes of her cloak. Unsheathing it she held it tight, using her grip on its leathered hilt to give her courage.

She was being tracked; hunted by someone who was attempting to be stealthy in their approach.

That probably meant there was only one of them.

Beatha was always vigilant when out on her foraging missions. She kept to the main tracks and ridgeways where possible, but when she had to venture into remote areas then she was careful to ensure no sign of bandits or the Red. Yet, clearly she had not been careful enough this time.

Someone had spotted her, following her to this glade within the woods.

It concerned her that she had been tracked so easily. Her usual precautions had been swept aside by a stranger who was confident enough to go it alone. That suggested it was not the Romans who sought her but somebody else.

A skilled tracker.

Cautiously, she slipped between the trunks of pine and birch, making her way to where the light was unobstructed. Another sound caught her ear, louder this time. While she had delayed her pursuer must have kept moving. She brought herself up behind one of the pines, pulling her skirts close in to avoid detection. Once more, she strained to hear, desperately trying to fix the position of her pursuer in relation to her own. The sound of pursuit stopped and she realised that he must be doing the same thing.

Beatha was brave, but, none the less, a rising panic was striving to take hold. Already she could feel the tendrils of fear bring a weak numbness to her limbs. There was still no sound; pursuer and quarry alike using all their senses to detect the other. Risking a look, she peered from behind the bole of the tree. The rough bark grazed her cheek causing her to flinch. She retreated back, stung by both pain and fear.

The view had looked clear.

She could wait it out, get a fix on his position and then move, but fear seldom tolerates patience. Besides, very soon dusk would fall and she did not want to find herself alone, lost in the dark and at the mercy of night animals. She had already heard the cry of wolves, albeit distant, but nonetheless a danger.

Her instinct was telling her to move, escape the woods whilst she could still navigate, recover her horse and flee as fast as she could. Only briefly did her mind try and interrupt the impulse.

Instinct overcame logic as fear succeeded reason. She hitched her skirts and ran as hard as she could. Reaching the edge of the woods she stopped for a second, expecting to hear the sound of feet crashing through the undergrowth behind her but there was only silence.

Maybe she had miscalculated how close he had been to her.

The forest could play tricks on the senses and she was experienced enough to know how sound could deceive. She carried on, keeping just inside the tree line as she had planned. Somewhere in the back of her mind a voice was desperately trying to tell her something, warn her, but hope had risen within and hope does not tolerate threats to its throne.

The voice within tried again, but she quashed it as her desperation spurred her on. Suddenly, she was out, back to the clearing where the horse stood exactly where she had left it. Relief flooded over her as her hopes lifted. Maybe now she would permit the voice to speak.

The horse! How do you think he found you?

Too late, realization dawned. The heavy bough cracked across the back of her head so hard that as she flew forward her last image was of the ground rushing up to meet her.

Her attacker threw down the blooded club. 'Stupid girl! Do you not think I have tracked greater quarry than you in my time?'

The man knelt down searching for a pulse on the girl's neck. Satisfied she still lived, he tied a woven bag over her head, bound her hands and feet before tossing her over his shoulder. He whistled, a pre-agreed signal.

An accomplice emerged from concealment, leading two horses forward to where the man stood with his prize. Beatha was thrown over the larger of the beasts and secured with rope looped underneath its belly back through the bindings of her hands and feet.

His accomplice noticed the drip of blood fall from Beatha's scalp onto the ground. 'There was no need to injure her. You could have restrained her instead.'

'If I want a commentary on my actions I'll ask for it. Now shut your fucking mouth and take her to where I told you.' He grabbed his accomplice roughly by the arm, deliberately digging his fingers into the exposed skin. 'Make sure nobody sees you. Fail me and you know what will happen tonight.'

The accomplice pulled away, knowing through experience that silence rather than crying out was the easiest way to avoid more pain. He would always react to crying or yelling with more vindictiveness. Silently, the accomplice lead the horse and its limp passenger away.

The man smiled to himself.

'A warrior should know his enemy's weakness Alba and I have just found yours. That little bitch has just become my insurance.'

CHAPTER XIII

'I can see the great fort at Bredon,' Argyll exclaimed, standing upright on his mount.

Alba and Rigari followed his outstretched hand. Sure enough, just visible through the morning mist rose the hill fort that dominated the landscape for miles.

'We are almost at the point where we must go our separate ways,' noted Rigari.

'Argyll and I have enjoyed your company these last two days,' answered Alba.

Rigari nodded at the compliment. 'It is good our two peoples should strike such a close accord. Should our shared enemy succeed, then we will need all our resources to resist.'

'Hopefully, it does not come to that, but I am glad we are met well. I am sure Rendrr will be reassured knowing we have such firm friends to the east of our borders.'

Rigari's party, including the two Cornovii men numbered a dozen men at arms. As they were all mounted, their progress northwards towards Alba's home territory had been fairly swift and, as yet, uneventful. At the head of the column were two scouts who would periodically disappear then reappear after checking the route ahead. Already today, they had been out and back four times. No one anticipated the fifth would be different.

Once more the two scouts approached, their horses kicking up dust as they rode in. This time their approach seemed faster and more urgent. The lead scout, a warrior named Arco, rode straight up to Rigari and bowed.

'We found a party of native warriors, all dead, cut down in a small clearing not two leagues from here.'

'A Roman attack?'

'It looks like they killed each other. Some still have the weapon of death embedded in their bodies. We saw no evidence of Roman involvement. This appears to be a brawl or other dispute which got out of hand.'

Rigari looked across to Alba. 'Is this common in these parts?'

'Occasionally, rival groups do get into a skirmish, but it is unusual for this level of violence.'

'There is something else,' reported the second scout. 'One of the warriors still lives. He may yet tell us something if we have the means to aid him.'

'I may be able to help with that, 'Alba volunteered. 'I carry medicine which may be of some use, depending on the extent of his wounds and how quickly we can get to him.'

'Alba, this smells of a trap. Remember, how Tadc's death was staged? This may be a similar attempt,' Argyll warned.

'We will all go,' Rigari cut in. 'Your friend is right to be cautious. I too find it convenient that this occurs directly in our path. Therefore, let us go forward in what numbers we have.'

'One moment,' Horva cut in, addressing the scout. 'Describe the terrain where you found these men?'

'It is a small patch of grassland surrounded by fern and bracken,' the scout replied.

'And the ferns,' Horva persisted, 'are they thick enough to conceal an enemy?'

'The foliage is extensive. Though we saw no other, it could conceal many men.'

Horva turned to Rigari and Alba. 'I suggest dividing our forces so that a few of us enter the area first, with the rest holding back in reserve should we need additional support.'

'That sounds reasonable,' Alba approved. Argyll nodded too.

'Chieftain, I will accompany Alba together with three others. If all is well then I will send one of our men back. If not, then he will not return and we will be dead, but you will be safe.'

Alba laughed. 'Horva, I hope it does not come to that!'

Horva selected one of the scouts before calling up two other warriors. 'These are Sheal and Braycll. They will accompany us, together with Arco who will lead.'

Alba and Horva kicked off, leaving Rigari, Argyll and the remaining men.

'I hope they're careful,' Argyll grumbled, unhappy not to be with Alba.

'Let us hope our concerns are unwarranted,' Rigari answered. 'One of the challenges of being chieftain is to question everything that I am told and sometimes even the evidence of my own eyes. It can be tiring constantly seeing threat when there is often none. Of course, it only takes one lapse on my part to bring disaster. That is why I must be forever vigilant.'

'I never thought of it like that,' Argyll answered. 'The responsibility must weigh heavy. I do not believe I would ever wish to be in your place, as a chieftain I mean.'

'My people look to me to be perfect, Argyll,' Rigari replied. 'I am not allowed to make mistakes. That would show weakness and subvert my authority. Yet, I think they forget that I am of flesh and blood, just like them.'

Argyll realised he had seen a brief glimpse into Rigari's life. That of a man burdened with the responsibility of leadership and the expectation of infallibility. He wondered if all chieftains felt the same burden or whether the drive to lead overcame the emotional baggage.

'In the meantime,' Rigari added, 'let us get to our position so that should we be needed then we can respond quickly.'

They moved off, the chieftain's mask back in place.

The journey to the dead warriors was short, the horses covering the ground in good order. Here the soil was poor, punctuated only by a hopeful sapling or hardy birch. Either side lay a thick blanket of bracken and tall ferns.

Alba was nervous. 'This land is perfect for an enemy to hide in. I did not realise this vegetation would be quite so thick or so tall.'

In response, Horva raised his hand for them to stop.

'Arco, are we close?'

'The killing ground lies just beyond this slight rise,' Arco replied.

'Then, we will continue on foot,' Horva commanded.

The warriors dismounted, following the same discipline as Alba, using the horses as protection. Cautiously, they crept forward, passing over the small ridge Arco had indicated. Before them lay some twenty bodies, just as the scout had reported. They looked on in silence, trying to work out why so many men had died here.

Up till now, they had grown accustomed to the background sound of nature accompanying their journey. Here, where death had struck, there was none. The imprint of violence, of stolen endings, was still fresh. There was a sense of aberration, the fabric of nature's innocence tainted by what had occurred. They could all feel it. Animals would not return to this place for some time.

Alba surveyed the layout of the bodies. As far as he could determine, it looked like Arco had described. Two groups of rival warriors that had run up against each other, found argument, slaughtered to the man.

The only thing was, it looked two perfect and conflict is seldom so neat. He moved over to the nearest body, noting that a sword thrust to the chest had ended this life. The next man he checked was the same, killed by a single strike to the torso. When the third corpse matched the others he stood up, alarmed.

'There is something wrong here.'

Horva came over to him. 'What do you see?'

'The wounds on these three bodies are all remarkably similar. I find it hard to accept that they were all killed in the same way during the heat of battle. It does not go like that, as you know.'

'Two of the others bear similar wounds also.'

'This begins to smell of a corruption not just of the dead flesh.'

'A set up?'

'Either that or someone is trying to detract from laying blame for this action. But if that were so, I do not think we would see such similar wound patterns. These men may well have been murdered *before* being laid out as we see them.'

'Horva, here is the man who still lives!' Arco shouted, kneeling beside a warrior who lay just outside the wall of fern.

'Quickly, whilst he still has life in him,' encouraged Alba, leaving the dead, hoping to save the whisper of life that remained at Arco's feet.

They had only moved a couple of paces when Arco lurched toward them, suddenly unsteady upon his feet. Horrified, they watched as a strangled gurgle came from his throat whilst his eyes became wide, staring at them in disbelief. A long wooden shaft with a bloody iron head protruded from his mouth. To get there, it had travelled through the back of his neck. Arco's dying eyes locked onto the cruel barb, painted with his own blood, as a last breath exited the punctured mouth. His lifeless body seemed suspended for one tormented second before finally tipping forward.

'Ambush!' yelled Horva.

A loud roar went up either side as two rows of Roman soldiers materialised out of the undergrowth.

The Romans held their line several paces away. Alba estimated that they were outnumbered four to one. Fighting their way out would be impossible. Their options were to fight and die or play for time, hoping Argyll and Rigari would come to their aid.

The Britons stood back-to-back, anticipating an assault from both sides. The disciplined Roman legionaries ignored the Britons, keeping their eyes fixed forward, shields locked with their neighbour. One side of their line parted and an officer appeared, resplendent in plumed helmet and mirrored plate.

'You will drop your weapons.'

The Britons held fast. Surrender, even against these odds would be a desertion of all they held true. Alba recognised the voice all too well.

'Come now, do you wish death so soon?' Lucius prompted. 'You are outnumbered and surrounded. Resistance is futile. Save yourselves a pointless death.'

Nobody moved.

Lucius smiled, enjoying the stage he had prepared. He was already congratulating himself on springing a successful trap. Even the delay in his appearance had been carefully choregraphed.

'As I am sure you know, I seek the one called Alba. Hand him over and you can go on your way. There is no need for more blood to be spent.'

The Britons stared back, unmoved. Alba wondered how long they would have before Lucius commanded his men to attack. The fact they were not already fighting told him that Lucius wanted them alive, or, at least, *him* alive. If he could draw this out long enough, duel verbally with the centurion, then they might be able to hold out long enough for Rigari's men to arrive. With any luck, Argyll would already be concerned that something had gone awry when he had not received word.

'We do not know of this Alba who you speak of,' Horva replied.

'Then what are you doing here?' Lucius retorted. 'I see five Britons before me with no apparent reason to be wandering around or are you just admiring the scenery?'

He laughed at his own quip, spreading his hands out to encompass the death below. His men laughed with him, a learned behaviour to enforce cohesion and earn favour.

'Do we need a reason? These are our lands, not yours and if you must know we are a hunting party from Bredon Fort,' declared Horva. 'We are returning there now.'

'Bollocks are you!' shouted back Lucius. 'I know you did not come from Bredon Fort because we have *already* been there. The chieftain of that particular blot on the landscape knows nothing of you. Now, I say again, surrender Alba or die. The choice is yours.'

'Perhaps if you told us why you seek this man, then we could reach some accord? It is conceivable that we may have come across him in our travels.'

Alba was impressed with Rigari's second. Like him, Horva had determined that playing for time was their best option.

'Questions, questions…,' Lucius flounced. 'Do you care why I seek him. It is enough to know that I do, surely?'

'If you threaten us with death, then surely we have the right to know why?' Horva persisted.

Don't push it Horva, Alba thought.

Too late, Lucius lifted his arm. Sheal fell. The arrow had hit him in the same spot as Arco.

Killed by an expert shot.

'I really do not care if I kill you one by one,' Lucius

remarked nonchalantly. He sauntered over to the wounded warrior Arco had tried to help. The man was clinging to life, a low moan emanating from his throat.

'Just so we understand each other,' Lucius continued, 'I enjoy killing. It matters not to me whether my enemy is standing on two feet or lying half dead on the ground.'

At this point Lucius placed the tip of his gladius in the dying man's mouth. The warrior's eyes widened. 'In my world Briton, you are barbarian, sub-human scum. I would wipe your kind off the face of this accursed land.'

He looked straight at Horva whilst slowly pushing down. Beneath him, the warrior gagged, his body arching in one final convulsion. Lucius continued pushing as the blade exited the man's neck and bit into the ground beneath. Only when he could go no further, did he pull back and kick the body off the crimson steel in one motion.

He held his hand up again. 'Now, for the last time, deliver Alba and live or stay silent and die.'

Their time had run out.

Alba had no intention of leaving Horva and Braycll to die. He was about to surrender himself when suddenly the shrill cry of a hawk carried across the air.

Argyll's signal!

But were they in position? Had Argyll signalled only that they were close? He would have to take that chance.

'I am Alba,' he announced, stepping forward.

Lucius looked elated. 'At last! Well, you have led us a merry dance haven't you. My Legatus is especially looking forward to meeting you.'

He walked over to Alba, triumph energising his walk. Standing directly in front of him, he drew himself up to his full height.

'I do not take kindly to be made a fool of, Briton.'

'You seem to do it well enough on your own,' Alba retorted.

'Funny,' Lucius mocked him. 'Well, we will see how long your good humour lasts when we have finished with you shan't we.'

He beckoned to his men. Two soldiers left the Roman line, advancing either side of Alba. They never reached him as two thuds echoed across the clearing followed by two dead bodies hitting the ground. From each of the soldiers' necks a native arrow protruded. Before anyone could react a third legionary emerged from the ferns flailing both hands in front of him. An arrow was buried between his shoulder blades and as they watched another struck him through the back of the neck. The irony of the marksmanship was not lost on Lucius.

'I'm afraid I will have to decline your invitation,' Alba smiled.

'How dare you kill soldiers of Rome,' stormed Lucius. 'I will have your head for this. Your body will be hauled up and I will cut the entrails from your stomach whilst your heart still beats. I will . . .'

'Enough!' yelled back Alba. 'I care not for your

threats, Roman. And it is I who should be promising *you* retribution.'

'You bluff,' retorted Lucius. 'How do I know that you have no more than one or two men beyond what I see before me?'

'You don't, but would you risk your life and that of your men?'

'We would die together.'

'Yes.'

'I could order my men to charge.'

'You could.'

Lucius flushed red. Alba stared him out, enjoying the frustration playing across the centurion's ruddied features.

'We will meet again, Briton.'

'Of that, I am sure, Roman.'

Lucius signalled his men. The Romans closed ranks, retreating in defensive formation. For several moments, Lucius remained exposed, in front of the defensive line, staring back in their direction before finally disappearing behind the shield wall. Alba surmised that his anger or pride had overwhelmed his military training, a fact that might come in useful for any future encounters.

Argyll followed by the rest of Rigari's men ran forward.

'You left it a little late there, my friend,' said Alba.

'Sorry. We had to make sure they did not hear our approach, plus it took an age before the archers could get a clean shot without going through one of you.'

'Then I am glad you waited,' laughed Alba.

'That centurion has it in for you. I think you've just made it personal.'

'He's certainly full of himself, but he is also dangerous. It showed a level of ingenuity to create the stage upon which we have just played. I'm not even sure where they found all these Britons. My guess would be they were captured men turned slave or just innocents which they dressed up to look the part. They have done similar before.'

'Retribution is well earned by this Roman, Alba. He must be dealt with.'

While they were talking Horva had moved across to where Arco's body lay on the ground. With surprising reverence, he knelt beside the dead man's head, held it firm in the one hand and snapped the arrow shaft before pulling both ends out. He laid the head down gently, bending his own in acknowledgement of the warrior's passing.

'I am sorry,' Alba said quietly.

'Arco was my sister's man,' Horva replied. He sighed deeply, closing Arco's eyes with his palms. 'He was a good man. He treated my sister well and did not digress from her. I do not know how to tell her, Alba. She was much in love with him, as he was in return. This will hit her hard.'

'No words can subdue the pain of a loved one's passing,' Alba replied. 'However, he died a warrior's death, with honour. I hope that will go some way to helping your sister through his loss. We will celebrate his life and that of Sheal tonight as we toast their passage to the gods.'

CHAPTER XIV

The cave was well concealed, invisible to those who were not aware of its existence. Knowledge of its location was guarded, limited to all but a few. The entrance, such that it was, merely a slit in the rock face where one edge lipped over the other, effectively concealing the gap unless you stood to the side angling yourself to the entry. In the winter months, streamers of moss cascaded over the external faces adding another layer of camouflage.

It was not deep, stretching back approximately sixty paces from entrance to rear. Barely larger than a grotto, there was headroom to accommodate a man near the entrance decreasing to a quarter of that by the time the far end had been reached. A single hollow in the side of a sandstone ridge, it bore no adjacent tunnels or caverns. Only the occasional weasel or stoat ventured into its recess. The floor was uneven and barren, except for the skeletons of several unwary birds who had found their way in but not their way out. Against one side lay more remains, the physical remnants of a warrior long past. The rusting hilt of the dagger that ended him protruded from the exposed rib cage.

Long dead,
Long forgotten,
Long murdered.

Within this hidden space lay another form, out of place, deposited with no sense of care. The body had been here for over a day. A low wail echoed within the cavern as it fought a path back to the realm of light, unaware that it lay concealed from the world outside.

Beatha flitted in and out of consciousness as her mind strove to fight through the veil of darkness. Each time her awareness took hold, the tempest within her skull drummed out a deafening beat which tore from one side of her brain to the other.

Her captors had left the coarse bag over her head, loose, so she had enough air to breathe, but, nonetheless, a deliberate act of indifference. Her limbs were tightly bound, forbidding escape. No fire was lit and whilst tolerable by day, the temperature would drop sharply with the retreat of the sun.

As she struggled to wake, an intense pain seared across her head forcing her submission to the sanctity of unconsciousness for the first few times of stirring. Strong of spirit, Beatha's innate energy fought hard to break through. The tether that held the connection between soul and physical wound back, until finally her eyelids flickered open.

The pain fought back, attempting to drag her

back to oblivion. It would have been easy to allow it, yet within her a voice told her that she was through the storm.

It was alright to live, to awake and be whole.

The expected image of her captivity did not materialise. She was still in darkness. A rising panic overtook her in those first few moments until the feeling of her body began to return.

Were her eyes not working?
Had she been blinded?
Was she dead after all?

When she moved her head, something else moved too.

Her face was covered; there was reason for her blindness.

The realisation forced the panic away. She could concentrate on other parts of her body without the encumbrance of fear. Feeling returned as her heart pumped harder. She could move her arms now.

Just enough to get a grip with her fingers.

After a struggle, she managed to free herself of the bag, but there was little reward for she remained in darkness.

Perhaps she could free her limbs instead?

Whoever had bound her was no stranger to knots. Even if she bent her hand back against the floor, her fingers would not reach the bindings. Exasperated, she tried the same with her feet. Leaning forward proved ineffective; she could reach the rope but before long her back would pain. A better solution was lying on her side, bringing her knees up to her chest. She could remain in that position for longer and her fingers could attend the bindings. However, her abductor had been just as thorough. There was no way she could loosen the knot.

She tried shouting for help, holding little hope of success, as someone who had been so diligent with her bindings would hardly leave her ungagged if there was a chance anyone would hear. A banshee screamed back in reply, as her corrupted voice bounced and mutated between every exposed plane.

She was quite alone. Spent with the effort, hoarse and frustrated, she lay back deciding instead to ascertain her surroundings in more detail. Her efforts to free herself had allowed her to deduce that she lay on a rocky floor. That there was no breeze and no light from anywhere led her to suspect she was in a subterranean space. She had no way of ascertaining how far or how deep underground she was; the free world maybe a few paces away or many hundreds hence.

She continued to lay back, straining to pick up on any sound or movement that could help her. As her senses reached out she began to discern sounds, faint but definitely present. Strange barks filtered through the darkness, whistles and howls that would wax and wane. At first, she was bewildered, frightened that she may indeed be in a sub-realm caught between the living and the dead. Yet as she listened, she worked out that what she was actually picking up were the sounds of fox, hare, owl and deer. Relief flooded over her. To be within earshot of such creatures meant she remained in the material realm. The underworld had not yet claimed her soul.

Her biggest fear was that she would be just left, forgotten and never found, destined for a slow lingering death of starvation. But if she had been left alive, then surely it was for some purpose, else why not kill her back in the woods?

This question vexed her deeply. To her knowledge, she posed no threat to anyone nor had she any enemies to speak of. Her people respected and valued her skills in the healing arts. That led her to another line of thinking. Maybe she wasn't the target but was being used to get at somebody else. Alba was the only one she could think of that made any sense. She was being used to get at him; the bait to destroy her lover.

The only thing was, she could not think of anyone that would do that or who had any motive to. Yet, here she was, trussed up like a bale of straw, waiting for . . .

Waiting for what?

On what she calculated was her third day of incarceration, she heard a different sound. Someone was shuffling through the entrance. She lay still, hardly daring to breathe.

'Are you there?'

A woman's voice.

'Do you live?'

'I am here,' Beatha replied.

The woman shuffled toward her without a torch.

'Why do you not carry a light?' Beatha asked. 'Do you fear me so much, bound and alone, that you do not light your way?'

'I fear for both of us,' came the reply. 'Should it be known that I have visited you, then I would be sorely abused, even killed.'

'Then free me so I can get help!' Beatha implored.

'No!'

'But I have friends.'

'He is too powerful, in ways you cannot comprehend. I have brought you some fruit. It is not much, but it will sustain you until . . .'

'Until what?'

'Until, hopefully, I can come again.'

'But who are you? Your voice is vaguely familiar to me.'

'It is best you do not know.'

'But how . . .'

'No more! I must go before I am missed.'

The woman threw something on the floor. 'The fruit is in a small bag. When you are done conceal the bag. If he knows someone is helping you then he will become angry. He does evil things when he is angry.'

With that she left Beatha alone, but, at least, with food. Her mind was running over what she had learned. The woman's voice not completely alien. She knew she had heard it before but from where?

***

The young adjutant saluted and handed Servius a tablet. A senator's son, but with a pronounced bent limp, his father had begged Servius to find a position for him in the army.

'Any position,' the Senator had begged. *'If you do not take him, my family will wear the shame of a cripple for ages to come.'*

Servius had eventually agreed, his concession sweetened by the transfer of a large quantity of silver into his family vault. The youth, Laelius, had proved adequate as an aid but was not extraordinary. He did not fit in and was often the butt of his peers' practical jokes. Were he not Servius's adjutant then the Legatus wouldn't have been at all surprised to see him met with some tragic end. As it was, it was only fear of the Legatus's retribution that probably kept him in one piece.

'What is this?' Servius demanded.

'Sir, it is a message just received by courier from centurion Lucius Glaucus.'

'And?'

Laelius cleared his throat nervously. 'Sir, I believe it best if you read it personally.'

The Legatus glared at him, sensing unwelcome news.

'Have you read my private correspondence already Laelius?

Sir, no, I . . .'

Servius well knew that courier's notes were often read before their intended recipients set eyes on them. He was just enjoying making the boy suffer some more. No doubt Laelius' so-called friends would have suggested such a thing to him, knowing he would land in trouble with his superior.

The youth was perspiring like a pig and was likely to wet himself if pushed much further.

'My eyes grow tired. Read it for me,' Servius commanded, deciding it better to hear the contents of the tablet than have his quarters reeking of piss.

Laelius took back the tablet and nervously began to read.

'To Legatus Servius Maximus, from Lucius Glaucus. We caught up and intercepted a party of Britons returning from the South. I believe the barbarian Alba to be amongst them. A small party of my men sprung a trap on the Britons. In the battle that ensued, forty Britons were despatched for the loss of two of our own. We made good our great victory, despite enemy numbers exceeding our own by some degree. By careful investigation I apprehended the barbarian Alba and had begun to make good our withdrawal when a second, even greater force of Britons numbering some eighty men came upon us. Despite valiant efforts by the entire troop, we had to retire (in good order). The barbarian Alba was snatched from our hands by this more powerful force. I therefore decided to regroup and plot another interception. I may beg of the Legatus that due to the increased numbers of the enemy forces if he would be so good to send a further Centuria to fall under my direct command

in assurance of the apprehension or elimination of the barbarians. Yours Respectfully, Lucius Glaucus, Commander Legio XX Valeria Victrix.'

Servius stared at the tablet dumbstruck. Lucius had failed in his plan to trap the Britons. He had even seized the barbarian Alba into his grasp but had then lost him. The scale of Lucius's alleged *great victory* followed by retreat in lieu of a greater enemy force was clearly exaggeration. Yet the fact remained that Lucius had failed. The ramifications of this failure made the Legatus go cold.

Recovering himself, he addressed the youth.

'Have you shown this to anyone else?'

'No, sir.'

'Anyone at all?'

'Nobody Legatus.'

'Did anyone see it before the courier gave it to you?'

'I don't think so, sir.'

'You don't think?'

'I am sure not,' cried the panicked youth.

'Where is the courier now?' Servius asked, relaxing slightly.

'Outside, sir. I instructed him to wait for your reply.'

The youth had the sense to recognise urgency, at least.

The Legatus grabbed a blank tablet and hastily scribbled some orders. Then he wrote another note, this time for Lucius, folded it over and gave both to the adjutant.

'Now listen boy. This one goes to the Praefectus Castrorum, this one to the courier. Make sure the courier talks to no-one; no-one do you hear? It is a matter of life and death. Your life or death to be precise. Do not fail me. Go!'

Servius leaned both hands onto his desk. If he were lucky, he could keep this away from Favius, let Lucius succeed on his next attempt to capture or kill Alba and still come out of it well. He had acceded to his request for more men. On the other hand, if Favius found out about this further failure then it would not just be himself that would pay the price but that of his family as well. He doubted there would be a corner in the empire where any one of them would be safe.

He sat down heavily and poured himself a large glass of wine. His body warmed to the grape and soon he had exhausted not only the glass but the jug that fed it.

'How strange that fear makes for an exquisite taste,' he thought. 'If only I could bottle it then I would have the perfect vintage.'

CHAPTER XV

They had parted from Rigari's men just north of Bredon hill fort as planned. The remaining journey back to their own stronghold had been uneventful, despite the fear that Lucius might have been lying in wait for them. For now, the Roman centurion appeared to be absent, perhaps licking his wounds or plotting his next attempt. Alba doubted he would be gone for long. A man like Lucius would take it as a personal afront that he had been thwarted by a barbarian.

They did not fully relax until they passed through between the ramparts of their own fort. Exiting the main gate, they handed over their tired horses to a stable hand before heading off to see if Rendrr was available. Despite Argyll's protestations, Alba had decided they should report in first before seeking respite for their long journey.

Rues, Rendrr's personal guard, was stationed outside the chieftain's roundhouse. Seeing the two warriors approach he motioned for them to wait before disappearing inside. Reaching the entrance they waited for the guard's return. To their surprise, when the door opened it was Rendrr facing them rather than the guard.

'Come in, you two. Rues, have my wife prepare food and beer for our two warriors. You will find her at the well, I believe.'

Rues nodded and disappeared to expedite his orders.

'Sit down,' Rendrr commanded. 'You must tell me all about your adventures. But first, we will eat, drink and toast your return.'

'It has certainly been an experience we will not forget,' Alba replied, seating himself on the straw floor. Rendrr's house always had a thick straw bedding, heavier than most, one of the perks of being chieftain.

'We have survived multiple attempts to kill us, both by man and sorcery,' Argyll chipped in.

'I see,' Rendrr replied, but was interrupted by the appearance of Enica who hastily set about preparing their refreshments. Not for the first time did Alba cast an eye about Rendrr's wife.

This woman has high status yet remains a mystery.

Enica was flustered, no doubt embarrassed to have been caught absent at the very time she was expected to be in attendance. Alba doubted she ever strayed far from the roundhouse.

Impatient, Rendrr hurried her to serve their food. 'Wife, these men are hungry and thirsty. Do you embarrass me by your lack of urgency?'

She hastened without even a glance at her chiding husband. Having sliced some cuts of beef onto a board she quickly poured beer into three beakers and set about handing them out. Approaching Alba she stooped to hand him the platter of meat but stumbled, so that the plate flew off discharging its flesh deep within the straw lattice.

Enica flushed, bending down to recover the lost plate. 'My apologies. I will get you a replacement,' she said hastily.

'It's alright,' said Alba, kindly.

Her sleeve rode up as she extended her hand, exposing a patch of discoloured skin. Seeing him notice, she hastily grabbed the soiled meat and withdrew. When she returned with the replacement platter the usual stoic face mask of the chieftain's wife was back in place.

Once they had eaten and drunk their fill Rendrr asked them for a full report on their exploits. He listened keenly, asking questions here and there. He seemed most surprised when they relayed the encounter with the demon in the valley.

'I did not know such creatures existed,' he remarked.

'It is unusual to find such malevolent darkness in the world of man,' Alba replied.

'Do you think there are any more of these things lurking in the dark recesses of the world?'

'I sincerely hope not.'

'And you do not believe this thing was

deliberately created or *conjured* to attack you?'

'I think someone had knowledge of it and used the location to lure us in, but I do not think it was conjured. My impression was that it had been there a long time.'

'What about the other attack on you, the one which impersonated your woman?'

Alba ignored the reference to Beatha being just 'his woman'. Rendrr was often impersonal in others' affairs.

'That was different, a deliberate attack by someone with magickal ability. I have yet to meet the owner of those skills.'

'But you believe that it was instigated at the command of the Red?'

'I do.'

'Let us hope they do not have any other sorcerers that they stand against you.'

'Indeed so, but it is concerning they have people with such abilities at all. Such people are rare and therefore costly. These are not the actions of the standard Roman army. It implies some other entity or organisation is at work, outside of Imperial governance.'

'You mean, not within control of the Emperor?' Argyll interrupted.

'Think about it, Argyll. Imperial Rome is a machine. It has a playbook on how to do things. Their world may be alien to us but they are ordered in everything they do. Their cities follow a standard layout, as do their forts. Their governance is the same whether it is in Gaul or Britannia. Even how they fight is by a rulebook. And yet, set against this standard way of doing things, they employ a sorcerer, lure us into a cursed valley, send one of their centurions all around Britannia to capture us. It does not have the pattern of the *standard* Roman rule book.'

'I wonder how they got onto your track so quickly?' Rendrr asked.

'That is a key question to which we still do not know the answer,' Alba replied. 'The list of people that knew of our quest at the outset was not large. However, our discovery of Doube and subsequent departure from this fort would easily have been noted and reported back to the Red by the traitor.'

Rendrr considered for a moment. 'What about Toryn. You have bad blood between you. He could have informed the Romans about your movements even if he wasn't involved in the murder of Doube.'

'I have considered that,' replied Alba. 'Toryn would probably enjoy any misdemeanours which the Red cause me. However, I do not think he would do so second hand.'

'Second hand?'

'Despite our differences Toryn is a man of honour. If he were to have me beaten up or even murdered, it would be by his own hand. He does not strike me as a man to employ agents in matters of personal effrontery.'

'I see,' Rendrr mused. 'And what of Doube's killing; would you put that past him if it served his interests, personal or otherwise?'

'Toryn would, of course, have had the opportunity to kill Doube and could easily have followed him from the Great Council. But one thing bothers me about that.'

'Oh, what is that?'

'Well, if Toryn planned to kill Doube, why not do it at the Great Council. It was held within his fort. He could easily have sent him to the underworld by slipping a knife between his ribs while he slept. Easier to shift the blame amongst more obvious suspects that way. Remember the delegates had two nights under his protection prior to the debate. Why wait till Doube set off home, risking discovery or somebody seeing you leave?'

'Yet, the fact remains that Toryn had the opportunity. Also, by visiting him he became aware of your involvement early on and could have informed the Red as to your movements.'

'That is true, but what we must also consider is motive,' Alba continued. 'The question of *why?*'

'Surely, Toryn is the easiest to fathom,' continued Rendrr. 'The leader of the Great Council would be the ideal spy. He would know every tribe's position on the Red and which leaders had strong leanings either for them or against them. I cannot conceive of a better position to hide their agent. Toryn could have informed them that Doube represented a threat to their plans. Hence, he was given orders to kill him. Sometimes, Alba, the simplest explanations are the right ones.'

'Don't forget Toryn hates you,' Argyll added. 'If he has got the ear of the Red then he could have had us followed from the moment we left his fort. Whether Cor is or is not, Tadc's bastard daughter, I wouldn't put it past him to get his leg over anything that was sold or given to him.'

'All of this could be true,' Alba replied. 'Yet, my instincts tell me that it is too tidy an explanation.'

'So, what do your *instincts* tell you instead?' Rendrr asked, irked that Alba was too dismissive of his own explanation.

'We know Doube was likely killed because of his opposition to the incursion of the Red across our lands. Tadc's views and allegiance had been bought by the Red which put him in conflict with Doube. Whether he was the one who murdered him is unclear, but he certainly had opportunity, motive and sufficient anger to do so.'

'But you are not sure?' Rendrr interrupted. 'You do not think this could just be a simple disagreement, a violent opposition to someone's opinion, even an affront to such?'

'It certainly could be viewed in that way, but there are other points such as the continuing attacks on myself and Argyll, despite Doube's death and which continued *after* Tadc's demise. And don't forget the Red centurion is still after us.'

'Yet, you refuse to consider Toryn as the hand behind it all?' Rendrr persisted.

'I suppose Toryn could have been in league with Tadc,' considered Alba. 'My views on Toryn are clouded by his personal enmity against me. It is possible he uses that to cloak his darker motive. But I still sense another influence at play, one which remains hidden, shielding those that work hard to conceal themselves.'

'Then you must cast your net yet wider.'

'Wider?'

'You must consider associates, friends, even lovers of the circle of suspects that you have.'

'I am not certain what you mean, Rendrr?'

'I mean, that we must consider those nearest to us to be potential suspects. For example, your own woman, Beatha.'

Argyll made to protest but Alba held his hand up. 'It is a sensible question given the leakage of our mission. No Rendrr, I do not believe Beatha would betray me. Furthermore, when we returned with Doube's body she was away on one of her foraging expeditions. I have not seen her for some time.'

'But that is exactly my point, Alba. If she has been absent on her so-called foraging trips, could she not have given information to the Red about our disposition, including knowledge of when Doube was going to attend the Great Council or when you and Argyll were absent from the fort?'

'I hardly think Beatha would talk to the Red, let alone betray us or me.'

'But it is possible, you will admit that?'

'Anything is possible. However, it is also conceivable that other warriors or their spouses may just have easily passed that knowledge. I think it unwise to fixate on Beatha, a woman who I know well and trust.'

'Maybe you think you know her well but your eyes are blinded by her beauty. It has happened to many a man before.'

'Rendrr, this is pointless. There is no evidence to support Beatha being a spy for the Red.'

'That remains to be seen, Alba.'

'Surely, the point is that we *do* have a spy in our midst who is passing information to the Red,' Argyll interrupted. 'Whoever may fall under our respective suspicions, we must look for clear evidence of treachery, not just speculation.'

Alba decided to change tack. 'Rendrr, does the rest of the community know about what is going on and how Doube was murdered?'

'Word has leaked out that it was not a simple killing,' Rendrr replied. 'There is talk of retribution in the air. Some call for a war council.'

'A war council!' exclaimed Alba astonished. 'Just who do they think they are going to war with?'

'Before you returned, word came to us that your friend Rigari had been consorting with the Red in return for expanding his territory.'

'What! Expanding it where?'

'Can't you guess?'

'Into our lands? You can't be serious! Rigari is honourable, true to the old ways. I fear these are malicious lies aimed to set us against each other.'

'I have to take such a possibility seriously.'

Alba shook his head. 'This is all wrong. I tell you,

Rendrr, there is deceit here. I would stake my life on it that Rigari is true.'

'One day soon, you may very well have to.'

Rendrr stood up. The audience was at an end.

'You have both done well. Go now, take rest and we will talk further soon.'

As the two warriors made to leave, Rendrr called Alba back.

'Alba, I still have my doubts about Beatha. Maybe you should find her and challenge her to account for her movements. Do not forget that we have both a traitor and a murderer in our midst'

But . . .'

'That is not a request, Alba. I *insist* that you seek out your woman and bring her before us to answer these questions formally in audience of her peers.'

'That sounds like you are putting her on trial?'

'I have a responsibility to get at the truth. *You* have the responsibility to obey my decision.'

Rendrr waved him away and called Rues. Exasperated, Alba nodded curtly, leaving before the guard could get close enough to intimidate. Rues did, after all, take his duties seriously.

When they had put sufficient distance between themselves and Rendrr's house, Alba pulled Argyll to one side, speaking quietly so they could not be overheard. 'Rendrr is wrong about Beatha. I know her too well to consider her capable of such treachery.'

'I expected him to instruct us to interrogate the rest of the fort,' Argyll replied. 'That way we could build up a picture of everyone's movements. Mind you, he's probably worried that we'd find out what that scum bag Rues gets up to. But I am surprised he has fixated on Beatha. That does not make any sense to me.'

'It is strange, as though he has made up his mind of her involvement. However, I will go to her and convince her to attend his questions. I am sure we can eliminate her from Rendrr's suspicions quickly enough.'

'Do you want me to accompany you?'

'No, Argyll. You get some rest. Tomorrow we will meet and see if we can pick out any piece of information that we may have missed. Anything that may give us a lead on where to direct our investigations next.'

Argyll nodded, secretly pleased that Alba did not need him for several hours. He was looking forward to returning to his own wife and daughter. Despite the fact that he was always a free spirit, enjoying the freedom to warrior and adventure with Alba, he was always glad to return home. His wife, Yana, always told him:

'Husband, there is no hearth like your own hearth,

No bed like your own bed,

No woman like your own woman,

All of these things bless you with warmth and love.'

Alba bade Argyll farewell, deciding to go to Beatha now rather than wait till morning. Reaching the door of her roundhouse he called her name. Obtaining no reply he called again, louder this time. Still nothing. It was unusual for Beatha to be absent for so long. Her family were not at home either which was also strange. A familiar feeling began to prickle at the back of his mind, diving down to his stomach as his concern became manifest.

He grabbed the door and strode in. As expected, the roundhouse was empty. The hearth was clear, unused since at least the morning. Her family had not even prepared wood and kindling for the evening fire. In fact, there was no sign of a recent meal or preparation for anything. The beds had not even had a change of straw and it looked like no one had been here all day.

He made a brief search, looking for any clue that could help him decipher their absence. All the time that worrisome feeling grew in intensity. There was nothing to indicate where they had gone or even if they had departed together. He did note all the weapons were missing. That suggested they had gone out as a group. Whatever the cause, it must have been localised to Beatha's family, otherwise Rendrr would have mentioned it when they had been debriefed.

Finding nothing, he exited the roundhouse, deciding instead to go speak to some of the adjacent families in case they had seen or heard anything of Beatha or her relatives.

He visited five roundhouses, each time meeting with disappointment. No-one reported anything out of the ordinary. Only one person said they could not recall seeing Beatha for several days. They had seen her other relatives up until yesterday though. It was not much to go on, but a theory began to coalesce in his mind, one that suggested Beatha had been missing for an extended period. Maybe that was why her relatives were also absent.

He was making his way over to the next dwelling when he heard someone shouting his name. Turning, he looked to see Sego, Beatha's grandfather, who was waving urgently to get his attention. Alongside him was her mother.

Catching up with them he saw that they were covered from head to toe in dust. They must have been out riding for most of the day as, behind them, a boy was leading away two horses. Even through the soiled face mask the mother looked anxious.

'Morvanae, I have been searching for Beatha but found no one home. I am concerned that some dark event has occurred,' Alba opened.

Beatha's mother stared open eyed at him for a second before bursting into tears. Her father came alongside her, lending his arm. 'Come daughter, do not despair. Young Alba is here now. All will be well. You will see.'

Morvanae shook her head, tears streaming down her face. Alba put his hands on her shoulders, pulling her to his chest. Warm tears irrigated his neck as she cried out the fear of losing her child. He would not get anything out of her until she had emptied her worry.

'Morvanae, I am here now. I will do all I can to help but you must tell me all you know.'

Still sobbing, she lifted her head, trying to control her tears. 'Oh Alba, I have been so worried. She has been gone for days with no sign. We have not even found her horse. Surely, if she had met with an accident we would have found Arealia? Instead, we are met with emptiness each time we search. I fear the worst and I am at my wits end.'

She sobbed uncontrollably, shaking as the emotion tore through her.

'We are used to my granddaughter being away for the odd night,' said Sego, 'but this is different. She told us that she was going to Wyeval wood for some fungus she wanted for her healing remedies. Four days ago that was and not a word or sighting of her since.'

'And you have been searching every day?'

'When she did not return by the second night we determined to try and find her.'

'You have searched the wood, of course?'

'There was no sign of her or her mount. We fear she may have been kidnapped or worse.'

Morvanae sobbed again. 'Alba, my dreams at night; I see her face down to the ground, the colour of life drained from her skin. What if it is true, that she is dead or violated, or . . .'

'She lives!' Alba stated firmly. 'I feel it. You are aware I have the gift. I would know if she were dead.'

That seemed to acquiesce Morvanae. Still sobbing, she nodded in acknowledgement before grabbing Alba's hand. 'Find my daughter. All our hopes are on you now.'

She squeezed his arm before lightly kissing his cheek.

'I will take her back,' said Sego. As he turned Morvanae away, he whispered into Alba's ear. 'If Beatha is with the gods, then revenge her for us.'

Beatha's grandfather had seen through his ruse to calm Morvanae, but, in truth, Alba was lacerated with his own worry. Realising that they threatened to overcome him, he pulled himself up, stiffening both his resolve and body posture. He was a warrior and a sorcerer who would use all of his skills to find Beatha. Woe betide those which had done her any harm for his retribution would be devasting.

With an effort, he steadied himself, forcing his mind to think. He considered what he had learned. It was possible Beatha had fallen victim to a chance attack, but the feeling in his gut said otherwise. He could not help but wonder if Beatha's disappearance was planned, premeditated by persons unknown.

Or maybe not so unknown as some would have him believe.

The wise thing to do would be to rest, take some refreshment and head out with Argyll in the morning. But this was Beatha, his woman and the one he loved more than any other.

That would be the right thing to do. But sometimes, the wisest path isn't the clearest.

His eyes refocused. A grey mare stood nearby,

its eyes, curiously, fixed upon his own. He had the distinct impression it knew what he was thinking. Experience informed him that some horses did form an empathic bond with their rider. This one seemed able to do so despite not being his own.

He called over to the stable hand. 'Is the grey mare fresh?'

'She last went out a couple of days ago so is well rested. Do you want me to saddle her?'

'I'll do it myself, thanks,' Alba replied.

Saddled and bridled, he led the mare by hand towards the main gate. Signalling the guard, he mounted, pausing to take one last look behind him. Argyll would be pissed that he had gone alone. He exited the fort and kicked the mare straight into a gallop. With luck he would reach Wyeval wood by nightfall.

CHAPTER XVI

Somebody was climbing through the entrance.

'Are you there?'

The woman's voice again. Beatha let out her breath.

'Over here.'

'Keep talking.'

Once more, her benefactor bore no flame, preferring to locate her by voice. Reaching her, the woman bent down until her scrambling fingers found Beatha's leg.

'I am sorry it has been so long, but I could not get away. Even now I must be quick, for I fear he suspects.'

'You haven't told me who this man is,' replied Beatha.

'Nor will I. You must not ask.'

'I am sorry. I know you take a great risk. Forgive me.'

'It is no matter. I have brought you more fruit plus some scraps I stole from the stable. It is all I could chance.'

'Thank you,' Beatha replied, feeling around for the woman's hand and the bag it contained. She tried a different tack. 'What will he do with me?'

The woman hesitated. 'I do not know. He needs you for something, else you would not still live. Beyond that, I cannot say.'

'Does he desire coin, for I have little?'

'No questions. For now, be grateful that you live.'

'You are a brave woman, I think.'

'I am not brave,' spat the woman. 'I live in fear, not knowing when the next beating will come.'

'Do you have no family to help you?'

'I am alone here.'

Beatha not only heard but felt the bitterness in her voice. She seemed desperate but trapped.

'I must go now.'

'Please, is there no way you could get a message to someone?'

'No!'

'Not even a message to my man?'

'Not least to Alba,' the woman replied.

Silence fell between them. Both realised the mistake.

'You know Alba?'

'I know nothing. Now be quiet and I will come again when it is safe.'

'Who are you?' Beatha implored. 'Please tell me. Alba can help, maybe protect you.'

In the darkness she heard a cynical laugh. 'No-one can help those who are lost.'

The woman left as Beatha's world, once more, descended into solitude and darkness. She had learned one thing in this encounter. The mystery woman knew of Alba, maybe even personally, but who was she so afraid of that she would not risk rescue?

There was also the fact that she was still alive. The woman reasoned she was needed for something. Beatha was not so sure. If her abductor did not know of his accomplice's visits to feed Beatha then surely he did not care if she still lived?

Or, maybe he was counting on not having her around for long enough to worry about feeding her. Whichever way she looked at it, her prospects seemed thin. Her only hope seemed to be able to convince her mystery benefactor to help and that appeared unlikely as things stood.

Beatha swallowed hard. Not for the first time did her panic threaten to overwhelm. Briefly, she gave vent to it, releasing a loud wail that echoed and reverberated around the black chamber. Outside, a nearby fox picked up a strange sound that it did not recognise. It stood still for a moment, trying to identify if it was a threat or prey. When the sound faded it put its head back down and continued its hunt. There were more palatable meals worth tracking than to be distracted by the phantom that fluttered briefly upon the evening air.

Hurrying through the undergrowth Beatha's benefactor feared the time she had been gone. With luck she could make it back before she was needed but it would be close. Fear and panic drove her on until with relief she spotted her horse, concealed within a thicket of hazel. Quickly, she untied the reins and pulled the beast's head around sharply, kicking it at its flanks at the same time. As she left, her thoughts wondered to whether the prisoner would find the other item she had left in the bag.

***

Alba approached the perimeter of Wyeval woods cautiously. Though he had left in haste, pushing the grey mare hard along the journey, he still took precautions. As far as he could tell he had not been followed. That did not mean that the woods themselves did not pose a threat. If Beatha had been taken here then her abductors may still be nearby or keeping a watch to see if anyone of interest turned up.

Her relatives had already searched here so maybe that meant it was safe. Furthermore, he did not know for certain that Beatha had been abducted here. She could have been taken along the way, either coming or going.

Caution was called for, despite his strong feelings. And they were strong, threatening to breach his reason. He had not quite realised until this moment just how much Beatha meant to him. She had always been a lover, a friend, even a confidante. Yet now, with the prospect of losing her, he realised that she was more than that. The realisation hit him hard; he had not understood it before.

Concentration was required, using his skills to read the ground and his intellect to interpret. This had led him to strike off from the main trackways following a path where the level of disturbance indicated a point of divergence. There may have been others but he knew he was roughly in the right area and it seemed as good as place to start as any.

The gamble had paid off, rewarding him with a trail of multiple hoof prints which had brought him to the same clearing where Beatha had left her own mare. Scanning the ground he detected several distinct tracks. It took him a while to sort them out but there were definitely two sets of prints heading into the woods plus another which seemed to loiter near the horses.

Beatha's prints were easy to identify, characterised by the random changes in direction as she searched for herb and flower. A second set had come later, definitely following, joining hers deeper into the wood. He followed Beatha's tracks carefully looking for the tell-tale signs of her stride and weight changing, an indication of flight. They were not difficult to pick up. Beneath the canopy of trees the tracks were easy to read as the ground remained damper in the shade. He followed them till he saw her break cover and run along the perimeter heading back to the clearing. Her pursuer had not followed, guessing correctly, that she was intent on recovering to her horse. Back at the clearing he saw the tracks converge once more, three sets now. This

THE CORNOVII MYSTERY

was where the other person, an accomplice, had come to assist.

He went cold when he saw the signs of where a body had lain. Not far off was the heavy log her assailant had used to incapacitate her, still darkly stained with blood. His only relief was that there was not too much blood. Hopefully, that meant her skull had not been split open. He continued studying the earth, able to discern by the heavier impressions that the original pursuer had picked the body up and most likely laid it across one of the three horses. After that, the signs became confusing. The horses had left but the tracks were muddied and confused. Plus, there was evidence of scrapping – a ploy where a large branch is towed behind a horse to disturb or eradicate the tracks.

Clearly, Beatha's abductors were sufficiently skilled to attempt such a deception. The problem was, it had worked well enough so that any remaining tracks had been sufficiently concealed making an informed pursuit impossible. Even Beatha's mare had been taken, either hidden or killed elsewhere. The care taken to follow, apprehend and conceal this foul deed bothered him. In fact, all the way through the series of events from Doube's murder to Beatha's abduction there was the impression of an intelligent mind at work. None of it appeared to be random, all of it felt planned. He couldn't shake the impression that he was a pawn in someone else's game.

By the time he reached the main trackway

the first hues of evening were breaching the sky. Deciding to strike camp he carried on until he spotted a small copse sufficiently laid off the road where he could shelter with some degree of security. The area was not extensive, with only a sporadic sprinkling of birch offsetting the mossy heathland. He tied the mare directly adjacent to where he decamped. The day was clear with no chance of rain but he had left in haste, only carrying the clothes he wore plus weapons. With no cloud cover the night would be cold.

He remained confident he was alone, but, as a precaution, before every change of direction he had doubled back on himself. He decided against striking a fire, his experience never quite willing to give way to the evidence of his senses. Were he with his own horse he would have laid next to her for warmth, but this mare was young so he couldn't risk she might kick him or try to bolt.

As the sun bade farewell, the nighttime cold seeped into his bones, finding a partner with the weariness of the last few weeks. For a while he slept the half sleep that comes to those who are over tired through physical or emotional exhaustion. By midnight, he was in and out of consciousness. Within both worlds he was tortured. In the conscious world he was beset by worry and guilt; a feeling that he would never find Beatha or that she would be dead before he could reach her. In the dreamworld, the valley demon pursued him across the land, trapping him in the roundhouse where the sorcerer had conjured Beatha within the flames. In one image she was herself, reaching out to hold his hand, only for him to look down and see his hand melt into hers as the fire consumed them both.

His salvation from the horrors of liminal space came from the mare. His eyes blinked open, unsure for a moment as to which world he was in. Yet the feel of the earth, the peculiar sense that nature was alive, told him he was awake. The mare was unsettled, moving her front feet, tossing her head to both sides. He lay still, straining to make out any movement or sound which might be the cause of the mare's discomfort. By now, the light of morning was returning, although the great sun disc had not yet revealed itself over to the east. He had not moved his body at all, fearing any sudden movement would cause a potential attacker to act before he was ready. Whilst he lay still he was giving his eyes time to adjust plus, more importantly, tensing and relaxing his muscles to be in a state where he could act.

Whoever or whatever was nearby was making no sound or movement. Maybe they were waiting to see if the mare's discomfort had woken him up? The main risk he ran by staying still was if his adversary had a bow. It was a chance he had to take, besides the light was not enough to ensure accuracy. After what seemed an age, he caught the faintest of movement, somewhere to his front and left. It was so slight, that had he not been awake already he would not have heard it. He had the mare to thank for that, one of the reasons he had stationed the horse close to where he lay.

Alba had been careful, taken all the usual precautions and yet it had not been enough. Whoever was following him must have skill, which meant they had probably done this sort of thing before; a professional.

Very slowly he moved his arm down off his chest toward where his sword lay, barely a hand span away from his side. The subdued light should conceal his intent, but it was an effort keeping his movements so slight. Reassurance came when his fingers finally brushed up against the leathered hilt.

'I wouldn't do that if I was you!' came a shout. 'I have had an arrow trained on you since you awoke.'

'If you had, then I would be dead already,' Alba replied. 'Someone with your obvious skill would not waste time bandying pleasantries.'

A hoarse laugh came from the shadows. 'Good point. Then we can dispense with any foreplay. My payment does not depend on how you die, merely that you do.'

Alba jumped to his feet at the same time as his pursuer broke cover albeit in a very relaxed manner. It bothered him that the man was so confident, reinforcing his suspicion of a professional assassin. Yet, he seemed familiar. He was sure he had seen him before.

'I must admit,' broke the man, 'you are quite skilled yourself. It was a pleasure tracking you. I prefer more difficult quarry, else my work can get rather boring.'

'I am happy to have brightened up your otherwise sad existence,' Alba retorted.

The man laughed again, supremely confident in his position. ' I am glad we can share such humour before I send you to the underworld. That is good, very good.'

'Why *are* you here? Surely a condemned man deserves to know why he must leave this world?'

'Do I care?' came the quick reply. 'You are just another job to me. I know not or care not *why*.'

The man's confidence bothered Alba. His own skill with a blade was good, but this man seemed unphased. Therefore, if he fought him in the conventional sense he could well lose. *Such confidence does not bode well for my chances.*

It was too late to try anything magickal so that left *the unconventional*. To survive he must be unpredictable. His analysis of his adversary had only yielded one slight flaw. When the man shifted weight he spent less time on his right side than the left.

A possible weakness on his left side.

That was all he had. He hoped it would be enough.

The man yawned, 'I think, Alba, it is time to get on with things, don't you?'

Alba smiled, treating his opponent in an equally nonchalant way, a device to sow even the tiniest of doubt . 'It's your party my friend. I'm ready to dance when you are.'

He expected another retort but the man moved like lightning. He parried the blow with a hairs breadth to spare. He was astonished anyone could move so fast. No wonder he was confident. Reflexes like that must subdue your enemies very quickly.

'Good!' his adversary exclaimed. 'It is so disappointing when they don't survive the first blow. I do try and enjoy my work.'

The blade flashed again, this time closer, splitting the yarn across his arm. He didn't dare look away, but he could feel the trickle of blood breaking across his wrist. The man was so fast that if he tried the usual ploys of fakery and attack he was sure it would be his last. All he could do was try and keep his distance and move. Movement was his friend in this battle.

Movement and time, said the voice in his head.

He did not often have his spirit guide break through into his conscious mind. In fact, he could only remember once when it had happened before, when as an adolescent he had attempted to climb a sheer cliff with his best friend. They had crawled their way two thirds up a crumbling rock face, only to realise in their youthful inexperience that the cliff outmatched them. They had become stuck, unable to move up or down. His friend had grown impatient and, in haste, tried to climb back down. When Alba was eventually rescued by the elders, he had seen his friend's broken body at the base of the cliff. Whilst he had been clinging to the rockface, alone and scarred, a voice had come into his head. A voice like no other. It was strong, warrior like but with a strange *feel* to it. He remembered it as almost *fatherly*.

It was the same voice in his head now.

Keep moving as the sands of time keep flowing.

Alba, stepped back a foot, alternating his posture, circling left and right, keeping out of range. Once more the strike came with precision and speed. Surprised, Alba looked down to see another cut across his chest.

The man laughed. 'I like your strategy my friend. You play well. I can carry on opening you up bit by bit or you can submit and I will make your passing quick.'

'I'm afraid you'll have to do better than that,' Alba retorted. 'To be honest, I am disappointed. I thought you would have been on your way by now. A man of your ability should be . . .'

The movement came. In an instant Alba dived down to the floor, skidding along the ground and moving his own sword in a wide semicircle. The blade hit home, tearing through flesh and ligament. His opponent released a howl of anguish. Alba had not stopped to look. Just as well, for even as he threw himself off and to the right the expected parry came with such speed that it still managed to nick his arm.

He recovered himself back to his former distance, appraising his opponent for damage. He had struck at the man's left ankle, exactly the side he had detected weakness. His blade had not gone too deep, but it had done enough to force a limp.

Time, time, time, repeated the voice in his head.

He understood, knowing that even a small wound would upset the delicate balance of the assassin. If he could keep baiting him, play for time, then he would tire, maybe force an opening. He was not stupid enough to realise that his opponent would also know exactly what he was about.

Use the ground.

I am using the ground, Alba repeated back.

Use the ground. It is loose like the cliff.

Another strike came, just as fast but slightly less precise. Dare he hope that his opponent was tiring? He kept moving and circling, attempting to draw an attack whilst evading and conserving his own energy.

Then he made a mistake.

He had been foolish to hope that the man would tire so easily. Instead, the assassin had not only lulled him into misreading his stamina but had also anticipated Alba's next move. The blade struck at where he was going, not where he was. Cold metal sunk into his shoulder and he cried out. The majority of warriors would have spent a fraction of a second recovering from such a blow but Alba, realising his mistake, threw himself at the ground, rolling over and away just as the follow up stabbed at where his neck had been.

The man's precision, even this far into the battle, was incredible.

He picked himself up, spitting out the dirt

which had filled his mouth. He reverted to circling, randomising his movements even more. His shoulder throbbed heavily. The wound was deep and would sap his strength if he did not win this battle soon.

The dirt is in your mouth.

I know the dirt's in my mouth, he thought back.

Then he realised. *Use the ground.*

He had to plan his move carefully, all the while avoiding those strikes and feints. He would only get one opportunity; one chance to strike with the same precision as his opponent. He faked a stumble, grabbing the loose ground into his fist whilst just avoiding the expected thrust. Another rip opened on his torso, yet the wound was light. He pretended to lightly stumble a few more times, trying to lull his opponent into believing he was weakening. Subtlety was the key to deceit and deceit was key to victory.

But could he carry it off?

The best lie is a half-truth, boomed the voice in his head.

As he parried the next blow he faked a stumble to his right. In reality, he *did* stumble, but he projected the seriousness just a touch more than it really was. The expected follow up came and Alba parried throwing the grit at the man's face. He was closer now, having committed to the follow up. Protecting your eyes is an involuntary movement, despite how well trained a man is. The assassin's arms flew up halfway before he realised his mistake. It was a split second too late. Alba struck at his left side, piecing his chest deeply to half the length of his blade. None the less, he jumped back expecting another counter.

But the damage was done. Open eyed the assassin's sword dropped from quickly numbing fingers. Staggering forward, he fell against the blanched trunk of a birch. Slowly, he sank to the ground, fouling the tree with crimson trail.

'You fought dirty,' he croaked, swallowing back the blood that was already overwhelming his lungs.

'You of all people should know there is no such thing as a *clean* fight.'

The man nodded, the effort to speak becoming great.

'Who sent you?' demanded Alba.

'Does it matter?'

'It matters. If you have any honour, even that of an assassin, then tell me now for your time is short.'

The man's breaths were becoming increasingly laboured as his eyes threatened to block off his consciousness forever.

'Quickly!' demanded Alba. 'Who sent you?'

His opponent started to speak, only for the words to be throttled by a geyser of blood which burbled out of his mouth. He had moments left.

Alba leant beside his mouth. 'Tell me and go to the underworld with what honour you have left.'

His reply was a loud thump followed by the jolt of the assassins body slamming into death. Alba jumped back in shock. A Roman pilum was shuddering from the centre of the man's chest. The point had pulverised the heart, embedding itself deeply into the tree.

Alba spun around, not in any real state to defend himself for a second time. A dozen Roman soldiers were marching slowly towards him, shields down, swords drawn with Lucius at front and centre.

'Sorry to disturb your play,' laughed Lucius. 'It was quite entertaining. I thought he would best you Alba, but you were more resourceful than he anticipated.'

'I am glad you enjoyed it,' Alba replied, struggling to cope with the pain in his shoulder which threatened to overwhelm the capacity of his nerves. Swaying, it took all his effort to stay upright.

'You are wounded, I see,' the centurion continued. 'That is well for me. It saves me the time of opening you up given you are already holed in several places.'

He motioned to his men. Four soldiers ran up to Alba grabbing him roughly by the arms before facing him towards the jubilant centurion.

'Well, let us dispense with any more pleasantries shall we.'

'Yes lets,' Alba replied weakly. 'Why don't you tell me why you're here and why you have been on our trail for so long?'

Lucius laughed again. 'I see you for what you are barbarian. You are nothing, yet my superiors believe you to be a threat.'

'A threat to what?'

'Oh, they believe in some idealistic future, an Empire that persists when all others wither. You represent a threat to that vision. There are others amongst your barbarian friends that think alike. My commanders, mistakenly in my view, believe they can turn them into good, reliable Roman citizens.'

'Who?' Alba demanded. 'Who among my people would betray their own kind?'

'Enough!' Lucius shouted. 'No more talk.'

'You're just going to kill me?'

'Those are my orders.'

'Then why all the attempts to take me alive.'

'Why isn't that obvious? I don't give a fuck why they want you dead Alba. I want you breathing whilst I take my revenge on you. You and that associate of yours have led us across half of Britannia. That does not put me in a very good light.'

Lucius moved closer to Alba, motioning to his men to hold him tight. 'No, it does not make me look good at all. So, now you will pay in pain and suffer until you are on your knees grovelling, begging me to thrust my sword down that shithole neck of yours.'

Without warning, Lucius punched him in the mouth followed by a withering blow to his wounded shoulder. The pain from the impact was so intense that, despite himself, he shouted out in agony. Lucius laughed, playing to his audience. In return, his men laughed back, eager to see retribution. Alba spat out fresh blood. Defiant, he grinned at Lucius through bloodied teeth.

'There is a thin veneer to your civilisation, Roman. You call me barbarian and yet beneath your technology, your great cities, there is only brutality.'

Once more Lucius struck at him, this time with the hilt of his gladius. Pain seared through Alba's shoulder as he sank to the floor barely holding on to consciousness. A straight kick to his head followed. The impact flung Alba backwards and onto his side. Dirt and grit adhered to his shoulder as the gash discharged a red river down his tunic.

'Beg for your life barbarian.'

Alba managed a barely discernible shake of the head.

'Get him up!' barked Lucius.

Once more he was man handled to his feet. This time for added drama Lucius took a run up, jumping into the air and aiming both legs at Alba's shoulder. His men applauded the drama enjoying the spectacle before them. Catapulted back, Alba crashed down hard against a dead stump. Consciousness came intermittently, but Lucius had not yet had his fill.

'Give him water,' he commanded. Two other soldiers walked forward and threw a sack of water into Alba's face. It brought him too slightly before he was brought to his feet, limply hanging between the two legionaries.

'Why, this is fun!' laughed Lucius. 'I could do this all day and not tire. However, I think it only fair that my men, who have also had to suffer your cunning, should take turns. Unless, of course, you wish me to end you now?'

He put his ear to Alba's torn mouth, teasing a response.

'No? 'Are you sure Alba?'

Getting no reply he motioned to another of his men to take a turn. The man walked up to Alba, urged on by his comrades. Reaching the Briton's limp form he held Alba's head by grabbing a great clump of his hair, withdrawing his arm and thumping Alba so hard that several teeth flew out of his mouth as he was sent spinning to the ground. This was met by huge approval by the rest of his company. Emboldened for more, he grabbed the semi- conscious Alba, looked back at his comrades for encouragement and began to withdraw his arm for the next blow. His audience cheered in anticipation.

Barely conscious, Alba felt himself suddenly released. He was too far gone to feel the impact of the ground as his body collapsed. He had not even felt the blow. Somewhere distant there was noise, a great deal of noise, but his body had had enough by now.

As his head dropped to the side, a bizarre image materialised in front of his battered face. A Roman soldier was staring at him, a frozen death mask of astonishment etched onto his features. As he finally lost consciousness the last thing he saw was the barb of an arrow jutting out of the man's forehead. Then darkness closed in and everything winked out.

CHAPTER XVII

Emptiness was all about him.
Is this it, came his first thought. *Is this where I end?*

As awareness returned the blackness began to change. Here and there a pinpoint of light appeared. More lights blinked on. Behind him a trail of particles led away into the distance forming what looked like a long winding path of stardust. As he walked, the path extended ahead, weaving its way out into infinity.

Huge galactic clouds, the great mists of the heavens, swirled about him punctuated by billions of tiny suns deep within their midst. The wonderment of his location was overwhelming. A sense of peace and euphoria intertwined and flowed through his Being.

I must have died.

'*You are in the space between realms,*' came the answer. It was the same voice that he had heard earlier; that which had spoken to him as a young boy.

'Who are you?'

'I am He who knows you better than you know yourself.'

'You talk in riddles.'

'There is much truth in riddles.'

'That's no answer.'

'Truth is not bound by convention.'

Confused, Alba looked about him once more. The stellar clouds continued to swirl, beautiful hues of blues, purples and colours he could not even describe. As he watched, some seemed to coalesce into recognisable shapes. Forms appeared, reminiscent of warriors, friends and family he had once known. They surrounded him, gently moving within their variant form. Beyond, he watched galaxies and vast nebulas move into a strange rhythm.

'You see the dance of the universe.'

'The what?'

'In this space, you are closer to the rhythm of all life than your physical world.'

'So, I am dead?'

'You are between realms.'

'You said that before.'

'I did.'

One of the warrior forms moved closer. Armed with sword and shield, he also carried a staff, much like Alba's.

'You are a sorcerer?'

'Was a sorcerer; I am more now.'

The man's face was that of someone who had seen forty seasons, lined not with age, but with experience.

'That is correct.'

'What is?'

There was a chuckle. *'That I am lined with experience rather than age.'*

'Why am I here?'

'An introduction.'

'To you?'

'Yes and No.'

'That's not very helpful.'

'I speak . . .'

'The truth. I understand.'

The warrior nodded. *'Our communication will be easier now.'*

'So, I am going back?'

'Yes.'

Before Alba could respond the picture before him began to change. The mists began to swirl and he felt like he was being pulled backwards. His last image was that of a great eye floating in the stellar void, looking directly at him.

***

'Shit, he's in a mess.'

'The shoulder wound was deep. Much blood has been lost.'

'Will he pull through?'

'I have done what is in my skill to do. He must decide whether to return or join his ancestors.'

'Fuck!'

Argyll stood up, concern for his friend etched across his features. 'I should have known he'd go off on his own. Damn it!'

Toryn stood next to him. Both had watched the wise woman attend Alba.

'If he dies, then he will have fought and died with honour. A warriors death. No-one can ask more,' Toryn stated bluntly. 'Argyll, we must talk. I have important information to share which has a bearing on your investigation. Come.'

Argyll nodded but carried on looking at Alba's body. Battered, bleeding and with his face badly bruised he wondered his friend was not dead already.

'Leave the witch with him. She knows what she's doing.'

Reluctantly, Argyll turned away. Together they marched over to where Toryn's men had struck camp. One of the men present seemed out of place, head down, disinterested in what was going on around him.

'Who's he?' Argyll asked.

'*He* is why I am here.'

'I do not recognise him,' Argyll began, but Toryn interrupted. 'Patience. Let me tell you how we came to be here so you might understand.'

'Very well.'

'Firstly, I will make one thing clear Argyll. When you and Alba turned up at my fort, I was enraged that your friend had the balls to show up at all. I have never forgiven him about the slur on my daughter. But this you know. Sometimes anger obscurers that which is important. So it was with me. My rage clouded my judgment, but some of what you said did sink in. Over the coming days I thought more on the events at the Great Council and one thing bothered me more than anything else.'

'What was that?'

'I told Alba that there was much shouting and brawling on that night in council.'

'Yes?'

'I also mentioned that I thought it odd that one leader had said nothing.'

'I remember,' replied Argyll, the inkling of a suspicion beginning to form in his mind.

'Well, that fact kept tuning over and over in my head. It was so out of character for the chieftain of the Brigantes, Artek, not to engage that it arose my suspicions.'

'So, what did you do?'

'I sent word to Artek, inviting him to a private audience at my fort.'

'I'm guessing you received no reply?'

'You guess correctly. I sent three messages and each was ignored.'

Argyll shot a glance over at the other man.

'Is that him over there?'

Toryn ignored the question, choosing to continue his narrative. 'When I received no reply, not even an excuse, I became certain there was more to my suspicions. I then travelled with twenty of my own warriors up to Brigantes land to interrogate him.'

'That was risky.'

'True, but I had to know. I had left word that if we did not return then a messenger would be sent to find you and Alba to inform you of my suspicions.'

'So what happened?'

'We reached Artek's fort to find his people in disarray. Artek had disappeared and there was disagreement over what should be done.'

'I assume he left to escape from accounting for his actions. However, he could have chosen to fight by wiping out you and your men before you got close to his fort. I wonder why he did not?'

'When we arrived, most of his senior warriors were still there. Only a handful had left with their chieftain. It seemed he miscalculated the depth of his support.'

'Support for what?'

'Those that remained told us that over the preceding weeks Artek had been increasingly absent. That is unusual. As you know, a chieftain stays with his people. Other than when in battle, he should be a constant, a rallying point in times of hardship, a figurehead who is always present.'

'So, where had he been?'

'None of them knew. However, when he returned from the Great Council he did call an extraordinary meeting. There he insisted that a great debate had taken place amongst the chieftains and elders resulting in a decision to welcome the Romans into both the Cornovii and Brigantes lands. He told them that only the Corieltauvi stood against it, painting Rigari's people as warmongers who would account for great bloodshed rather than joining peacefully with the Red.'

Argyll was silent for a minute. A worry danced at the back of his mind. 'Artek is not the only one to single out Rigari.'

'What do you mean?'

'Rendrr was also talking of Rigari as a threat, though he did not paint it in the same way. He accused the eastern tribes of incursion into our lands and spoke of convening a war council. He seemed very sure the Corieltauvi were the guilty party even though Alba and I did not agree.'

'That is indeed curious.'

'Alba always looks for patterns,' Argyll added, looking across to his friend.

Toryn nodded slowly, following Argyll's eyes to where Alba lay. 'Anyway,' he continued, 'when I told Artek's warriors what really had transpired at council they were shocked. It confirmed their suspicions that Artek may have sold out on them. There was much anger after that.'

'What did you do?'

'It was decided that he should be tracked down and brought to my fort to face questioning at the Great Council. After that, we formed a hunting party and went in search of him.'

'It looks like you found him,' Argyll gestured to the Brigantes chieftain.

Artek lifted his head and spat toward them. 'You do not understand. None of you do. I do not wish to fester in stone huts and animal skins when there is another future. You are all blind. What is coming cannot be stopped. We will join with the Red peacefully or otherwise. Those that stand against us will be quashed. Only then, will there be . . .'

There was a loud crack as Artek crumpled to the ground.

Toryn replaced his staff. 'Treacherous bastard!'

'This conspiracy has run far and wide,' Argyll mulled, looking with disdain at the unconscious chieftain.

'It is difficult to sift friend from foe,' Toryn agreed.

'I'm afraid things are worse than that.'

'What do you mean. Is this not enough?'

'When I left to find Alba, Rendrr had just concluded his threatened war council. I protested as Alba had done, trying to convince him that there was no evidence of Rigari's guilt. He would not listen, repeating his claim of several raids on our eastern borders with many casualties. He went so far as to call me a coward for disagreeing. Now he's taken the majority of our warriors to find Rigari and give him a bloody nose.'

'Fuck! He'll start a war.'

'He will, right at the time when we are most exposed to the Red.

'If these raids had happened then I would have heard of it,' said Toryn. 'You will not be surprised if I tell you that I have *people* stationed in every hill fort throughout Cornovii lands. None of them reported such an event.'

'I fear he is wrong or has been ill advised. When I asked about our own fort no one else had heard of anyone being attacked, let alone killed or wounded.'

'We need to stop him, Argyll. If the Romans learn of this in fighting they might take advantage and then we are all in the shit.'

They were interrupted by a low moan. The wise woman motioned them to join her.

'He returns.'

CHAPTER XVIII

Alba was still very pale, but Argyll could see the colour of life returning.

'His heart and spirit are strong. He will mend quickly now,' the wise woman noted before bowing to Toryn and taking her leave.

'Argyll, we do not have time to wait for Alba to recover fully. If Rendrr is set upon his course, it is vital we intercept them before the two sides meet.'

'I know, but Alba may have vital information. For a start, why the Red were here and who this other body is.'

'Very well, but I will order my men to make ready to strike camp.'

Argyll knelt beside his friend. Alba's eyes were open now, the strength returning quickly. He tried to speak but coughed immediately.

'Pass me some water,' Argyll called to a nearby warrior.

The man unclipped a leather water satchel and passed it over. Argyll held it lightly to Alba's lips.

THE CORNOVII MYSTERY

'Slowly now. No large gulps.'

Alba sipped the fluid. His lips were torn, stinging as the water passed over them, yet it tasted sweet and wonderful. He desperately wanted to drink his fill, but his mouth hurt where his teeth had been knocked out and he would need to lubricate his throat before he could satiate his thirst properly.

He took his time, allowing his body time to hydrate. As feeling returned, so too did the pain of his shoulder. A compress of leaves and ointment had been bandaged against the wound where the wise woman had attended him. The pain served to remind him that he was alive, back in the world of man. He remembered the great eye that had watched him return and then, refocusing, he handed the satchel back to Argyll.

'Thankyou. I did not believe I would see my friend's face again.'

'You should have waited for me.'

'I know.'

Alba took in his surrounding, straining to focus through bruised eyes. 'The Romans, did you kill them?'

'We drove them off. Once they saw they were outnumbered your centurion friend left the field in short order.'

Alba nodded. 'Pity. I fear he is one that will be a persistent thorn in our side. Now, listen Argyll, I must tell you . . .'

Without warning his head started spinning so violently he almost passed out. The colour, which had been returning, drained away from his face. Alarmed, Argyll reached a hand to his shoulder, holding him lest he should keel over.

'Take it easy or you will be out again.'

'This is more important. That man over there was an assassin, sent to kill me.'

'I am glad he failed.'

'He nearly did not. He was an expert at his trade who almost bested me.'

'But how did he know where you would be? You left quietly, without a word even to me.'

'I was foolish going it alone, but I wanted to find Beatha. She has been missing for many days. Her family fear for her safety.'

'You think she has been taken or . . .'

'I do not know her fate as yet,' Alba interrupted quickly. 'However, this one was paid to kill me.'

'Do you know who he is or who sent him?'

'When I first saw him he seemed vaguely familiar; perhaps a face I have seen yet have not noticed. But I have remembered since my journey to the other realm.'

'Other realm?'

'I will tell you some other time. Argyll, this man has been living in our own fort, amongst us!'

'I do not think I have noticed him before.'

'That is his trade, to live amongst his prey, being seen but not being noticed. Anyway, the only reason I recall seeing him at all is because of whose company he was in.'

'Go on.'

'Rendrr's personal guard, Rues. I remember seeing the two of them together. It was just before we set off to see Toryn. They were hanging around the stables drinking beer. I thought nothing of it then. I don't even know why I remember it other than there was no one else other than the stable boy and ourselves present.'

'You think they were loitering deliberately?'

'I don't know what they were doing other than it stayed in my mind.'

'I wonder whether Rendrr knew of his personal guard's taste in friends?'

'Either way, we have a leak, a traitor within our ramparts,' Alba said grimly.

'I just said to Toryn this thing seeps wider and wider.'

'Toryn is here?'

'Our paths crossed on the way to find you. He has Artek in tow as well, although, to be more precise, he has Artek unconscious on the ground.'

He motioned over to where the Brigantes chieftain still lay sprawled in the dirt.

'Toryn is innocent in all this then, you are sure?'

'He is sure enough Alba!' Toryn's voice boomed. 'Despite your suspicions, I am here and I have a gift for you in the form of our friend from up north. It appears that he sold himself out to the Red via another acquaintance of yours.'

'I seem to have too many friends of poor character,' Alba joked weakly.

'This one's tale you will want to hear. I have

told Argyll part of it but not all. In particular, the involvement with . . .'

'He was working with Tadc?' Argyll guessed.

Toryn scowled at the interruption but contained his annoyance. His fingers rippled ominously over the grip on his staff as he carried on. 'Artek's warriors identified Tadc as one of the emissaries he had received on numerous occasions over the preceding months. He even made no secret of it, passing it off as cooperation between the north and south. His senior council initially thought he was encouraging greater trade between the two communities. There was hope of increased wealth coming across their borders with the advantages the south brings through their access to the ports. However, they were deceived.'

'That explains why he was so silent at the Great Council,' Argyll chipped in. 'He would not wish to side with Doube nor draw unnecessary attention by cheering on Tadc either.'

'It seems clear that the two were working together, but, so far, I only have evidence that Tadc was the one interacting directly with the Red,' replied Toryn.

'There must be more,' said Alba. 'The pieces come together but there are gaps. Did Artek's people say anything else?'

'There was one thing,' Toryn answered. 'One of their warriors overheard Artek bargaining with Tadc. He was seeking some kind of payment, presumably for his cooperation with Tadc's scheme. I would imagine this insipid little snake would not be shy in his demands. Anyway, Tadc did not want to pay him more coin but mentioned he could get other forms of recompense. Artek was quick to suggest women could form part of the trade. Apparently, his exploits with the womenfolk of his tribe were well known. He was accused on several occasions of having it off with other mens' wives or their daughters, but each time the accusation would be withdrawn before it could reach public council. I digress, but the point is Tadc took him up on his suggestion, referred to women being one kind of currency he could transact. He was overheard telling Artek that he had already traded his daughter to forward the cause, selling her to a tribal chieftain up north.'

'Up north, does he mean the Picts?'

'It wasn't clear, but I doubt he would go too far from the main sphere of Roman power.'

'Interesting. We heard similar from Gruenval, the new chieftain of the Dobunni. He too spoke of a girl, a daughter, who disappeared. They suspected she may have been sold.'

'Seems they were right,' Toryn snorted.

Alba and Argyll were looking at him. He read the challenge in their eyes and, for a moment, there was silence between the three of them.

'For fucks sake, Cor was not sold to me by Tadc!' Toryn protested. 'I have enough witnesses to our affair who can vouch for that.'

Alba and Argyll nodded quietly. 'We may never know what became of the daughter,' Alba continued. 'However, it does tell us the lengths someone like Tadc would go to. Like attracts like, so if he was prepared to sell his own daughter, who knows what else he or others in his circle, would do. We do have some clarity on other matters. For instance, I am inclined to look to Rues and his dead acquaintance over there for answers as to how the Red discovered our whereabouts so quickly.'

'It would explain many things,' Argyll agreed. 'Being so close to Rendrr, Rues would have been perfectly positioned to pass on any intelligence concerning our mission either to the Red or to an assassin.'

'Yes and I bet it was Rues who started the rumours about Rigari's men causing trouble. If he had our dead friend there tailing us, who was a proficient tracker by the way, then he would have seen us meet up with Rigari. That is what probably gave them the idea to prompt Rendrr to convene a war council. We need to get this information to Rendrr before he makes a big mistake.'

Argyll and Toryn looked at each other.

'What have you not told me?' Alba said, catching their look.

'Rendrr is *already* leading a large party of our warriors against Rigari,' Argyll answered.

'Didn't you try and stop him!' exclaimed Alba.

'He would not listen and accused me of cowardice. Of all people, Alba, he accused me!'

'Rendrr is a stubborn man once his mind is set,' Toryn remarked.

Alba reached a hand toward his friend. 'I am sorry, Argyll. I meant no insult and I know you would have done all you could. Matters proceed apace despite our best efforts and I am still without Beatha.'

'You've played your part in this,' said Toryn. 'Let Argyll accompany you to secure your woman. In the meantime, I will take my men to try and avert a slaughter.'

'Thank you,' Alba replied, still weak but feeling the strength return.

Toryn nodded. 'One last thing. I assume you have settled on Tadc being the murderer of Doube?'

'Maybe,' answered Alba. 'I am not yet fully certain of that.'

'You are not sure, despite all we know?'

'I still have doubts.'

'You are a hard man to convince. Very well then, I leave you to your doubts.' Toryn motioned to his men and moments later they had moved out leaving Alba and Argyll alone.

'I hope they make it in time,' said Argyll, as the last of Toryn's warriors disappeared from sight.

CHAPTER XIX

When Alba and Argyll rode through the gates of their own fort, it was all but deserted. Only a handful of warriors remained, mainly sentries posted atop the palisades. To any would-be attacker it would look a normal compliment. But this was deceit, for only women, the young and elderly remained within the interior. Rendrr had taken the rest on his mission to intercept Rigari.

'Let's hope the Red don't attack here instead,' said Alba, noticing the lack of men.

'If they do, it's going to be one short fight,' Argyll replied.

They made their way inside, intending to investigate the roundhouse where Rues resided. They had not got far before Morvanae, Beatha's mother, spotted Alba and hurried over.

'Alba, you must come. Quickly, for there is little time.'

'What is the matter Morvanae? Have you found Beatha?'

'It is Rendrr's wife, Enica. She is dying but asks for you. Come.'

She took a step back, only now noticing Alba's condition.

'You are hurt, Alba. Is Beatha . . .?'

'I have not yet found her, Morvanae. She may yet live.'

She put her hand to her mouth, emotion overwhelming her. 'Oh Alba, I fear any moment I may have news she is dead and now you are wounded. I look to you as I would you were of my own flesh and Beatha loves you. I could not bear to lose you both.'

With a struggle, Alba limped over to Morvanae, pulling her close, allowing her to exhaust tears which dampened upon his tunic. She recovered herself, dried her face with her palms before grabbing his hand.

'I forget myself. We must hurry!'

They made haste to Rendrr's house. Within, several people including Beatha's grandfather were gathered in a semi-circle around a body on the floor.

Alba was aghast at the sight that met him. Enica was propped up against the inner wall, her head slumped onto her chest, which rose with shallow breaths. Buried into her belly was an unusual weapon, a vicious narrow bladed dagger which made up in length what it lacked in breadth. The straw around her was soaked in so much blood he wondered she still lived. A cloak was draped loosely over the top half of her body.

'By the gods!' Argyll exclaimed.

Alba knelt down. His eyes moved from the dagger to the grandfather. 'Is there nothing to be done?'

'The blade is long and has penetrated through her. The damage internally is too great. Were we to remove it she would go immediately. I am sorry.'

Alba nodded, understanding. He leant close to Enica's ear.

'Enica, it is Alba. I am here.'

She lifted her head slowly, struggling to focus. It took several laboured breaths before her eyes settled upon his face with recognition.

'Alba . . .'

'Take it easy, you are badly wounded.'

'I am not important. You must look. '

She paused, allowing her head to drop once more.

'What does she mean?' Alba asked the others.

'I think she is speaking of her this,' spoke Morvanae softly. 'She wants you to see.'

Slowly, Morvanae reached forward and pulled the cloak from Enica's naked body. The blade had been pushed in just below her navel, an old blade speckled with rust. Alba reasoned it was a spare, kept hidden for emergencies. What made Alba and Argyll draw their breath at, was the sight of Enica's exposed skin. She was covered in cuts and bruises, some old, others very new. The worst wounds were about her chest. Alba was convinced he was looking at bite marks on both breasts. The pattern suggested they had been made by human teeth.

Gathering the cloak he covered her over gently, before laying a hand on her brow.

'I am so sorry Enica. I think I understand now.'

Argyll was beside himself. 'But Alba, who the fuck did this. Is this Rues's doing?'

'I don't think so,' Alba replied sharply. He leaned close to Enica, compassion replacing the anger which had briefly coalesced upon his face. 'Enica, that is not your given name is it? Am I right, that you are Eith, daughter of Arietha?'

'But that's Tadc's daughter!' burst Argyll.

Enica nodded. 'I am glad you know me truly at the end, Alba. I have suffered much under Rendrr. He is a traitor you know?'

'I am beginning to.'

'He bought me from Tadc, who I will not call a father, for to him I was only a commodity. He did not know love, only profit and power. Rendrr, to my dismay, was the same. Oh, he was more discrete than Tadc. He used agents, like Rues and other men who could be bought for coin. He thought himself so clever, but he could not hide his activities from me. I was beaten, bitten and bullied into a silent life of duty and servitude.'

She coughed as the exertion of speaking sapped her dwindling strength. Alba tried not to obviously notice the trickle of blood which appeared at the side of her mouth.

'Would you like some water? he spoke softly.

'I will have a little, please.'

Morvanae passed him a beaker. Gently, he held it

up to Enica's lips, careful not to let too much pass. She nodded in thanks.

'He is a deceiver, the viper that hides in the shadows, the one who sent you on this quest. Oh, he laughed so much during the weeks you were away. He thought himself so clever that it was he who had betrayed you.'

Alba looked across at Argyll. His friend looked aghast, struggling to comprehend what he was hearing.

'Enica, think carefully now. During the time of the Great Council meeting, was Rendrr ever away from here or the guard Rues?'

Enica nodded, the effort to lift her head becoming too great. Speech became difficult, each word a triumph of determination to pronounce. 'He made excuse over one night that he had to meet an emissary from the west. He was gone for four days. When he returned he claimed that he had been negotiating a new trade agreement. '

'Did anyone not query this?' Argyll asked.

'Whilst he was gone, he told Rues to inform anyone that came by that he was with fever and not to be disturbed.'

'What about the sentries? They would have seen him leave surely?' Argyll persisted.

'I do not know. Maybe he paid them off or Rues did. I only know he managed to come and go unseen. But I saw him on his return. He could not hide from me particularly when I saw the state of his clothes.'

'They were covered in blood?' suggested Alba.

'Yes. It looked like he had gutted a beast by the amount that was upon him. The next day he made me bury it.'

'Rendrr killed Doube, . . . I can't believe it!' Argyll exclaimed.

'With the aid of the Red,' finished Alba. 'Now we have our answers.'

Enica coughed again. Alba noticed more blood at her mouth, coursing down her chin. She did not have long. Already the sallow colour of death was upon her skin, even to those areas hidden by bruise and lesion. Her head lolled to one side and for one moment he thought she had gone, but Enica was not done yet.

With great effort she tried to speak once more. Her words were almost inaudible, so that Alba had to lean close to her mouth. She spoke only one word. Then Enica, daughter of the union between Tadc and Arietha, died. There was silence in the roundhouse for several moments after her passing. Alba gently closed her eyes.

'Rest now Eith. Rest and be with your ancestors.'

Morvanae looked up at him, her face once more moistened by sadness. 'We will look after her. Go Alba. Find Rendrr and my daughter.'

Alba nodded, pulling himself up.

'And Alba?'

'Yes Morvanae?'

'I only expect one of them to be brought back here alive.'

They exited the roundhouse. Alba looked puzzled.

'What did she say?' Argyll enquired.

She only spoke one word.'

'Anything that can help us?'

'*Cave.* That is all she said.'

'I do not know of any cave hereabout.'

'Neither do I, but it was obviously important enough for her to expend her last breath on.'

'Do you believe that could be where Beatha is?'

'Either that or where Rendrr is hiding out, but the problem is where to look. We have a location without context.'

'I think we may have another problem,' Argyll replied. 'Over there!'

Alba followed Argyll's gaze. Near the main gate a rider was extracting a spear from the stomach of a guard. Alba half expected him to make a run at them, but instead the killer kicked his mount savagely, bolted through the gates and was gone. The wounded guard lay writhing in the mud, clutching at his torn abdomen. Argyll ran over to him leaving Alba to catch up. The guard, a young warrior of only eighteen seasons, looked pleadingly at Argyll. Blood gurgled out of his mouth. Argyll knelt beside him, grasping the boy's hand tightly.

'Courage my friend. Hold on to your bravery. Tight now!'

The boy stared at him hard, forcing his last reserve away from fear to a determination to die with honour.'

Alba reached them as Argyll laid his hands upon the boy's face.

'These bastards will have their reckoning Alba. I swear it.'

'He died doing his duty. He will be honoured when this is over,' Alba replied. 'The one that escaped must have been one of Rendrr's men. He probably had orders to report to him if anything happened that could threaten his return. The boy probably challenged him when he made to leave his post.'

'What do we do now?'

'We go and find Rendrr before Toryn kills him.'

Argyll looked aghast at Alba as though he had lost his senses. 'After all this, you would have us save Rendrr from Toryn's blade?'

Alba nodded slowly. 'I need him to find Beatha.'

'Surely, the cave cannot be that difficult to find?'

'We do not know where it is or even where to begin looking. Listen, I know the land pretty well between here and Wyeval woods, but I have no clue to the location of this secret cavern. We must assume that this place is well hidden and only locatable to those that know of its existence. My guess would be that it was discovered by accident, remaining a secret to all but a few.'

'But Alba, after all he has done. Enica, Doube . . .'

'He will account for his deeds, but I need him alive to tell us where this place is. Also, remember Beatha has been gone for many days and may starve if we do not find her soon.'

'You are assuming, of course, that she is not dead already?'

Alba winced. 'I am my friend. I am betting that Rendrr is cunning enough to have left himself the option if all goes wrong.'

'What option?'

'Well think about it. Rendrr is leading our warriors into a battle with Rigari's men. I doubt he would not have told his Red masters. Having two British tribes warring with each other in open battle gives the Romans a perfect opportunity to turn up at the right moment and remove a large portion of their opposition. Rendrr would find a way of using the battle between the Corieltauvi as an excuse to bring in Roman rule, probably on the premise of providing peace and stability.'

'Doesn't he run the risk of being killed in the battle?'

'Rendrr does not want to die in the battle or be seen to have been *saved* by the Red. He is more subtle than that. My guess, is that he will provide an excuse, something believable that allows him to leave the field early and wait it out until the dust settles.'

'And go where?'

'Where do you think?'

'The cave?'

'It's the perfect hiding place and even if his plan goes wrong then he has Beatha as a hostage. He has considered every eventuality. As Enica said, he is cunning, leaving little to chance.'

CHAPTER XX

Lucius looked back across the two columns of soldiers behind him. His forces had been buoyed by the centuria which Servius had granted. He had already congratulated himself on winning this concession of more men, despite the setback of the barbarian Alba escaping him for a second time. He smiled to himself, not for the first time recalling the words his first commander in the field had told him:

'There is never a battle that is lost,
Defeat can be turned to victory;
The point of your stylus,
Is as sharp as that of your sword.'

The smile became a chuckle as he recalled how he had turned that back upon his commander. Eager to advance, Lucius had been held back from promotion in those early years. His Tribune had pushed other officers ahead of him, citing his self-indulgence as a trait that threatened his effectiveness as an officer.

During a skirmish with the Gaul Lucius had taken his chance. Whilst his Tribune was engaged in close quarter combat, Lucius had turned his sword against him, sending an upper cut through his arse and into his guts. In the confusion of battle no one had seen. Lucius had already prepared a tablet where he had forged his superiors signature. After the battle, he ensured this tablet was the one that was sent back to Rome. Within a month, Lucius had been promoted.

He turned back around, flicking a non-existent insect from his tunic. Resplendent in his armour, as befitted his status and the responsibility of commanding such a large force, his only surprise at receiving the influx of additional manpower was that Servius had not come in person. An Optio called Quintus had led the centuria from their fort to where Lucius was camped. He had handed Lucius a tablet, written in the Legatus's hand, ordering him to make haste eastwards where he was to intercept a large force of Britons. His orders had been quite specific on one point.

He was not to engage until the Britons had depleted themselves.

Servius's orders suggested that the Britons were set to fight amongst themselves and despite the opportunity for valour and honour to be obtained, Lucius was only to engage in order to eliminate the survivors.

'Are the scouts back yet?' Lucius asked of Quintus.
'They are expected shortly, sir.'
'You told them to ensure they were not seen?'
'Of course, sir.'

'Good. Once we know where the Britons are likely to engage we can arrange our forces accordingly. I doubt this will be much more than a sweep up exercise.'

'Our strength is more than enough to despatch a few scrambled barbarians,' agreed the Optio.

'The problem with the barbarian mind, Quintus,' pondered Lucius, 'is that it does not know when it is already defeated.'

'Once they feel our blades in their flesh, they will know, sir.'

Two riders approached the column, scouts which Lucius had despatched earlier. They galloped forward, jarring their mounts to a standstill in a cloud of dust. Lucius brushed the fine particles away from his tunic, annoyed at the impudence and dramatics the two riders had displayed.

'Report!' he ordered angrily.

The nearest saluted and began his report. 'Sir, we rode out, as you ordered, eastwards to intercept the Britons.'

'Yes?'

'Well sir, it was strange.'

'What do you mean *strange?*'

'The barbarian army was heading eastwards.'

'Your point?'

'We were led to believe they would be *coming from the east*, not heading back that way. They appear unaware of the force of Britons coming up on them from the west.'

'All the better their surprise when our agent

catches them,' Lucius laughed.

The scout looked puzzled. 'Sir, the barbarians we observed did not number many. We counted only about twenty warriors in their party.'

'I was led to believe this would be a clash of armies,' Quintus chipped in. 'This sounds more like a tribal dispute.'

'Neither of you need concern yourselves over the trivia,' said Lucius. 'What matters is *who* will be present. Amongst those twenty warriors you observed is Rigari, chieftain of the Corieltauvi. When he dies, together with others from the Cornovii, then there will be a power vacuum amongst the barbarians. They will be in disarray, ripe for the picking.'

'I see,' Quintus observed quietly. 'Then our victory will lead to a new era of Roman rule in central Britannia?'

'It will and *we* will be celebrated as the men who helped bring it in. Now tell me about the barbarians approaching from the west.'

'Their force was much larger. They numbered around one hundred and twenty warriors.'

'Did you identify our agent amongst them?'

'We did, sir.'

'Is everything prepared as arranged?'

'Yes, sir. Six of our men are tracking his party. When he breaks off, they will escort him back to the secret location. Once there, they will wait with him until they receive message that it is safe to return. I also passed on your *other* orders, sir.'

'Do they understand what they must do?'

'Perfectly, sir. Should the barbarian Alba turn up they are to eliminate both him and the girl.'

'Excellent! Then I believe all contingencies are covered.'

Supremely confident, Lucius bade the Optio to give the command to march. As the Roman force went forward Lucius allowed himself to imagine the honours Servius would bestow on him. Unknown to Lucius and his men, a third force of Britons, under Toryn's command, were racing to catchup with Rendrr's army. Someway behind them two horses bearing Alba and Argyll were also galloping forward to catch up with both parties.

***

Up ahead Rendrr's scouts were reporting back.

'Chieftain Rendrr, the Corieltauvi warriors continue eastwards. They are not far ahead of us.'

'Good. Once we are upon them they will learn that the only reward from raiding our lands is one of death,' Rendrr declared.

'They are proceeding at quite a leisurely pace unaware that we are pursuing them,' the scout added, a puzzled look upon his face.

'Something bothers you about that?'

'Rigari's men only scout ahead of their path.'

'What about it?' Rendrr answered impatiently.

'Would they not be covering their retreat if they had been raiding?'

'Do not worry yourself with the motives of

criminals,' Rendrr answered. 'They are confident they have gotten away with their foul deeds, that is all.'

'You are sure this is the band that has slaughtered our men?' spoke up one of the other warriors.

'Do you doubt my word?' Rendrr countered, annoyed. 'These scum from the east have invaded our territory, murdered our people and plundered our livestock. They must pay the price. Is that understood or do I take challenge from you?'

The warrior looked surprised Rendrr had reacted so forcefully. 'I merely point out that we have no hard evidence confirming these are the men responsible. Would it not be wiser to take this up with Elder Toryn of the Great Council first, to get at the facts? The Council is the traditional place to settle disputes, after all.'

Rendrr drew his sword so quickly that the warrior who had questioned him took a step back just as the blade pierced his neck. His hands sprang upwards in an attempt to stem the death flow, but even as they moved his legs buckled. He was dead by the time his body fell to the floor.

'Does anyone else have quarrel with my decision?' Rendrr shouted, wide eyed, drilling his challenge into the shocked faces of his warriors. A silent consent came in reply, as each man stared at the corpse which lay at his feet. 'Good, then prepare to attack the Corieltauvi criminals and tonight we will bask in the honour of our victory.'

***

'Well?' Toryn questioned his chief scout, Eenir.

'Rendrr's men lie ahead of us. Once we located them, we did as you suggested and swept in a south-easterly arc.'

'And what did you find?'

'We saw a large force of Roman soldiers, at least one hundred strong, shadowing a second group of twenty or so Britons heading eastwards.'

'That must be Rigari's men. Can we catch Rendrr before he intercepts them?'

'Not in my opinion. Unless they delay for some reason, the Corieltauvi will find themselves under attack very soon.'

'And Rigari's men will not last long if they are outnumbered some five to one,' Toryn continued. 'Options?'

His question was met by blank faces. As it stood, they risked losing the race. By the time they arrived both Rigari and Rendrr's men would lie dead.

'There is one possibility,' spoke Eenir. 'We could risk riding through Saverford Bog.'

'Without a guide we will founder in the peat,' spoke another of Toryn's warriors. 'One misstep by man or beast and the black death sucks you down to oblivion. We cannot risk it!'

'Yet, unless we get there we will have nothing to fight for anyway,' Toryn mused. 'It seems we have no choice. We will have to take our chances through the bog. Eenir, do you know the path?'

Eenir looked down. 'I do not.'

'Then we are lost,' another shouted.

'You are not lost!'

They span around to see Argyll and Alba, trotting up behind them. Toryn noticed the sweat on the flanks of their mounts.

'By the gods, you must have wings instead of hooves on those beasts!'

'Wings would have been preferable Toryn,' Alba replied, holding his hand to his shoulder.

'You are welcome,' Toryn continued, 'but unless you have a map of Saverford Bog then there is no way we can catch up with Rendrr before he attacks.'

'I may have the next best thing to a map.'

'I knew the bog as a boy,' Argyll announced. 'I believe I can find the path.'

Toryn's other warriors murmured amongst themselves. They were brave men, but most could not swim and had a deep fear of drowning.

'Can he do it?' Toryn whispered to Alba.

'If he says he can then I would stake my life on it.'

'You have just staked *all* our lives on it!' Toryn answered grimly.

CHAPTER XXI

'Chieftain Rendrr, we are within attack range of the Corieltauvi. We can strike on your command.'

Rendrr did not seem to hear his second. Siegel was the tribe's weapons training expert, usually occupied with teaching the youth of the community how to handle spear and catapult alongside sword practice. Now he was anxious to set about his task, lest they should lose their advantage.

'Chieftain, do you not hear?'

Rendrr seemed preoccupied, more concerned with the rear of the column than what his second was saying. 'Of course I hear,' he replied irritably.

'Then shall we attack?'

They were interrupted by the appearance of a rider approaching at breakneck speed, from the direction they had come.

'Ah Rues, what news?' Rendrr asked as his personal guard skidded up to them.

'There has been a raid on the fort in your absence.

More bandits from the east we suspect.'

'And?' Rendrr asked impatiently.

'Several civilians and four of our guards were killed before we drove them off. I am afraid your wife, Enica, is one of the casualties. She lies mortally wounded and calls for you. I regret she does not have long.'

Siegel observed this with some curiosity, particularly as Rendrr appeared strangely unsurprised at his guard's sudden appearance.

'Very well, then I must return. Siegel, our force is superior to the Corieltauvi scum so I leave it to you to exact revenge upon our enemy. Be sure to kill them all and leave no one alive.'

'As you command, my chieftain,' Siegel answered, taken aback. 'But you will need an escort in case there are more Corieltauvi rebels at large. Quickly, he chose six warriors who formed up in a line behind Rendrr and Rues.

Rendrr looked like he was about to protest, but without further word he turned his horse and galloped away followed by Rues and their escort. Siegel watched them leave with a confused shake of the head.

'Siegel, this is most irregular,' spoke one of the other warriors. 'Wife or not, Rendrr's place is here on the field of battle.'

'I hear you Ofrid,' Siegel replied. 'Would you have me challenge him? You saw his anger earlier on. He is set upon this course and he is our chieftain. Let us be about this task and get it over with.'

'As you wish. I just find it odd.'

'It is our *chieftain's* wish,' Siegel corrected. 'Draw up your men into four groups. We will attack on all sides.'

'We could always shoot them down with bow and spear?' Ofrid suggested.

'Given our numerical advantage, that would be dishonourable. We will fight them man to man, shield against shield until there are none left standing.'

'But if they murdered and stole from our own, do they deserve an honourable death?'

'That is *my* will Ofrid. Now do as I say. I have not the appetite for this business a moment more than is necessary. When your men are in position sound the horn to attack!'

***

Up ahead, Rigari, Horva and the remaining contingent that had survived the battle with Lucius were completely unaware of the trap that was about to be sprung.

'By my reckoning, we should be on the borders of our own lands before sunset,' Horva reported to Rigari.

'That is good my friend. Too long have we been absent from our own fort.'

'I confess that I look forward to mounting the ramparts of my woman as soon as I get home,' Horva spoke wistfully.

'Let us hope she has missed the heat of your cock

as much as you have missed the heat of her thighs,' Rigari laughed.

Their laughter was cut short as a horn suddenly blasted through the air. From all sides, warriors charged, swords waving madly in the air as the force under Siegel descended upon them.

'Defend your chieftain!' Horva shouted, turning his horse to repel the first attacker. A skilled swordsman, Horva despatched his opponent with a lateral strike which removed the head of the attacking warrior. The horse had been charging so fast that he had the briefest view of it disappearing off the field with its headless rider still saddled.

The Corieltauvi warriors attempted to form a defensive circle around their chieftain, but their line was thin and gaps were already opening up. Beyond the first line of attackers other Cornovii warriors circled waiting to throw spear and axe through any breaches of the line.

Horva spotted another warrior who had crept around their flank. Spear raised, this one had spotted Rigari, and was desperately trying to get a clean shot. Horva reeled his horse around, digging deep into its flanks to urge it toward the Cornovii spearman, simultaneously deflecting sword and spear from both sides. The man had seen his opportunity and pulled his arm back to release the missile. Horva was almost upon him when he collided with another rider, the impact almost dismounting him. Regaining his balance, he looked across at Rigari, relieved to see he fought on without injury. Fortunately, the horse he had collided with bore a Corieltauvi warrior who had spotted the danger and charged the attacking spearman. The enemy warrior was on the ground, a bloody geyser jetting out of what was left of his arm. Nearby, the severed limb still bore the spear in its fingers.

Quickly, he was surrounded by three more of the opposing warriors. At this rate they would be reduced very quickly. He killed one of the surrounding three with a stab to the chest, noting the man's markings denoted him as Cornovii. The other two, who were more cautious in their attack, wore the same.

'Why do you attack us?' Horva yelled, defending a slash to his head. 'We have no quarrel with the Cornovii. Why this madness?'

'You lie!' answered one of his attackers. 'You attack our forts, murder innocents and steal our crops.'

'You are mistaken,' retorted Horva, parrying another blow to his chest. 'We are neighbours and friends to the Cornovii. We have not raided your lands.'

His answer came with a tear along his arm as he parried one attack but was too slow to avoid the second. Immediately, blood bubbled up through the tear, soaking his arm until it dripped off the end of his sleeve.

And then, suddenly, over the din of battle came the call of another. 'Stop fighting! You are deceived. Stop I say!'

For a moment, it looked like the fighting would stop, swords paused mid-flight as each man sought to understand the source of the distraction. The respite did not last and within seconds the clash of metal against metal resumed. More men fell. The circle around Rigari had reduced to only eight warriors.

'Enough!' boomed the voice once more. 'I am Toryn, Chief Elder of the Great Council and I command you cease. Now!'

This time the sound and name of Toryn's voice got through. Blades were stayed, axes lowered. Toryn rode into the centre, holding his staff of office for all to see. Alba followed, reigning up beside him.

'Warriors of the Cornovii, you are betrayed! Your chieftain acts with the Red. I tell you that Rendrr is a traitor and a murderer. He is the one who killed Elder Doube and he would sell you, your lands and your very souls to further his own ends.'

Shouting and anger rippled through Siegel's men.

'Lies!' shouted one. 'Rendrr defends our lands,' said another. The Cornovii warriors still had their blood up, eager to finish off Rigari's remaining men.

'Then where is he, this great defender?' retorted Toryn. 'I do not see him before me, fighting with you, as is his place. Did he spin you a tale, I wonder, of some trumped up emergency that demanded his presence?'

There were murmurings among the Cornovii warriors at Toryn's words. Many were still angered at

Rendrr's absence, but could they believe that their own chieftain was a traitor?

Toryn forced his way through to where Siegel still had the tip of his blade against a man's throat. 'I know you, Siegel and you know Alba, one of your own. Listen to how he discovered Rendrr's deceit. If you still doubt after that, then you may finish what you have started.'

'It is true,' confirmed Alba. 'Rendrr has betrayed us all.'

'But we were told our fort had been attacked and that his wife lay dying!' Siegel challenged.

'Argyll and I have come direct from our fort. It is true that Enica is dead, but she was killed by Rendrr's hand, not any of these Corieltauvi men. In front of others and with her dying breath she told me of his treachery.'

Siegel's men looked at each other, doubt finally staying their blood lust. Weapons slowly lowered as they gave distance to the remainder of Rigari's men.

Siegel grabbed Alba's arm. 'Why would Rendrr do such a thing? He has given us no cause to doubt him over the many years of his leadership. I do not understand.'

'He has connived with the Red and other tribal leaders to bring about the end of our way of life. He seeks power in a different world to ours, Siegel.'

'Alba, time is against us,' interrupted Toryn. 'We must retreat to a more defensible position.'

'Toryn is right. We are in very great danger remaining here,' Alba continued, lifting his voice so that all could hear. 'A Roman force of a hundred plus men has been tailing you. Their plan was probably to wait until you had killed as many of each other as possible, then ride in and slaughter those that remained.'

A Corieltauvi warrior approached Alba. Through the blood lined features he made out Horva's face.

'My gratitude Alba. Had you not arrived with Toryn when you did I doubt I would be talking with you now.'

'Horva!' Alba exclaimed, grabbing the warrior by the arm and greeting him warmly. 'It is good to see you still alive my friend.'

'It seems your chieftain has much to account for. I would see retribution for this. We have lost many good warriors today.'

Rigari pushed his way forward. 'I too would see justice for this trickery.'

Siegel manoeuvred his horse till he was side by side with the Corieltauvi chieftain. 'We were told the Corieltauvi had been raiding our lands. It seems we were betrayed. I offer you my hand in peace and, if you accept, my warriors in service.'

'We have all been deceived and there is no slur on you Siegel. Together, as allies, we will fight with honour and bring this traitor to justice,' Rigari answered, grabbing Siegel's outstretched arm.

'Let us clear the field and organise our retreat,' agreed Siegel.

Toryn had remained silent throughout this exchange. His attention was focused away from the accord between the two tribesmen and instead was directed towards the ridge of land which skirted the field of battle. Following his gaze, Alba quickly discovered the reason for his distraction.

'I'm afraid, it is too late for retreat,' spoke Toryn. 'The Red are upon us!'

CHAPTER XXII

Rendrr together with Rues and the escort of six other Britons had sped westwards away from the battle. They had pushed the horses hard, but just outside of a pine wood Rendrr brought his horse up sharply. One of the escort warriors rode up to Rendrr to investigate.

'Is there a problem chieftain?'

'I think he has thrown a shoe.'

'I will check.'

The warrior passed the reins to Rendrr and dismounted. Rues waited until the man's attention was focused on inspecting the shoe, then brought himself alongside, shielding the warrior's view from the rest of the Britons.

Rendrr raised his arm, held it momentarily, before bringing it down sharply. In response, a silent volley of arrows shot from their concealment within the trees.

The man who had bent to check Rendrr's horse looked up at the thud of bodies hitting the ground. It was the last thing he registered as Rendrr's sword slid through his gaping mouth and out the back of his neck. From his mount, Rendrr kicked the gagging warrior away in disgust.

One of the other guards had survived an arrow to his side and was attempting to crawl away to safety. Rendrr motioned to Rues who quickly walked behind the injured man, turned him over and dispassionately shoved his sword into the man's heart.

Emerging from the trees, six Roman soldiers led out their horses, joining Rendrr and Rues.

'Your orders are to accompany me to the safe place?' Rendrr asked.

'Those are our orders.'

'Then let us get to it. There's a girl waiting for me who if all goes well you can have some fun with. I'm sure you Romans are not averse to fucking a *barbarian* bitch?'

***

The ridge of land which overlooked the battle between the Cornovii and the Corieltauvi had been the perfect topography for Lucius to bring up his troops unseen. From here, he had enjoyed watching the barbarians fight until the appearance of another smaller group of Britons had put an end to the conflict. Though they shared not the same discipline as the Roman army, it was always entertaining watching men slaughter each other. The smell of blood carried on the air and he licked his lips appreciatively, confident that he would have more before the day was done.

Lucius was most pleased, if not surprised, to see that the barbarian Alba had made it to the field. He suspected that it was his influence that had ended the battle prematurely, which meant the Britons were likely aware of their presence. He would take particular pleasure completing Alba's journey to the underworld, especially as he had been robbed of that privilege on their previous encounter.

Despite his scheming, Lucius was not the best tactician in the field. He had drawn up all of his forces on the ridge, supremely confident that both his numerical advantage and imperial discipline would carry the day. Quintus seemed less sure.

'Sir, may it not be wiser to send some of our men around their flank? An enemy engaged on two fronts is easier to overcome.'

'Nonsense!' Lucius shouted him down. 'We are almost twice their number.'

'A cornered man will always fight hardest,' Quintus reminded him..

Lucius flushed angrily. 'Quintus, any more cowardly suggestions and I will have you demoted and sent to the nearest Games.'

'As you command,' Quintus conceded.

'Well get on with it man!' Lucius barked impatiently. 'Attack them, now!'

***

'I have an idea,' Alba said to Toryn.

'Fuck Alba, we're about to get our arses kicked

and you have an idea?'

Alba scowled.

'Out with it then,' Toryn commanded.

'I am certain that the centurion who commands them is the same man who has tracked us since we began our investigation. He has a habit of springing traps and this has his smell all over it.'

'How does that help us?'

'He is cunning and sure of himself, but he only thinks in two dimensions.'

'What the fuck does that mean?' Toryn shouted exasperated.

'It means he will be over-confident. He knows he has us at a disadvantage and I suspect he will be so overwhelmed with the prospect of victory that he will attack head on.'

'That is usually the way of things,' Toryn continued, not getting at what Alba was driving at.

'I mean, Toryn, that he will likely send his entire force towards us in one go. We can use that to our advantage, maybe outmanoeuvre him.'

'Go on.'

'When his forces come down that ridge we must be ready to split into two columns, circle out left and right, and turn back on them before they can regroup. That way they will be fighting us on both sides. It will even the odds a little and negate some of their numerical advantage.'

Toryn considered for a moment. 'It might, you are right, but what if they do not commit all their forces in one go?.'

'I'm afraid, that is my plan,' Alba shrugged.

'Then as I cannot think of a better one , that is what we will go with. Besides, it may buy us enough time.'

'For what?' Alba asked, puzzled.

'You are not the only one with plans,' came the reply.

***

Quintus positioned himself at the head of the Roman column. He looked back to check his men were ready. All seemed in order. His gaze flicked back to where Lucius, surrounded by four legionaries, had decided to stay back.

'To watch the slaughter,' he had said.

All very well, thought Quintus, *if you did not get your blade sullied with blood but took the honours for the victory.*

He did not have a lot of faith in Lucius. He had heard rumour, of course, but this was his first time under the centurion's direct command. Right now, his opinion on what he had heard among other officers seemed about right. While no-one thought Lucius a coward, he was regarded as a dangerous man to serve under. The type of dangerous that would get you killed as no more than collateral damage on the centurion's march to greatness.

Quintus had ordered his men to form either side of his charge, moving the whole column into the classic wedge shape to smash through the Britons. Lucius had initially baulked at his plan, before

Quintus reminded him that their victory would be all the greater if they could report it had been won *by the book*. That hit home and Lucius had relented.

He looked down at the Britons. They had recovered some of their order but remained on the low ground. It would have been futile for them to try and assault the Romans positioned as they were on the ridge. At least they were not *that* stupid. Part of him was surprised they had not made a run for it. He would have much preferred to have split his formation in the way he had suggested, but Lucius had been adamant. Besides, the centurion was correct in one respect. The Britons were outnumbered, bore wounded, and were really no match for the fresh Roman troops about to smash into their ranks.

He raised his hand. The call to advance was given and the column began to move forward at a slow walk accelerating into a controlled canter. One third down, the horn sounded once more, signalling battle speed. As they closed on their target below Quintus checked to see that both flanks were moving out to form the wedge. Everything was in order and he glanced across at the Eagle bearer, swelling with pride at the sight of the Imperial Eagle charging toward its prey below. The excitement of battle fanned fire through his veins as the distance closed. The entire troop was thundering at full gallop towards the hapless Britons, each man revelling in the expected slaughter and glory to come.

They were within two hundred yards when the Britons suddenly did something unexpected. They had looked in disarray a moment before, but now they were moving, forming two columns very quickly.

Too quickly.

Too late, he realized what they were about. Somewhere deep in his mind a surprised admiration at their tactics briefly flickered but was instantly quashed as he forced his mind to act.

They came crashing through empty space where moments before the Britons had been circling in confused disorder. Quintus, yanked his mount around to recover the column but the Britons had already turned back. He marvelled at their horsemanship to manoeuvre so quickly. Hand to hand combat had already begun and it was pointless trying to give orders in the din. They would just have to get on with it, and besides, they still had the superior numbers.

Up on the ridge, Lucius watched the battle with little emotion. He had seen the Britons pull off their tactic, astonishing since they were not skilled in military theory. None the less, he remained supremely confident of victory. Quintus and his men were fighting hard, though it was difficult to see any serious progress. He was surprised to see some Roman bodies amongst the fallen but some losses were to be expected, even against barbarians.

The four legionaries stationed with him remained impassive, but he could tell that they were ill at ease. He had already informed them that they would share the honours of victory even though they were not engaged in combat. He could not understand when despite acknowledging his words, they did not appear reassured.

Lucius wondered how he could retell the upcoming victory in its best light. He would need to recall the key details, of course. Embellishments could always be added later.

'Fetch me a tablet and stylus,' he ordered the nearest legionary.

'Sir?'

'Tablet and stylus. Now!'

'Yes, sir.'

Puzzled, the legionary walked back to where Lucius had set up his command tent. Within, a folding wooden table served as a battlefield planner. Spotting a stack of spare lead tablets at the side, he moved across and grabbed the nearest. Annoyingly, the styluses were not with the tablets so he had to search further. Finally, he found them, contained in a small leather bag hanging off one of the tent supports.

Stupid place to keep them, he thought.

He heard a noise behind him, no doubt another legionary sent to hurry him up.

The pompous bastard will blame me for not finding his stupid styluses.

'I'm fucking coming!' he blurted.

The legionary turned around, annoyed at being hurried. He had a brief view of a barbarian's face smiling at him before he realised his belly had been opened up. With disbelief, he sank to his knees, watching the obscene image of his intestines slithering along the floor of the tent.

Up on the ridge, Lucius was getting impatient. 'Go and see what that lazy fuck is doing in my tent,' he ordered. There was no reply, so turning to the legionary on his left, he repeated the order. 'Did you not hear?'

The legionary was staring at him open eyed. Lucius saw the blade extracted from his belly as the man fell to the floor. In his place was a grinning barbarian. Behind him, a small army of Britons walked slowly forward.

'Shit!' exclaimed Lucius.

CHAPTER XXIII

Down below, the Britons had won an advantage by their earlier tactic of separating and encircling the initial Roman charge. The fighting had since become one of attrition. Roman and Briton alike fought both on horseback and on their own two feet.

Alba sensed the Romans were gaining the advantage. Both his and what was left of Rigari's men were tiring, whilst the Roman force looked fresher and though he could not see Lucius amongst them, they appeared to be in good order. He was all too aware that this open field warfare favoured the Romans who were moving and fighting as a concerted unit. Their own warriors were more loosely engaged, favouring one on one combat. It was not a recipe for success.

'Toryn!' he shouted.

The Chief Elder of the Great Council was busying himself with both staff and sword. Alba only made himself heard after Toryn decapitated a legionary who had been lulled into a mistake. The whites of

Toryn's eyes shone gleefully as the soldiers blood coated his face in a fresh collage of blood and grime. The severed head dropped at his feet where a well-aimed kick sent it flying through the air toward the roman ranks.

'Toryn! We are playing to their strengths, not ours. We must pull back and regroup.'

'No!'

'*No* for pulling back or *No* to regroup?'

'Both.'

Toryn disappeared again as more red soldiers filled the gap from their headless comrade. Despite their predicament, Alba had the distinct impression he was enjoying himself. Exasperated he tried again, timing his call for when Toryn's head resurfaced.

'Toryn! We are being ground down. We must break off else we will be overrun.'

'Hold Alba. Hold and fight!'

'Hold on for what?' Alba shouted back. 'There is nothing left to hold on for.'

'How about that.' Toryn yelled, removing his blade from another Roman torso and pointing the dripping steel forward.

Alba followed the direction of the sullied blade towards the ridge where the Romans had first charged. Pouring over it were more men, running full pelt down the slope towards the battle below. His first thought was that they were done for. There was no way they could withstand a further assault of such magnitude. Then his eyes registered that the attackers were not in Roman dress.

They were Britons!

Other warriors hesitated as they spotted the wave of men racing towards them. The Romans noticed too. Their commander formed his troops into a defensive square, a desperate measure for now they were the outnumbered.

Alba expected the new force of Britons to slam into the red square but instead they formed a rotating circle around their quarry, jeering at the Romans from behind their shield wall. Each side waited for the other to make a move. When it came, it was heralded by the Britons stopping as one, jarring the battlefield into a sudden silence. In the pause, Rigari and Horva made their way over to Alba. Both carried minor wounds but none that were serious.

'Any idea who our new friends are?' Rigari asked.

'I'm hoping that they *are* friends.'

They watched as the circle of Britons parted. A lone figure was propelled forward, followed by his native captor. The warrior kicked the back of the prisoner's knees so that to great cheering the soldier crumpled to the ground. Lucius picked himself up, only to be immediately recovered by the man who had thrown him, a knife held closely to his throat.

'Gevoh, you old dog!' greeted Toryn. 'I wondered when you'd turn up!'

The warrior holding Lucius grinned back. 'Chief Elder Toryn, it is good to see you still able to fight. I thought you too weak to hold a blade these days.'

'Not too weak to teach you a lesson, eh?' Toryn

laughed. 'I see you bring us a gift as well.'

'I found this Red scum hiding back on the ridge. For some reason he did not want to join you. I persuaded him that it would be in his best interests to do so.'

'Oh, how did you manage to convince him?'

'Well, to be honest, it was his own men. When they saw our army approaching they . . . , let's just say they lost their heads.'

At that moment, three severed heads arced through the sky landing in front of the Roman line. A slim trail of blood leaked a winding pattern in the dirt as they skittled to an uneven halt. A great roar of appreciation went up from the Britons at this brutal display.

A warrior emerged from the line carrying a fourth head. This one was mounted atop a long spear to which strips of torn Roman tunic had been bound. Holding the spear in front of him, the warrior faked a Roman march and strode up to Toryn.

'Toryn, I present you with our Imperial Standard.'

The man bowed and made a roman salute before rejoining his comrades. Toryn turned towards Lucius, laughing at the trophy in his hands. As he walked up to the centurion he became suddenly serious.

'Well Roman, it seems you have gifted us our own imperial battle standard.'

A murmur of appreciation went up within the British ranks.

'A friend of yours was he? Here, why don't you

take a closer look.'

He thrust the spearhead at Lucius so hard that it caught the Roman in the forehead forcing him to stagger backwards.

'Why look, he doesn't like you does he!' laughed Toryn.

'You barbarian bastard. You will die a pathetic death!' screamed Lucius.

The Britons roared with laughter at this exchange. Within the Roman formation, men looked nervously at each other, wondering if they were destined to the same fate.

Toryn was thoroughly enjoying himself. 'To be honest, I think your friend here has had enough for one day. He just told me that his head was hurting.' More laughter followed, as he continued. 'I once knew a wise woman that said the only real cure for a headache is to relieve the pressure on the brain so I will be merciful and put your friend out of his misery.'

There was an abhorrent crack as Toryn pushed the decapitated head down sharply, forcing the spear point up through the neck and out the top of the skull. Pieces of hair and bone adhered to the point as he forced it all the way down the shaft before removing it.

'Here you go, I give your fallen comrade back to your men.' He took a step back before kicking the mutilated head into the Roman square.

'Why you barbarian scum,' yelled Lucius, red with rage. 'You will pay for this outrage.'

'I think not,' Toryn laughed. In a split second he whirled around landing Lucius with a jarring blow to the head with the infamous staff. Once more the Britons yelled in delight. Lucius, struggled to his feet, blood running out of a gash to his left temple.

'Why don't you stay down Roman?' Toryn taunted, before following up with a shuddering blow to the centurion's groin.

Lucius collapsed to his knees, rocking back and forth in an effort to distract from the agony that had exploded within his balls.

'He wails like a baby!' taunted Toryn.

'I didn't think babies had big enough balls?' laughed Gevoh in return.

More laughter followed from the ascendent Britons, but Toryn held up his hand for quiet. 'I've always wondered if you hit a man hard enough whether you can send his balls up his tubes and out the other end.'

He walked up to Lucius and grabbed his bollocks, twisting them hard so that despite the fire already in his balls the Roman gasped.

'What say you Roman? Shall we see if we can pop them out of your fucking mouth?'

Despite the pain, Lucius looked up in horror.

'Stand him up and spread his legs,' ordered Toryn, menacingly swapping the staff from one hand to the other.

The Britons kicked Lucius's legs wider. Panic registered in the centurion's eyes.

'Enough Toryn,' Alba broke in.

'I am only just getting started Alba,' Toryn replied. 'This little shit has been a pain in our collective arses for too long. I intend to have my fun with him.'

Alba stepped close enough to Toryn so that no other could hear. 'Toryn, I beg you, I need this man alive. Much that I would like to see him upon your sword or staff, he has yet a part to play.'

'Do I care?' Toryn retorted. 'If you mean your woman, then we come down to it don't we. I willingly fight to protect our lands from this Red scourge, but now you ask that I aid you for a woman you favoured over my own daughter?'

'Alright then,' replied Alba, thinking on his feet. 'Are you willing to let Rendrr escape. He is more of a shitbag than this Roman stood before us. He is the traitor Toryn, the one who sold out on all of us.'

His words hit their mark but it was not over. Still high with adrenaline and bloodlust, Toryn teetered between killing Lucius and vengeance against Rendrr. Most of the warriors were still goading him on, desperate to see if he really could do what he threatened.

Toryn looked straight at Alba, before the staff flashed again catapulting Lucius onto his back. For an instant, Alba thought he had killed him before a low groan came from the prostrate form on the ground.

'Fuck!' Toryn yelled. ''You better find that bastard Alba.'

Alba nodded, relieved that Toryn had abated. 'I

will find him.'

'What will you do with the rest of them?' Argyll cut in, indicating the legionaries still formed up within their defensive square.

'What do you think I'm going to do with them? Give them a fucking pat on the back and send them on their merry way?' taunted Toryn.

'Can I suggest something?' Alba replied.

'You seem expert at coming up with shit, Alba. What now?'

'Let them go.'

'Let them go, are you fucking joking?'

'Leave me the centurion. Let the others go but send them with a message.'

'Anything else? Shall I feed and water them as well?'

'Listen Toryn. You could slaughter them all but they still number fifty or so men. They are well disciplined and we would no doubt lose some of our own warriors in satisfying nothing but a need to blood let. We have already won the field. Besides, I have an idea.'

Without waiting for Toryn's response, Alba called over to the main body of Roman soldiers.

'Send out your commander. If you do not, then you will all die. Decide now.'

There was a moments pause where the Romans held fast. Alba considered that their commander may already have been killed, in which case he would need another plan. As it was, the front ranks withdrew their shields creating a narrow gap through which stepped their senior officer. Despite himself, Alba marvelled at their discipline. The gap had formed as though the geometry of the square had morphed rather than men simply moving position.

Face darkened with the grime and gore of battle, but still in one piece, Quintus halted a couple of paces distant. He glanced down at the stricken Lucius, barely conscious and still groaning in the dirt. Then he brought his attention back to Alba.

'I am Quintus, Optio to Lucius Glaucus of the Legio XX Valeria Victrix,' he replied.

'I am Alba.'

'I know who you are Briton.'

'Good. Then that makes this easier. I am going to keep your centurion hostage. If you do as I say, you and your men can retire without reprisal.'

'And if we do not?'

'Firstly, you will be cut down, your bodies disposed of without trace and your legion will be sullied by the dishonour of failure and defeat. In addition, once your friend here has ceased to be of use to me then I will hand him back to Toryn. I am sure you understand what will happen to him should Toryn see his ball sack in his sights again.'

'How do I know that you or he,' he motioned toward Toryn, 'will keep your word?'

'I give you mine.'

'The word of a barbarian?' spat Quintus.

Alba smiled. 'You take my word or none at all Roman. Retire with what is left of your honour or die with none. The choice is yours.'

'What will you do with my centurion?'

'I will release him once I have finished with him.'

'You expect me to believe that?'

'Do you have a choice?'

Quintus looked down at where his superior still lay incapacitated. The decision would have to be his own.

'Apparently not. You seem to hold the advantage, Briton.'

'One other thing. I require you to deliver a letter to your superiors which I will dictate before we leave.' He paused and looked Quintus squarely in the eye. 'Do I have your agreement?'

CHAPTER XXIV

'Are you going to tell me what you put in that note?' Argyll enquired, once they were on their way.

Behind them, sandwiched between Argyll and Horva sat a battered and bound Lucius. The centurion's head hung limply to one side, bouncing in sync to each stride of the horse. Five other warriors brought up the rear.

Alba glanced back at him as they rode on. 'I sent a note to his commanding officer informing him that this was the third occasion he had let us slip through his fingers. I may even have suggested he held sympathies for the Britons, given that he seemed wholly incapable of catching us.'

Argyll laughed. 'Well, if you do release him he will certainly have some explaining to do. I'd love to see him get a dressing down from his superiors!'

'The thing about these Romans,' continued Alba, 'is that they like to vaunt their accomplishments but hide their failures. I thought it would be entertaining to imagine what such ignominy would do to such a pompous little shit as our friend here.'

'I'm still not sure why he's with us anyway.'

'We need some bargaining power; leverage, should Rendrr use Beatha against us.'

'That's assuming we are heading in the right direction. You are staking everything on what Toryn told you. He may be wrong.'

'It's all I have. A rough location is better than no location,' Alba replied, recalling his last conversation with Toryn. They had been preparing to leave the field, bundling a defeated Lucius towards a waiting horse. Toryn had belayed them.

'Where are you heading with this little viper?' Toryn had asked, grabbing a tuft of hair and yanking the centurion's head back sharply. Stepping forward, he stared wide eyed into the Roman's face, the two pinpoints of his pupils never wavering from the gaping black holes which gazed back in retreat.

Toryn fixed him, not for a moment averting his gaze. Lucius, for all of his training, looked lost, unused to such irrationality. Very slowly, Toryn pushed his tongue out so that its red tip halted but a finger width away from the Roman's face. Eyes locked, he retracted the snaking organ before flicking it out repeatedly, moving it around his lips as though in a prelude to some bizarre mating ritual. Then he bent closer and slowly raked both sides of Lucius's neck with long sweeps of his tongue. Satisfied, he turned around to the watching Britons and spat out in disgust.

'I thought so,' he announced. 'He not only looks like shit, he tastes like shit as well!'

A roar of laughter once more accompanied Toryn's antics. If Lucius had thought the moment over he was mistaken. Toryn returned, this time grabbing his jaw. Thick set, heavy hands swivelled the centurion's head from left to right. A dagger appeared in his hand, so quick the transformation as if conjured out of the air itself. The point teased a dance in front of the centurion's eyes.

'I may just fancy widening that shithole of a mouth for you,' he taunted, placing the edge of the dagger lightly against Lucius's lips before slowly drawing it across.

The blade was not pushed home and Lucius went limp with relief.

'Why the little prick has almost shit himself!' Toryn exclaimed. He slapped the Roman round the cheek as a parting shot before addressing Alba. 'The centurion may not help you. He is full of himself but not stupid. He knows if he tells you the location of your woman then his worth is done.'

'I gave my word,' Alba protested.

'Do you think a Red like him would believe it?'

Alba hesitated.

'I thought not,' continued Toryn. 'However, I might be able to help.'

'Go on.'

'Notwithstanding being an ignorant fuck for what you did to my daughter, for now, we have common cause.'

Alba wondered where this was going. Toryn had calmed down since the fighting had ceased. Some semblance of restraint or what passed for it in Toryn's case, had re-established itself.

'When you spoke about finding a cave it reminded me of something I had all but forgotten,' continued Toryn. 'A long time ago, I was close to Rendrr. We had both seen many battles in our youth and were beginning to turn our attention to other things as well as fighting. Well, Rendrr wanted to become an elder, figuring that he had proved his worth in battle enough times and that the other elders would accept him. He had only one opponent in the contest, a man by the name of Aesa. He was also an experienced warrior with just as good a claim as Rendrr. The problem was that neither of them could stand the other.'

'Surely, a bit of animosity in such a contest was to be expected?'

'This went beyond animosity and you could tell that they hated each other. I do not know why the feeling was so intense between them. Whether it was just the desire to win over the other or maybe a woman, who knows.'

'I assume Rendrr won given that he went on to become chieftain?'

'Correct, he did.'

'But?'

'He won by default.'

'By default?'

'He was elected as elder due to no-one standing

against him.'

Alba was confused. 'But I thought you just said . . .'

'I did, but on the day of voting, Aesa never showed up. In fact, he has never been seen up to this day.'

'You think something happened to him, some deed that lies at Rendrr's door?'

Toryn didn't answer.

'What else are you not telling me?' pushed Alba. 'Did you know about this?'

'I am ashamed to some extent over this affair, Alba. I did not know at the time but have thought often upon it since.'

'I am still unsure how this helps us locate Beatha,' Alba continued, puzzled.

'Look, I said Rendrr and I used to be good friends. That friendship started out when we were just boys. One day we were out messing about, a few leagues south of Wyeval wood. We came across an exposed rock face which upon any chance discovery looks just like any other piece of limestone. The rest of it disappears underground, beneath moss and heather. It was Rendrr who found the entrance; a narrow opening between the overlapping rock with a slit just big enough to squeeze through. Inside is a small cavern which became our secret camp. We used to disappear for days there. You'll also be interested to know that the acoustics of the cavern do a thorough job of muzzling any sound from within.'

'The perfect hiding place.'

'Yes.'

'And Aesa; do you suspect Rendrr disposed of him in the cave?'

Toryn winced. 'I do not know. I blanked my mind from it to be honest.'

'You did not go to check?' Alba asked astonished.

'To my shame I did not. Remember, I was close with Rendrr back then and I did not want to believe my best friend capable of such a thing.'

'Did the rest of the tribal elders believe Rendrr to be under suspicion?'

'There was other testimony which alluded to Aesa being seen near the western borders. Back then, border disputes were more frequent. It was not unusual for warriors to stray into another territory and not be seen or heard of again. The elders accepted that Aesa had probably fallen foul of such a fate.'

'Alba!'

Argyll's voice brought him back to the present. 'Look, tracks.'

They stopped the horses. Alba jumped down to inspect the ground, running his hands over the churned-up earth.

'Is it Rendrr?'

'I think so. We have been fortunate to pick up their trail. There are multiple tracks so he must have left with an escort.'

'The cowardly bastard!' spat Argyll.

'There is no effort to conceal,' puzzled Alba. 'Obviously flight and speed were more important to him than secrecy.'

'Or he didn't think anyone would be left alive to follow him.'

'There is another possibility.'

'That he wanted to be followed?'

'I mean, he may have wanted *me* to follow him. Remember, Rendrr has survived this long. He works to a plan but covers himself all the same.'

'Then, when we find him he could be expecting us?'

'We must assume he has a welcome planned for our arrival.'

'I guess we don't have much choice do we?'

'Not at this point,' Alba conceded. 'For now, we follow and see where it leads.'

'And Beatha?'

'She is additional leverage but I have no doubt his intention will be for none of us to draw breath once this is over.'

The other warriors had drawn around them, listening to the exchange.

'Let us continue,' Alba declared, 'but be on your guard. The trap does not necessarily get sprung at our destination.'

They reformed their line, Alba leading. The tracks were clear and easy to read. They followed them up to the edge of the pine wood where the sight of the dead warriors arrested their progress. Alba immediately commanded them to dismount, using the horses as shields. When they were sure no attack was imminent, Argyll approached the nearest corpse.

'Roman arrow. Archers were probably concealed just within the tree line.' He went from body to body, turning over those that were face down. 'Rendrr's not amongst them and this one has been stabbed as well. My guess is he was wounded and tried to crawl away. Thrust was straight to the heart.'

'If Rendrr is not amongst them then this may have been a planned ambush,' said Alba.

Argyll inspected another warrior, a distance away from the rest. 'This one is different. No arrow wound, but . . .' There was a pause whilst he absorbed the evidence of his eyes. 'Shit! He's been stuck through the mouth and neck. The angle suggests the killer was on horseback.'

'Rendrr's work I suspect,' Alba replied. 'He probably distracted him whilst the others were dispatched.'

'Another example where he works with his Roman friends,' Argyll said, disgusted.

'The Red obviously think he's worth it. I wonder how they intend to use his loyalty given they go to all this trouble?'

He let the question hang in the air. Argyll pointed at the dead warriors. 'What shall we do about them?'

'Nothing for now,' Alba replied. 'If we survive then we can organise a party to retrieve them. Time is against us now.'

CHAPTER XXV

Laelius walked back to his quarters. Though he was favoured by Servius, he was constantly ill at ease, a consequence of a difficult childhood. His Senator father had never shown him any affection whilst his mother seemed ashamed of him. He could never once recall being in the presence of others when his parents entertained company. He would be told to stay out of sight and remain silent with only slaves as company.

When his father had informed him of his attachment to Servius he was terrified. Not once had he set foot outside of Rome. The far reaches of the empire filled him with dread rather than awe. Yet, a part of him accepted that he may find purpose, become a man and make his father proud.

The reality had been somewhat different. Servius tolerated his presence but made no secret that he loathed him. Other officials and most of the soldiers insulted him whenever he was away from the Legatus. Everything about this assignment was hateful. Even the weather in this remote part of empire was wet and depressing. Despite everything, he missed the trappings of home or at least the luxury.

His quarters was a large tent and well furnished. Servius had seen to that. Any official of the Legatus did live in a modicum of luxury, one of the few things he could be grateful for. The interior was illuminated by a couple of candles he had lit before attending Servius for his last orders of the day.

He stopped, aware that something felt different. His eyes flitted around nervously, seeking the source of the disturbance.

'I have been waiting for you,' spoke a soft, feminine voice.

What was a woman doing in his quarters?

He moved further in, noticing another light illuminating his bed.

'Come over here.'

'Who are you?' he answered.

'I am your reward.'

'My reward?'

'The Legatus is pleased with you. I have been provided to give you pleasure.'

The drape separating his bed from the rest of his quarters moved. Laelius had never seen a woman before, naked and without fear. His eyes widened before moving over the landscape before him.

She smiled at his attention before walking slowly toward him. Involuntarily, he took a step back, unsure and fearful.

'You are a virgin? Do not be afraid. I will guide

you.'

She had reached him now. The beauty of her body was overwhelming and paired with a light perfume which teased of the far eastern reaches of empire.

She pressed her body against him before removing his tunic. The feel of her warm breasts upon his bare chest was like nothing he had experienced. Smiling, she raised her head and moved her lips to his own. Despite his seventeen years, he had never tasted a woman's lips before, enjoying the excitement of her tongue within his mouth.

Overwhelmed, Laelius never noticed the subtle movement as the concealed blade was positioned above his chest. Still kissing him, the assassin slid the blade into the youths pounding heart, killing both his passion and his life.

Laelius died instantly, his only time with a woman also his last. As the assassin lowered the body quietly to the floor she looked back at the sightless eyes frozen into a mask of surprise.

'A pity my friend but a job is a job. No loose ends.'

She left the tent and disappeared into the night, hoping that her next mission would be so easy.

***

'Are you still alive, little bitch?' Rendrr teased, before bringing himself fully into the cave.

His own words echoed in response and, for a moment, he wondered whether she may have starved before recalling his last conversation with Enica.

'I know my wife has been visiting you. Do not be shy. Besides, I have a little surprise outside waiting for you. A few of my Roman friends cannot wait to make your acquaintance. You'll have them all to yourself. Aren't you the lucky girl?'

Frustrated with no answer, he pulled out a flint and began to light the bundle of birch which he had thrown in ahead.

'Enica is dead by the way,' he goaded, striking the flint against a clump of dried moss.

'I suspected she had followed me so I set Rues to watch her. He told me she had visited you twice. I cannot allow treachery, particularly when it lies within my own fucking house.'

Still no answer.

The moss had become damp and was struggling to light. Annoyed, he struck harder at the flint.

'She was surprisingly unapologetic when I told her she had been observed. I'd normally give her a beating, but, to tell the truth, I've tired of her pathetic presence these last few months. It was quite satisfying burying my rusty old blade within that barren belly of hers. The stupid bitch couldn't even produce any offspring so probably just as well to put an end to her miserable existence.'

The moss suddenly flared up as the embers coalesced into flame. He threw it onto the torch, the fire quickly catching on the resin saturated branches. The cavern flickered to life. Irregular surfaces produced a collage of figures which shifted in a choreography of light and shadow as he moved. Cautiously, he stepped towards where he had left her but only emptiness and angular rock faces reflected back.

Most men would have paused just a moment to take in the empty space where Beatha had lain, but Rendrr's instinct was quick enough to anticipate an attack. He moved just as she brought the rock down at his head. Had it connected where intended then the top of his skull would have been crushed. The escape was not total; the rock caught the side of his neck gouging a bloody gorge.

Recovering quickly he dived at Beatha as she desperately scrambled for the entrance.

'Nice try bitch!' he yelled, grabbing at a shadow before him.

A clump of thick hair found its way into his grasp. Savagely, he wrenched it back. A scream pierced the darkness as she fell back against him. 'Now, you really have pissed me off,' he grated angrily in her ear.

As she staggered backwards, he brought his fist up against her left cheek sending her spinning to the ground. Flushed with anger, he leapt across and pulled her up by her hair, curling it around his wrist as he wrenched her battered face toward him.

'I would have thought Alba would have taught you some manners,' he spat, phlegm peppering her face. 'Now listen to me. You are only breathing because if by some chance that bastard of yours makes it here then you get to live a little longer. If he doesn't, then my Roman friends outside will be making friends with you in their own unique way.'

***

Out of the undergrowth Horva emerged, keeping low and quiet as he crept back to where Alba and Argyll were waiting.

'I followed the tracks as best I could whilst keeping to cover. They lead through a wooded area, not dense but close enough to conceal an enemy. Beyond it, there is nothing but a rock face covered in overhanging vines and moss. I saw no sign of an entrance, however.'

'And the tracks stopped there?' Alba asked.

'Yes, but there was plenty of disturbance in the ground within the woods.'

'I bet there was,' Alba mused.

'You think it is a trap?' Argyll asked.

'The disturbance in the ground is most likely an effort to conceal their intent. It makes a pursuer unsure whether to carry on ahead or spread out amongst the trees.'

'So what do we do?' Horva asked.

'We do both,' Alba replied. 'Rendrr will assume that we have followed him.'

'He may not know that the Romans were beaten,' said Argyll. 'If he thinks we are dead then surely he will not expect an attack?'

'But he will allow for it, Argyll. Remember, this man is used to planning for contingencies. That is why he has survived so long.'

'What do you command then?' Horva asked.

'Argyll and I will go ahead, through the woods, challenge him direct.'

'You will be killed,' protested Horva.

'We will go slowly and on foot. Once there is sufficient distance between us, you and the other warriors will split into two groups fanning out behind us, flanking left and right. With any luck you can take out any guards hidden in the trees before they get a chance to engage us.'

'That's a big risk,' Horva protested. 'We may not find their positions until they have shot at you. You could be killed before we can act.'

'It's a risk we have to take,' Alba said simply.

'You agree with this?' Horva questioned Argyll.

'I see no choice.'

Horva sighed. 'Then it will be done.'

'What about him?' Argyll pointed at Lucius. 'He's a liability Alba. Let us despatch him now and have riddance.'

'No Argyll! He may yet be useful. Take him off the horse and bind him to that oak over there.'

Reluctantly, Argyll strode over to Lucius. Once he had unbound his restraints, Argyll feinted holding his hand out. As soon as the Roman's eyes met his own he shoved hard, sending the centurion reeling over the other side of the horse. Lucius fell badly, cracking his head upon an old stump. Unfazed, Argyll
 grabbed the battered Roman by the back of the

neck and dragged him to the bole of the tree. Once secured, he spat in his face and returned to the other Britons.

'Had your fun?' Alba asked.

'Not nearly enough. I think it a mistake leaving him here, alive.'

'We'll see. Now, let us be about our business.'

'May the gods guide you to victory,' whispered Horva.

'You too,' Alba replied. 'Do not move until there is sufficient distance between us to convince them we are alone.'

***

Rendrr had been surprised at how Beatha had found a way to cut her bonds. She must have been lucky and found a piece of rock that had an edge. He had only bothered to retie her wrists as she would need the use of her legs for the next phase of his plan, albeit for a brief time.

Part of him still rejected the idea that Alba may have survived the trap he had laid with Lucius. In answer, the voice in his head replied that it was well to be prepared. He knew that really. It was just his mind over thinking, but the mental chatter did keep him alert to every possibility. Rendrr's entire existence was mind centric. It served him well, together with the illusion of empathy he had perfected to exist in his role for so long.

A noise came from near the entrance as Rues's voice reached out into the cavern.

'Rendrr! Alba and Argyll are approaching.'

'Are the men ready?'

'Everything is set.'

'Then greet them properly, but make sure that Alba is still alive when I bring his bitch out. I want his last moments to be spent watching the Romans having their way with her.'

'As you wish.'

Rues disappeared. Rendrr waited, surprised that Alba had both survived and caught up with them so quickly. There again, he had hardly made it difficult for them to follow.

Never underestimate an enemy.

He had learned that lesson very early on. Aesa, his opponent to become chief elder all those years ago had taught him that. His debates in open council were always heated and occasionally violent where Aesa was concerned. That was the way of things and to be expected. What he had not anticipated was to be ambushed whilst out hunting. Aesa had surprised him, nearly besting him not far from where he was now. His mistake had been to brag about it. A moment's lapse and Rendrr had turned the knife held against him and buried it into Aesa's own seedy little throat. He often chuckled when he remembered the look of complete surprise on Aesa's face when Rendrr had pushed the blade home. He looked over at the skeleton, remembering the moment of death. Briefly, Aesa's face seemed to superimpose itself over the discoloured skull.

'You risked all and lost Aesa,' he muttered.

Rendrr turned away, refocusing upon Beatha. 'Not long now and then you get to see Alba again. Of course, he may not be up to much when you do, but I promise I shall leave enough life in him to enjoy the spectacle.'

He yanked her closer, breathing heavily into her face. 'My Roman friends are looking forward to getting to know you more intimately. I am told they enjoy others looking on whilst they fuck their whores. I'm afraid in this case, your audience will be what's left of Alba and that shit of a friend of his.'

Beatha's wide eyes stared back at him. He laughed, enjoying the acoustics as the sound bounced around him in a medley of madness.

CHAPTER XXVI

'This should be far enough,' whispered Alba.

'And open enough,' worried Argyll. 'We are very exposed and Rendrr may not want to face you. He could have given orders to shoot us on sight.'

'I know, but hopefully Horva should be in position by now and we are committed.'

They halted, just beyond the cover of the trees. In front of them, the rock face concealing the cave entrance was only fifty paces away.

Alba took a step forward. 'Rendrr! It is Alba. Come out so we can talk.'

There was no answer.

'I don't like this Alba. We should retreat to cover.'

'Wait! It is his move.'

'Rendrr!' he called again. 'You invited me here didn't you? Well, here I am!'

As they watched, an illusion transformed before their eyes. As if emerging from the very rock itself Beatha appeared, followed by the Cornovii chieftain. They pushed through the moss and vines, stepping down the rockface until they were on the same level as the two warriors.

'I am glad to see you followed my trail Alba. I thought you would find a way out of the little surprise I had sprung. You are a lucky bastard after all.'

'Let Beatha go, Rendrr. You have me now.'

Rendrr laughed. 'That would be far too simple and besides, I expected a better play from you than that.'

'We have an army with us,' lied Argyll.

'The sidekick speaks,' sneered Rendrr. 'I think not, Argyll. The fact that you are here alone speaks the lie to your words.'

'Then what do you want?' Alba asked.

'Why, isn't it obvious? I'd have thought a man of your ability would have worked it out by now. I intend to kill you Alba, but not so soon that you won't be able to enjoy a little performance I have arranged.'

'Leave Beatha out of this,' guessed Alba. 'You've had your use of her to get at me. Let her and Argyll go free. You can take your spite out on me alone.'

'I have gone to a lot of trouble preparing for both your arrival and my escape, Alba. I'm afraid the three of you will be going nowhere other than the underworld very soon now. Your luck has finally run out and so my friend, it is so.'

Alba guessed Rendrr would have a word or action to signal the Romans who he was sure were concealed somewhere close. He had warned Argyll to be on his guard for such. Simultaneously, they both dived away in opposite directions. Argyll was a split second slower. A shower of arrows buried themselves in the ground where they had stood moments earlier. As he scrambled toward cover he heard his friend cry out.

Rendrr remained where he was, smiling. He held Beatha before him, a shield against any attack. Pressed tightly to her throat was a thin bladed dagger with a cruel curve at its end. His confidence and apparent disinterest in any threat posed by Alba was disconcerting.

The bastard always has a plan, thought Alba.

The sound of more fighting came from the trees behind him. Horva's men must have engaged the Romans stationed in the woods. Cries of killed or wounded breached the air, though he did not see either Roman or Briton from where he was crouched. He risked poking his head out to see if he could spot Argyll. Immediately, the tree bark splintered in front of him as a Roman arrow buried itself a hairs breadth away from his face.

Ducking down, he tried calling out instead.

'Argyll?'

There was no answer. For his friend not to reply could only mean he was unable to. He dared not countenance he was dead, but how could he reach him? He could make a rough guess of where Argyll would have most likely tried to recover to but getting there would risk another arrow. He briefly thought back on how many times they had saved each other's lives, knowing this would be no exception.

Alba ducked his head out to be rewarded by a second vibrating arrow shaft appearing in the trunk before him. Gambling that the archer would take a few seconds to re-nock his next arrow he sprinted over to cover just as two further missiles flew either side of him. One was close enough to graze his side. It stung but the wound was superficial. The archer had been faster than he had anticipated.

His approximation of Argyll's position had been correct. Not far away he spotted one of his feet poking out of the undergrowth. Fearing the worst, he crawled on his belly until he reached his friend's side.

'Argyll, do you live?'

Argyll's eyes flickered open. He had been hit twice, once in the left thigh, the other to his left shoulder. The shoulder wound was bleeding but not immediately dangerous. He could not tell with the leg, but the shaft was buried worryingly deep and there was already a pool of dark blood below him.

'Keep still and stay silent Argyll. I will return.'

Argyll's eyes closed. Alba slapped his face hard. 'No my friend! Do not sleep.'

There was little he could do to help Argyll until he had dealt with Rendrr and the remaining Romans. He would have to hope Horva was dealing with the latter, but Rendrr was his problem. The Cornovii chieftain had not moved an inch, despite the sounds of fighting further into the wood.

Alba quartered the area, keeping close to the ground and using the trees for cover. On the outskirts of the wood there were few trees with a thick enough trunk to protect him. The archer was well hidden and despite his efforts had maintained an annoying track of his progress sending several shafts within a hand's width of his body. He had the distinct impression he was being toyed with until his master called time.

'Why don't you come forward, Alba?' teased Rendrr. 'Your bitch is waiting for you. If you don't, then I may just slip a little with this blade.'

'Let her go then Rendrr,' Alba shouted. 'Fight me man to man or do you continue to hide behind a woman.'

'Come, come Alba. You know me by now. That is not how things are done.'

'You have nowhere to go Rendrr. Not only is your entire plot laid bare, but all of the tribal leaders know of your betrayal.'

'I assure you that my future looks far brighter than yours,' Rendrr barked back. 'You have no concept of just who you are dealing with, do you?'

'I know you sold your soul to the Red; that you probably negotiated safe passage to an area of empire where you can live as one of them.'

Rendrr threw his head back and laughed again. 'Oh, little pathetic Alba with his little pathetic bitch. You really do not see what is there before you. I do not want to live out my days as some wealthy, ex

Briton in a mountainside villa. I want to be part of a greater future, one which will endure for centuries.'

'You talk like one of them, Rendrr.'

'And why shouldn't I be one of them? I have outgrown you and your kind. I desire more than sitting in command of a desolate hill fort in the middle of nowhere.

'Then why did you not just leave? Why all of this plotting and murder?'

'I am not yet a Roman, Alba, but my mind is. I cannot simply leave the Cornovii to their own destiny, not when it can be part of something greater. Doube failed to see that. Night after night, he drooled on and on about self-determination and guarding the old ways. I can't tell you how satisfying it was ripping out his gutless innards with my blade. The old fool never realised where my true loyalties lay. Now, it is time for the Cornovii and the rest of the tribes of Britannia to understand their place in the new world to come.'

'And where would that be? Forced out of our lands, enslaved and subservient to your Roman masters?

'Only the strong can rule and bring technology, medicine and purpose to the masses. It is called civilisation; a natural order of things where intelligence presides over brawn.'

'Then you really are lost Rendrr. It is not just your mind that has turned red for your heart also runs red. Red with deceit, red with treachery and red with the blood of Doube and Enica. You will be banished by our gods, your soul forever to roam the underworld.'

'Enough!' Rendrr yelled back. 'I grow tired of this. I don't give a fuck about the gods anymore; they are no longer mine. Come forward now or I start to take the bitch apart, piece by piece. I'll start with one of her ears to incentivise you.'

Unable to establish what was going on behind him, Alba realised he had finally run out of time. He cast a look to where Argyll lay, unmoving. This time, his friend would not be able to save the day.

His only option would be to spot the hidden man, get to Rendrr before he cut Beatha and maybe use him as a shield. It wasn't much of a plan.

He left the cover of the trees and strode out to face the traitor.

'Come closer,' Rendrr encouraged. 'Don't you want to exchange a few last words with your beloved before you die? He smiled, completely sure of himself and enjoying the power. 'She made friends with my guards while you have been away. You understand that I cannot kill her before they vent their frustration on her. Fighting does do wonders for a man's lust and I'm sure she will appreciate some Roman cock between her legs before she joins you in the underworld.'

'You touch her and I promise you that you will not see the day out alive!'

'And who's going to stop me? You or your friend perhaps? I think that imbecilic simpleton is probably dead or dying, otherwise we wouldn't still be talking.'

'I promise you, Rendrr, by all the gods, I will have my vengeance upon you.'

'It has been enjoyable,' laughed Rendrr. 'Even that other dumb bastard, Toryn, had no idea I was the one you sought. I shall amuse myself on that for many years to come. Now, throw down your sword and the dagger I know you always keep.'

Reluctantly, Alba complied. He had no doubt that the hidden archer already had an arrow trained upon him. Though the sound of fighting from the woods had diminished there was no sign of Horva or his men. His options were reduced to one and he did not rate his chances. Jumping Rendrr, whilst avoiding the arrow he was certain would fly, was likely to result in his death, but better that, than to be slain doing nothing.

'Kick them away,' ordered Rendrr.

Alba kicked the weapons to one side.

'Well, our business is almost done. The only thing remaining is for you to enjoy this little vixen getting what she deserves.'

Quick as lightning he flicked the blade down Beatha's front. For a moment, Alba thought he had opened her up. Instead, Rendrr ripped her garments away exposing her nakedness. Alba leapt forward as the archer released.

The arrow buried itself into his right calf, forcing him to collapse at Rendrr's feet. The insanity and pleasure of victory mixed into one roar of delight as Rendrr aimed an upper cut with his leg to Alba's chin. It missed but caught Alba on his damaged shoulder instead. He was flung back, collapsing as pain radiated out from the reopened wound. Once more, his tunic became soaked with fresh blood.

'Bring the horses,' ordered Rendrr.

The soldier emerged from the trees, an eastern style recurve bow slung over his back. This had been the man Alba had so desperately sought, whilst the unusual bow explained why he had been able to fire so rapidly. He led two horses over to where Rendrr still had Beatha. His eyes widened at the sight of her exposed body, dwelling on her intimate womanhood.

Rendrr caught his look. 'You can pleasure yourself on her if you like. Just do not leave it too long in case they send reinforcements. Make sure you finish him, but only after you have fucked the girl. I want him to watch and know what it means to fail completely.'

The Roman looked like he was in two minds, but as Rendrr mounted his horse he hitched up his skirts and pushed Beatha roughly to the floor. Satisfied she couldn't resist he began to straddle her. Alba watched in horror as the Roman fumbled for his manhood.

'Enjoy the show, Alba!' Rendrr laughed. 'It will be the last thing you see before you die.' He spurred his horse and galloped away.

Still bound, Beatha screamed and tried to kick at her attacker. Angered, the soldier aimed a fist at the side of her head, almost causing her to pass out. Helpless, Alba watched in horror as the Roman finally released himself. Triumphant, he looked across at Alba, grinning as he held up his freed and engorged manhood, positioning himself to invade the dazed woman beneath.

There was a whoosh and a thud. The grin left the soldier's face as his gaze fixed upon an iron point which had suddenly extended an arm's length out of his chest. Beatha writhed below him, trying to get away even as his life blood dripped onto her skin. Finally, he fell to the side, his torso slowly slipping down the blood greased shaft which had killed him.

Beyond where the Roman had been hiding, Horva emerged, bloodied with battle but alive. He ran over to where Alba lay.

'Thank you my friend,' Alba exclaimed, relief flooding his features.

'I am sorry I was so long, but the Romans were well hidden and took some rooting out. We lost two men and another is wounded. I sent him back to keep an eye on the Roman centurion.'

'Rendrr has got away,' Alba said grasping Horva's outstretched hand before stumbling over to Beatha.

'I am sorry.'

'There is no fault with you. Beatha is safe, but Argyll is badly wounded.'

'I will attend him,' Horva replied and ran back to where Alba indicated his friend lay.

Alba took the gag off Beatha and released her wrists. Finally, he held her to him, as silently they reaffirmed their bond.

Horva returned. 'Your friend will live. The wound in the leg is deep but not life threatening. I have stemmed the bleeding until we can remove the arrow.'

'I will treat him but first you,' said Beatha, indicating Alba's leg.

'See to Argyll first. I can manage.'

'No, you cannot!' she replied sternly. 'You have an arrow through your own leg and despite the fact that the arrowhead has exited, the shaft remains inside. If you move the shaft could splinter and cause more damage. Therefore, you will listen and do exactly as I say.'

'I will do as you command,' Alba said sheepishly, raising his eyebrows towards Horva.

'Your friend will need to help as well,' Beatha said, catching his glance and then turning to Horva. 'You will need to hold him still when I pull it out.'

Horva nodded and passed Alba a piece of bark. 'Here, bite down on this.'

Alba put the wood into his mouth and clenched his teeth firmly against it. Gripping the exposed shaft, Beatha snapped off the fletched end first. Alba winced, knowing that this was just a prelude to what was to come.

'This will hurt a lot. Prepare yourself.'

Alba braced himself as Beatha curved her fingers around the rest of the arrow, below the head but above where it had exited the flesh. Horva held Alba firmly by the shoulders as in one swift motion she pulled the shaft out the other side. Searing hot pain fired through his already stretched nerves, and, despite himself, he bit down so hard that the wood broke in his mouth.

Blood leaked heavily from the wound from both entry and exit holes. Quickly, Beatha ripped her torn clothing into strips and tied it around his calf until the bandage held.

'This will do for now, but I will need to treat it to stay infection. Return to me once you have dealt with Rendrr for he must pay for his crimes. I would see retribution for what he did to Enica. She helped me at great risk and suffered greatly at his hand.'

'He will, Beatha. You have my word.'

Horva helped him to his feet. 'We should check on the centurion first. Then we can take him with us if you still think he is of use in hunting down Rendrr.'

Alba nodded and slowly they made their way back passing several corpses on the return. In one thicket, two Romans and one Briton had died together. They carried on, but, as they stepped over, Horva noticed a slight movement from one of the soldiers.

'Hold on.'

He knelt down next to the wounded legionary. The man was conscious but barely holding on to life. Horva removed his helmet to be confronted by a remarkably young face The soldier blinked rapidly as the extra light flooded into his darkening eyes.

'You fought bravely,' Horva spoke. 'There is no shame in meeting your gods.'

The soldier stared at Horva, an understanding

forming between them despite Horva speaking in his native tongue. A moment later he was gone.

'The Romans fought hard,' noted Horva. There was almost a hint of admiration in his voice, though Alba knew better than to comment on it.

They reached the place where they had left Lucius. A rope lay loose against the base of the trunk. Its former occupant was gone, while to one side lay the Briton who had guarded him. A neat line of red dribbled out of a cut across his throat.

'Shit!' exclaimed Alba.

'But how did he get loose?' Horva asked, bewildered.

Alba bent down and examined the warriors neck. 'Slit from behind. A cowardly attack on a warrior who was already wounded. This has the stench of Rues. My guess is that he had orders to release the centurion as soon as Rendrr was free. No doubt, they are on their way to join up with him at a pre-agreed meeting point.'

'If we hurry, we may be able to cut them off.'

'How many warriors do we have left?

'Myself and two others, though one is badly injured and may not survive.'

'That may not be enough and we don't know if he is meeting with the Red.' Alba clenched his fist, frustrated. 'Damn! Rendrr's strategy confounds us once again.'

'I will go and deal with the traitor,' Horva offered again.

'No Horva. I would not send you on this course

without the certainty of numbers. Rendrr survives by outthinking his enemies so we must do the same in order to bring him to justice.'

'Then it is a good job that I have saved you the trouble!' boomed another voice.

Alba and Horva whirled around. Before them stood Toryn flanked by two of his own warriors.

'What are you doing here?' Alba exclaimed, taken aback.

'I came to make Rendrr pay for his treachery,' Toryn replied. 'I followed behind you once Rigari and I had secured the field.'

'I told you that I would deal with Rendrr,' Alba protested, wincing as his leg threatened to give way.

'And yet, you let him escape.'

Alba ignored the insult. Toryn's words always seemed to bait him. 'Do you have Rendrr or not Toryn?'

'Fortunately for you, my men and I intercepted him on our way here. Curiously, he was not too keen to rejoin your little party so had to be *persuaded*.'

'And how exactly did you persuade him?'

'We shot his horse from under him.'

'So, where is he now?'

'Relaxing over there behind that big oak.'

They walked across to where Toryn had indicated. Alba knew Rendrr was dead before he reached him. The distinctive smell of blood and death had already carried on the light breeze. What he didn't expect was the scene of carnage and brutality that had been effected to the Cornovii chieftain's body.

The entire chest cavity had been cut away with entrails and other organs ripped out and thrown either side of the body. Blood around the groin suggested that his genitals had also met with the same fate. The face had not escaped either, and, as Alba lifted up the chin, he was met with two empty eye sockets and a mouth that had been sliced open from ear to ear. He stopped short of inspecting inside the mouth having a suspicion of what he might find. A dagger had been driven into the top of the head with only the handle still visible.

'I scooped out the cheating bastards innards and shoved them down his treacherous fucking throat,' grated Toryn. 'You might call it retribution for what he did to Doube and for the betrayal of his people.'

Alba was incensed. 'Damn you and your temper, Toryn! Had he lived, we could have learned much about the conspiracy and if anyone else is involved. You have wasted our opportunity to expose them and now we will never know.'

'You of all people should have cause to see him dead,' Toryn replied angrily.

'He should have been brought before the Great Council to face his crimes and for us to learn how far the conspiracy extended. You should have stayed your blade and waited. Instead, your anger or whatever you call this aberration has robbed us of the chance.'

'I did what must be done.'

'You did more than that! I wonder if there was reason for your haste?'

'You dare make accusation against me, despite the fact that I saved your scrawny neck back with Rigari. I have killed better men than you, Alba, for less.' Toryn turned his back and strode angrily towards his horse. Once mounted, he turned back to face him.

'It seems our dispute comes full circle.'

'It seems so.'

Toryn yanked the horse's head around in a melodrama of movement. 'In that case, you know where to find me,' he shouted, digging his heels deep into its flank. The beast snorted, flaring its nostrils in response, before leaping into a gallop flanked by the other two warriors.

Alba stared after Toryn for several long moments.

'At least it is over now,' said Horva. 'The traitor is dead and you have your woman.'

'For now,' replied Alba, shaking his head slowly and following Toryn till he disappeared from view.

EPILOGUE

'I have received this tablet,' said Favius.

The two men before him remained silent.

'It is from the barbarian Alba. The very same barbarian you were sent to eliminate.'

Lucius remained very still. Quintus, stood beside him, said nothing.

'Still you know that don't you Quintus? Given that it was you who penned it and delivered it into my hands.'

He paused, turning the tablet over and over. 'I confess that this is the first time I have seen an officer of the Imperial army reduced to a barbarian's lackey. But I digress. I have not yet got to the main highlight for it goes on to say how on three separate occasions that you, Lucius, let the barbarians slip out of your hands. He goes as far as to suggest, that given your ineptitude and inability to hold them, even when caught, that you must possess some sympathy for their plight.'

Favius looked up, the two black discs fixed on the

centurion. 'It would pain me, very much, if I thought that were so.'

Lucius made to respond, but in a flash Favius's hand shot up, commanding immediate silence. 'What we cannot have is for our authority to be made a mockery of.'

By now his voice had become a low, menacing hiss. Quintus, sensing Lucius was about to be made an example of, couldn't help a whisper of a smile hint at the side of his mouth.

'And you,' Favius turned, quick as a viper toward the Optio. 'You were sent to aid your senior officer, not enable both his capture and an embarrassing retreat.'

Quintus tensed, quite bewildered how Favius had sensed his enjoyment of Lucius's predicament. The man must have the senses of the gods.

'Pitiful! Both of you.'

'Sir, Legatus Servius was well aware of my plan to intercept the barbarian. He sanctioned the entire action…'

'Silence!' Favius commanded. 'I am well aware of the part Servius played in this. I would advise you, Lucius, not to shift the blame to your superior for your pathetic failure. Do not protest, for that is what it is, pathetic. However, the chain of command is clear. Your Legatus should have managed you and coordinated your actions more effectively. The blame lies squarely at his door.'

The two men before him visibly relaxed. It was the barest hint of the release of tension but Favius was upon it.

'The blame for this ineptitude will be upon Servius's shoulders. But, be in no doubt, for your failure on the field I should have you both publicly flogged and sent to the arena. There you would not even be granted an honourable death by combat but be offered up as meat to the lions!'

Favius walked behind the two men. He stopped, leaning his head so that it was between theirs. 'Your Legatus or ex-Legatus to be more precise, failed to comprehend just who he was dealing with. I would hate for you two to make the same mistake, so let me be clear. You are officers of the Roman army. I am not. You report to me, not to any career officer or some pumped up Senator's son but to me. Is that clear?'

'Yes, sir!' came the synchronised reply.

'Then we have an understanding.'

'Sir, our orders, will they not come from Rome?' queried Quintus, puzzled by exactly what rank Favius held.

'They will come from me and me alone. Oh, I do not hold a rank as you would know it Quintus. My superiors are positioned far above the ranks of the Imperial army. You just need to understand that my word is the only one you need listen to. Should you not listen, deviate or turn against my authority, well, both the regular army and my *organisation* have a code of conduct. Like the army we do not tolerate failure. If you fall short in the army you may face degradation, discharge or be told to open your veins. We do not need a lengthy list of punishments. Failure in our organisation simply results in death. Of course, interpretation of whether a particular action is a success or failure can be, shall we say, open to a degree of creativity. In other words, I write the reports. Remember that well.'

He let that sink in. Favius had not got to where he was without using silence as well as words to achieve the effect he desired. Satisfied, he leant forward, whispering into the ears of each man before him.

'Do you wish death Lucius?'

'No, sir!'

'Do you wish death Quintus?'

'No, sir!'

Favius withdrew from between the two men. Slowly and very deliberately he walked around to stand before them. The slit of his moth formed what passed for a smile as he regarded them, eyes resting from one to the other.

'I am glad we have straightened out any ambiguity. Your actions, I trust, will now be guided with the complete knowledge of how failure is rewarded.' Favius threw open his hands. 'But I talk only of the dark side of things. Be it known that success will also be rewarded. The organisation of which you are now a part is also generous. We acknowledge those who risk themselves to further our cause. As a result and despite your earlier, shall we say, shortcomings, I have been authorised to grant an immediate step up in rank for both of you.'

Quintus stole a glance at Lucius. The centurion stayed impassive.

'Lucius, you are hereby promoted to Legatus. Quintus, you are promoted to centurion under Lucius's direct command.'

Lucius shifted his weight. It was only a small movement, imperceptible to most but Favius seemed possessed of an ability to spot a man's inner thoughts.

'You are uncomfortable with something Lucius?'

'I am curious as to Servius?'

Favius smiled, the thin lips withdrawing to a slit. 'Do not burden your thoughts about Servius. His light is spent and as we speak, he is drowning his sorrows in that piss awful wine of his.'

Favius walked over to his desk, pouring himself a wine from a pitcher. 'This, on the other hand, is from one of my own vineyards,' he said casually. 'The quality of this grape far exceeds that of Servius's.'

He sipped the glass. As the red liquid touched his lips it seemed to secrete itself into his mouth rather than flow through the gap. 'Exquisite!' he approved.

Turning to the two men he waved them off. 'You may go.'

Lucius made his way over to the Legate's quarters. He hoped Servius would be gone by now to save any embarrassing confrontation. As he stepped inside, the smell of wine and something else assailed his nostrils.

Servius must have drunk himself silly.

The whole place reeked of piss and liquor. Lucius noticed that Servius's effects were still here. If the ex Legatus had been told to vacate then he was certainly in no rush. He stole himself for a confrontation and walked boldly over to Servius's office. To his surprise the Legatus was still there, slumped over his desk like a drunk.

'Servius?'

No answer came.

The idiots making himself even more of a laughingstock, thought Lucius.

'Servius?'

The form wasn't moving. Come to think of it, he couldn't hear him either. Drunks usually snored through their stupor. Suspicious, he moved closer and lifted his ex-superiors head up. It lolled limply before falling back down with a crash.

Lifting the head up again, Lucius noted the Legatus eyes were wide and unblinking, the pupils almost as large as the iris around them. A noise made him turn to see three slaves waiting expectantly.

'Yes?' he queried irritably.

'Sir, we were sent here to help you tidy up,' replied the nearest.

Lucius nodded slowly, guessing Favius had sent them. 'Very well. Clear everything. Nothing is to remain. When you have finished have my things brought from my quarters, my old quarters that is.'

The slave nodded and began to issue directions to the other two.

'One more thing.'

'Sir?'

'Get rid of this first,' he said, indicating Servius's corpse. 'And do not drink the wine; it has gone off.'

Favius helped himself to another glass of his own grape. Overall, he had tidied things up as best as could be hoped. The new orders from his superiors had been as impassive as ever, never once communicating anger. He knew them too well for that. Everything was simply *dealt with.*

His explanation and subsequent laying the blame on Servius had been accepted. Servius was to be removed from history. His corpse, estates, slaves, everything to which his name was given or owned was to be wiped from the face of the earth. Favius had no doubt the clean-up operation was already in progress back in Rome and wherever Servius had interests. The slaves he had sent to Servius's quarters had been told to take the corpse to the quicklime pits. There the ex Legatus would be stripped of his flesh as well as his name.

He had received several tablets outlining his next steps and future operations. One in particular had caught his attention. He read it again, for the third time.

Your elimination of the failed sorcerer Adrionix noted. We have arranged a replacement with capabilities suitable to combat the barbarian mystic. She will make herself known to you within the coming weeks. She is regarded as a reliable asset and is a native of Britannia. Do not underestimate her.

Favius set the tablet down. The asset when she arrived was just who he needed. A native sorcerer skilled in both the ways of the Britons and those of his own organisation.

'Then we will see just how good you are, Alba,' he muttered, before taking a seat and sipping the rest of his wine.

The End

Printed in Great Britain
by Amazon